. . . it was the   But Fiona's mouth   , he promptly forgo   emptation she offered. Yet, oddly enough, though he ached to feel the touch of her lips on his, it was not an ache born of mere lust—but rather a compelling need to pay homage to her compassion and courage and incredible optimism in the face of almost unbelievable odds. He reached across the narrow space between them to cup her chin in his fingers while his lips sought hers with a gentleness bordering on reverence.

"Forgive me, Mistress Haines, I should never have done that," he said, looking every bit as shocked as she felt. "I swear I do not know what came over me. I assure you I meant no disrespect, and I promise it will never happen again."

"I accept your apology; we shall forget it ever happened," Fiona lied. For, in truth, she felt certain she would remember till the day she died how it felt to be kissed by Adam Cresswell.

A Touch of Magic

Nadine Miller

A SIGNET BOOK

SIGNET
Published by the Penguin Group
Penguin Putnam Inc., 375 Hudson Street
New York, New York 10014, U.S.A.
Penguin Books Ltd, 27 Wrights Lane,
London W8 5TZ, England
Penguin Books Australia Ltd,
Ringwood, Victoria, Australia
Penguin Books Canada Ltd, 10 Alcorn Avenue
Toronto, Ontario, Canada M4V 3B2
Penguin Books (N.Z.) Ltd, 182–190 Wairau Road,
Auckland 10, New Zealand

Penguin Books Ltd, Registered Offices:
Harmondsworth, Middlesex, England

First published by Signet, an imprint of Dutton NAL,
a member of Penguin Putnam Inc.

First Printing, May, 1999
10 9 8 7 6 5 4 3 2 1

To Laverne Harris of Friendly Horse Acres,
a dear friend, whose love of the remarkable
Exmoor Ponies was the inspiration for this story.

Chapter One

"You cannot be serious! Surely you are not blaming yourself for the death of some country bumpkin simply because you happened to play a hand of cards with him." An angry flush flooded the Duke of Bellmont's sallow cheeks and crept upward toward his grizzled brows, but the expression in his pale eyes remained as glacial as ever. At the moment those eyes raked his second son, Lord Adam Cresswell, with undisguised disapproval.

Adam instinctively flinched beneath his father's censure. Old habits died hard and for one brief instant he felt more like a prankish schoolboy sent down from Eton than a thirty-two-year-old veteran of the Peninsular Wars. He cleared his throat, wishing he'd had the sense to defer this confrontation with his father until after the family had left the dinner table.

He glanced hopefully at his older brother, Ethan, willing him to help smooth the old man's ruffled feathers. Ethan merely elevated his left eyebrow, indicating that the subject was of no interest whatsoever to him.

Adam gritted his teeth. "The 'bumpkin' was a man, Father, with the same claim to a heart and a soul as you and I. His name was Buckley Haines—and true, I did not push him in front of the coach and four that crushed the life from him. Still, I doubt it was mere coincidence that he met his Maker just minutes after I won everything the fellow owned in a game of hazard."

"Nonsense. No man in his right mind would commit suicide over the loss of such a trifling sum of money."

Leave it to his father to reduce the sorry affair to a mere triviality. "I did not say he purposely stepped in front of the carriage—though, God forbid, I suppose it is possible. But he was distraught. Fifty pounds may seem a trifling sum to you; it is not

to a simple farmer from Exmoor. Plus the young fool put up the
deed to his farm to stay in the game—and therein lies my guilt.
If I'd had my wits about me I'd have refused to continue to play
then and there."

Ethan laid down his fork. "I have to concur with Father,
Adam. I find your thinking illogical on several points—as it so
often is." He effected the pedantic tone of voice Adam had come
to despise in the six months he'd been home from the Peninsula.
"For one thing, I suspect the farmer was seriously inebriated."

"Drunk as a wheelbarrow," Adam admitted grudgingly.

"And like most drunks, excessively maudlin."

"I suppose you could say that." A fresh wave of guilt swept
through Adam as he recalled how the burly fellow had forfeited
the slip of paper on which he'd scribbled the deed to his farm,
then burst into tears and blubbered something to his tall, red-
haired companion about having to break the news to his wife.

"Well then," the duke interjected, "he is not worth all this
bother, is he?"

"My point exactly." Ethan's disapproving scowl was a poor
facsimile of the duke's. "Nor is his unfortunate demise a suitable
topic of conversation for the dinner table—especially when
there are ladies present." With a curt nod, he acknowledged the
presence of his wife, Lady Eudora, and Lady Tansy Cresswell,
the duke's spinster sister.

Adam could see this discussion was growing more futile by
the minute. It was all-too apparent that both his father and
brother considered the death of a common farmer too inconse-
quential to accord it more than a passing comment.

Absentmindedly, he traced a finger along the thin, white scar
from a Frenchman's sabre that marred his left cheek—a constant
reminder of his own brush with the Grim Reaper. He had seen
enough of death in Spain to fill a thousand lifetimes, but he had
never become inured to the horror of it.

"For whatever reason, a man whose life briefly touched mine
is dead," he said grimly. "Under the circumstances, I feel
obliged to seek out his widow and assure her I want no part of
her husband's farm—fairly won or not."

"How ridiculous. You are under no such obligation. If you are
serious about relinquishing any claim to the farm, send one of
the grooms to Exmoor with a note to that effect." The duke's

scowl darkened. "What the devil was a farmer from the hinterlands doing in a gaming hell in London's East End anyway? For that matter, what were you doing there? I distinctly remember asking you to accompany Lady Felicity Blakesly and her parents to the Bramwells' musicale on that particular evening."

Adam took a deep breath, aware that the answer to his father's question would only further enrage the old tyrant. He glanced apologetically at the other members of his family, whom he'd inadvertently involved in the unpleasant business.

His older brother, Ethan, Viscount Sparling, was a younger, less dynamic copy of the duke, with the same blue-black hair and finely chiseled features that marked all the Cresswell men. Ethan wore his usual worried frown, though what was worrying him at the moment was a mystery to Adam. Beside him sat his wife, Eudora—a plain, gray mouse of a woman who always looked ready to burst into tears.

At the foot of the table, in the chair that had once been his mother's, sat his aunt, Lady Tansy Cresswell, an unusually perceptive woman with whom he shared a close relationship. More than once in the six months since he'd sold out his commission he'd felt her compassionate spirit reach out to him when one of his black moods was upon him.

Furthermore, he suspected she knew about the nightmares that still plagued him. He'd waked often enough to his own voice crying out to the friends he'd lost in the awful carnage of Ciudad Rodrigo and Salamanca—and her bedchamber was directly across the hall from his. Surreptitiously, she lowered one eyelid in a conspiratorial wink that let him know he had her support in anything he chose to do.

The duke's long, elegant fingers tapped an impatient rat-a-tat on the table. "I asked why you were not at the Bramwell's musicale," he repeated. "I have yet to hear your answer."

"I was there," Adam said, with a patience he was far from feeling. "But the affair was too tortuous to bear. The musicians were hopelessly mediocre and the featured soprano had a voice sharp enough to pierce armor. I left at the end of the first number and sought entertainment elsewhere."

"God's breath, you young fool, is that any way to treat the woman you plan to marry?" The duke slammed his fist on the table, upending his glass of wine. "What must the Earl of Sturnhaven think of you—publicly humiliating his daughter in such a fashion?" Impatiently, he waved off the footman who was attempting to mop up the soggy mess. "If you're not careful, he will change his mind about accepting your offer for her."

Adam shrugged. "Since I am not considering making such an offer, that is the least of my worries."

The duke struck the table another shattering blow. "Well, you had damned well better consider it, and get to work siring a healthy son or two. The future of the title is at stake, since it appears your brother's witless wife can produce nothing but females. Five daughters, for God's sake. What is the woman thinking of?" He cast a look of disgust at Lady Eudora and Adam watched the poor creature shrivel into a ball of quivering misery.

"There is plenty of time for Ethan and Eudora to produce the requisite heir," Adam said quietly. "As for me, I have just returned from four years of war and am far from ready to settle into domestic life."

"If you offered for Lady Felicity today, it would take her mother at least six months to plan a wedding and buy bride clothes—ample time for you to sow any wild oats you have in mind."

Adam stared mutely at his determined father. How could he explain that another round of the aimless entertainment he'd been pursuing since returning to London was the very thing he did not need. After years of living with the constant threat of death, he needed a purpose to his life. Otherwise, how could he justify surviving with nothing more than a scar his current mistress pronounced "devilishly attractive" when better men than he lay dead in foreign soil?

"You cannot afford to miss this opportunity," the duke continued, ignoring Adam's silence. "The Blakesly women are good breeders. Sturnhaven's wife presented him with four strapping sons before she produced a single daughter, and I am willing to wager Lady Felicity will do the same."

He paused to draw a breath. "What can you possibly have against the gel? She is not that bad to look at, and she comes with a dowry that would make any man's mouth water."

Adam shrugged. "I have nothing against her. She will probably make some man an excellent wife, if he does not mind being bored to death with her silly prattle."

"God's breath, is that all that bothers you? No one is asking you to talk to the chit. What man would be so lost to reason as to engage his wife, or any other female in his household, in serious conversation?"

Lady Tansy made a small, choking sound deep in her throat, and not for the first time, Adam found himself wondering why such an intelligent, warmhearted woman had never married. Surely no husband she could have chosen would have been as difficult to live with as his tyrannical father.

"Well that is settled then. We will say no more about this Exmoor nonsense," the duke declared. "I shall inform Sturnhaven he can expect you to call on him within the next day or two to make your formal offer."

Extracting his watch from the pocket of his waistcoat, he flipped open the gold hunter case and checked the time. "Devil take it, I've no time for an after-dinner brandy. I am already late for the card game at my club." So saying, he promptly rose from the table, bowed to the ladies, and strode from the room. A few moments later, Adam heard the hall footman close the outside door behind him.

Ethan was the first to break the silence that followed the duke's departure. "Your four years under Wellington have mellowed you, little brother. I have never before seen you give in to our father without an argument."

"What a ridiculous thing to say." Lady Tansy cast a sly smile in Adam's direction. "Adam has done no such thing. He has simply avoided a senseless quarrel with my impossible brother."

"Of course, how silly of me to forget that the Hero of Salamanca is entitled to do exactly what he wants, regardless of the effect his actions may have on the rest of us." Ethan studied Adam with narrowed eyes. "You are still planning to call on the grieving widow then, despite Father's disapproval."

"I am," Adam said gravely. "Honor demands it."

"Honor my foot. If you ask me, it is merely an excuse to escape London before you find yourself trapped into marrying that insipid creature Father has chosen for you."

"Well that too," Adam admitted. "But whatever the reason, John Bittner, my batman-cum-valet, is at this very minute packing my saddlebags so I can leave at dawn. Furthermore, the helpful fellow has agreed to lend me his old uniform. With times as hard as they are, I have decided to travel as a recently discharged foot soldier to avoid offering temptation to the thieves and cutthroats prowling the country's highways."

"Am I to take it you plan to walk to Exmoor then?" Ethan's voice was heavy with sarcasm. "The poor devils I have observed have all been traveling by shanks mare."

"I doubt it is necessary to take things to that extreme," Adam said dryly. "I plan to ride the mare I brought back from Spain."

Lady Tansy nodded enthusiastically, sending wisps of silver-gray hair floating around her small, heart-shaped face. "An excellent plan, dear boy, and in my opinion your concern for the farmer's widow does you great credit."

"An excellent plan for whom?" Ethan demanded. "The old man will be like a bear with a sore paw if his favorite son thwarts his attempt at matchmaking—and I will be the one on whom he vents his wrath. My life will be a living hell until Adam returns—and chances are he will still end up marrying the Blakesly chit. Once Father makes up his mind on something like this, there is nothing can stop him."

Adam saw the stricken look on Lady Eudora's face as she leapt to her feet and ran sobbing from the room—and suddenly remembered how, seven years earlier, his father had manipulated Ethan into marrying her even though everyone in the *ton* knew his heart belonged to another.

Ethan swore softly under his breath. "Now look what you've made me do. Eudora takes enough abuse from Father; she does not need it from me as well." He groaned. "I'd best go pacify her before she gets hysterical. It is not a pretty sight."

Rising to his feet, he tossed his linen serviette to the table. "Take care on this ill-conceived journey of yours, Adam," he said in a tight voice. "As usual, you are an unmitigated pain in the ass, but you are the only brother I have."

Adam watched his sibling stride from the room, a sick feeling in the pit of his stomach. With a wave of his hand, he dismissed the butler and footmen hovering discreetly in the background and moved to the chair nearest Lady Tansy. "I don't understand why Ethan hates me so much," he said once they were alone.

"We were great friends when we were boys but he has done nothing but snarl at me since I returned from Spain."

"Are you blind, dear boy? Your brother suffers from an acute case of sibling jealousy."

Adam stared at his aunt, shocked into silence by her unbelievable pronouncement. "But why?" he asked when he found his voice. "He is the heir to the title and estates. Were it not for my inheritance from my maternal grandmother, I would be penniless."

"But because of that inheritance, you enjoy the kind of independence Ethan will never have until your father dies. That, combined with the fact that you are everything he knows he can never be, is destroying him. Think back, Adam. You have excelled at everything you have ever done—leaving Ethan behind to wallow in his own ineptitude."

Lady Tansy raised her teacup to her lips and took a dainty sip. "Futhermore, you have had one woman or another in love with you for as long as I can remember; only one woman has ever loved Ethan and he was forbidden to marry her."

She sighed. "Of course, a great deal of his present resentment toward you is due to your father. Reginald has gone out of his way these past few years to show Ethan that you were his favorite son."

"His favorite? You cannot be serious. We have been at daggers drawn since the day I became old enough to rebel against his tyranny."

"Exactly, and perverse devil that he is, he finds your rebellion as commendable as it is annoying. I suspect you remind him of himself when he was young. He wasn't always a pompous old stick, you know."

She placed her cup in its saucer and folded her hands in her lap. "Your father was like a madman the four years you were gone— haunting the corridors of Whitehall to examine the monthly lists of dead and wounded submitted by the Duke of Wellington's aide-de-camp. Lord Castlereagh finally arranged to have copies delivered to him here at the townhouse just to be rid of him. I shall never forget the day he found your name listed amongst the wounded. No one could console him—least of all Ethan."

Adam swallowed the lump in his throat. "I never knew," he said in a voice hoarse with emotion. "I always believed I was a bitter disappointment to my father."

"Your choices might have disappointed him. Still, he cannot help but admire your mutinous spirit and fierce independence. Ethan, on the other hand, has earned nothing but his disgust by trying so hard to please. My heart aches for the poor fellow. More than once I have heard Reginald revile him for being born first, when you would make the better duke. Can you imagine how that makes your brother feel when he is already well aware of his many shortcomings?"

"Good Lord, no wonder he hates me." Adam had never deluded himself that his was the happiest of families, but he had hoped Ethan and he might at least learn to respect each other. Sick at heart, he propped his elbows on the table and held his aching head in his hands. "Maybe I should just quietly disappear on this trip to Exmoor—and never return."

"That would solve nothing. In fact, I suspect it would make things worse." Lady Tansy smiled. "But all is not lost. I have recently seen signs that Ethan's resentment toward your father is building to the point where he too will finally rebel. I pray to God he does, but it is something he must decide on his own or he will never find the strength to see it through."

She reached across the table and patted Adam's cheek, much as she had when he was a small boy. "In the meantime, my dear, go to Exmoor and make your peace with the farmer's widow. Then, God willing, you may at last find a way to make peace with yourself."

It had been a fine funeral.

Fiona Haines comforted herself with the thought that wherever Buckley was now, he must be pleased at how many of his friends and neighbors had turned out to pay their last respects.

But now, with more than a month passed since the unhappy event, it was time she stopped wallowing in her misery and got on with her life. The trouble was, she seemed incapable of deciding how to go about it.

Always before she'd had Buckley to back her up—solid and a bit slow-witted, but unswerving in his loyalty. Because she had been the clever one, the quick one, the one whose imagination soared to heights he could not begin to comprehend, she had never realized how much she depended on him. She knew it now and that realization left her with a terrible, guilt-ridden grief that numbed her mind and robbed her of her usual dauntless spirit.

Sadly, she acknowledged she could scarcely remember a time when Buckley hadn't loved her. She had been but seven years old the first time he had caught her stealing a fat hen from his father's chicken coop and lied to protect her from the local beadle. In one way or another, he had been protecting her from something or someone ever since.

She smiled to herself, remembering the saintly picture the vicar had painted of Buckley in his eulogy. The man she knew so well had never aspired to sainthood. Far from it. He was a simple, good-natured farmer with an incurable addiction to games of chance and a tendency to drink more than his share of the fine dark ale brewed by the owner of the Black Boar Inn.

Still, when all was said and done, he had plowed his fields in the spring and harvested his crops in the fall, attended his church on Sunday and was generally the same solid kind of fellow as countless generations of Exmoor farmers before him. The one and only time he had stepped out of character was the day he'd married her.

A less likely pair had never stood before the altar of the village church than Buckley Haines and Fiona Derry, the ragged, half-starved waif who was the illegitimate granddaughter of the woman known as the Witch of Exmoor. But even then, Buckley had loved her in the same uncomplicated way he'd loved his fields and his sheep and the sturdy moorland ponies that carried the brand of Larkspur Farm.

And she had cared for him—not with the mindless passion that had driven her mother and grandmother into reckless liaisons with fly-by-night rogues, but rather with a deep, abiding gratitude to the generous-hearted man who had given her the respectability and security she had always craved.

But now her husband was gone, and she was left with a farm that needed working and only one frail old man to help her. Ben Watson had worked for Buckley, and his father before him, and had long ago been accepted as part of the family. He could still manage much of the lighter work around the farm, but a younger, stronger man was needed for the heavy chores.

Oh, she'd had plenty of offers from men eager to help her manage Larkspur Farm. Before the last shovel of dirt had dropped on

Buckley's coffin, his friend, Dooley Twig, had made his offer—and after him, every single man between here and Withypool Common. For there was no finer piece of land in Exmoor and to a man they were willing to forget the Widow Haines's unsavory past and wed and bed her to get their hands on it.

But she needed a farmhand, not a husband. Never a husband. She had submitted to Buckley's clumsy martial demands because she'd been so grateful to him for marrying her. But she had soon learned that the intimacies of the marriage bed were not to her liking. The idea of doing *that* with any other man made her skin crawl.

Ordinarily she would ask for help from her half brother, Liam, but she had quarreled bitterly with him that terrible day when he'd driven a horse-drawn sledge into the farmyard and uncovered the oak casket in which he'd carried Buckley's broken body home from London.

Shock and grief had turned her into a screaming banshee. She'd called Liam every vile name she'd ever known, for if not for his tall tales of the wonders he'd seen in his travels, poor Buckley would never have thought to hare off to London with him, only to die beneath the wheels of a stranger's carriage.

Liam hadn't offered a word of rebuttal to her charges, which was most unlike the glib-tongued rogue. Nor had he looked her in the eye, as any man innocent of them might. He'd simply stared at his boots and mumbled some gibberish about a piece of paper Buckley had given to some high-and-mighty milord. As if a simple Exmoor farmer would ever know such a person.

Once she'd vented her spleen, she'd found she could no longer stand the sight of her brother's handsome face or his flame-colored hair, so like her own hated legacy from the unconscionable rake who'd sired them both. She'd sent him on his way, swearing she never wanted to lay eyes on him again.

So now here she was on a gray, drizzly day, watching the flower garden she'd tended so carefully turn into one huge mud puddle—and pondering the riddle of how to maintain Larkspur Farm in the manner Buckley would have wanted.

The solution was simple. Find a hardworking young fellow, preferably a stranger, with no ambitions above a decent wage, good food, and a bed in the attic room next to Ben Watson's.

The problem was how to find such a man.

Chapter Two

Adam wasn't certain what to expect of Exmoor. He'd heard the remote area in England's West Country variously described as a barren wasteland inhospitable to man or beast, as a domain of treacherous bogs, brooding tors, and ancient Celtic monoliths, and finally as an immense pastureland for the sturdy ponies descended from the wild horses that roamed the British Isles in ages past.

His first few hours there confirmed all three descriptions and more. He had never before seen a land of such wild, savage beauty and startling contrasts—nor one that called so strongly to his restless spirit. Everything about the vast, lonely moors fascinated him and at the same time, seemed oddly familiar, as if in a time too long ago to recall, he had traveled this way before.

For miles on end, the road beneath his horse's hooves traversed countryside as bleak as any godforsaken plain he'd crossed in Spain. Then topping a steep rise, he gazed upon a seemingly limitless stretch of pale, wind-tossed grass high as a man's knee and teeming with game.

Red deer gazed down from the slopes of gentle hills as he rode across the lush swale, and ruffed grouse, and small, brown hares scurried across the narrow, rutted roadway in front of him. Flights of birds he recognized as pipits and dippers and gray wagtails darkened the sky above, then wheeling and swooping like children at play disappeared over the horizon. He spied a pair of blue kingfishers perched in the branches of a scrub oak and in another such tree a woodpecker scolded noisily as he passed by. Once he even caught a glimpse of a small herd of the mysterious wild ponies for which Exmoor was famous.

Only now and then did he see signs that humans, too, inhabited the isolated region—a friendly curl of smoke from a distant cottage chimney, an abandoned cart with a broken axle, a fenced pasture filled with grazing ewes and newborn lambs.

The road through the grasslands was a sea of mud from a recent rain, and more than once his mare whinnied her frustration at sinking into the muck with each step she took. Luckily, the wind was at his back and with the sun low on the western horizon, Adam urged his weary mount on toward the Black Boar Inn, which he'd been told lay ahead. How far ahead, he'd neglected to ask.

Just as the flaming ball of the sun dipped below the horizon and he'd begun to think he was doomed to spend the night on the open moors, the road took a turn around the base of a towering black tor and he came upon a small village comprised of a church, a mercantile, a dozen or so weathered cottages, and a travelers' inn. But to his dismay, the two-story inn was gray with age and the outbuildings adjoining it appeared to be but a hair's breadth from total collapse.

He blinked, rubbed his eyes, and blinked again. Could this ugly blot on the landscape be the much-touted Black Boar Inn? Tired and famished though he was, the ramshackle collection was not his idea of an inviting refuge for weary travelers. Still, it was too late in the day to ride farther and his mare was exhausted; he would simply have to make do with what was at hand.

Half an hour later, when he'd tucked into a tasty mutton stew and washed it down with an exceptionally fine dark ale, he decided that despite its sorry appearance, the Black Boar Inn had much to recommend it.

Furthermore Hiram Blodgett, the elderly innkeeper, turned out to be a fund of helpful information. "If it be the Widow Haines ye're seeking, she bides at Larkspur Farm," the crusty old fellow declared. "Though there be them as says she has no rightful claim to poor Buckley's land, with her ne'er-do-well brother the one as spirited him off to London town to be run down in the street like a mongrel dog. But live and let live says I."

His eyes narrowed assessingly. "What be yer business with the widow, if ye never mind me asking?"

Adam pondered how to answer the innkeeper's question without divulging more than he wished the nosy fellow to know. "I have something that belonged to her husband," he said finally. "I wish to return it to the rightful owner."

"Have ye, indeed? Well ye've the sound of a Londoner, and that be a far piece to travel for a trifling reason. Must be an important thing ye're returning to the widow."

Adam shrugged. "Important enough, I guess."

"Ye and the widow be good friends then, fer ye to go to so much trouble."

"On the contrary, I was briefly acquainted with her husband, but I have never met her."

"Is that so? Well then, if it be courting ye come for, ye may be chasing after the wrong partridge. 'Tis already been tried by every young buck in the county."

"Courting?" Adam stared at the garrulous old man in disbelief. "Good God, the woman's husband is scarcely cold in his grave."

"But cold he be—and she a woman alone, and one as were not all she should be before Buckley wed her, if ye knows what I mean. There be no point waiting out a proper mourning period when such a woman comes into one of the finest farms between here and Cornwall—a farm she's no way of managing on her own."

From that telling statement, Adam deduced two things. Firstly, that Buckley Haines had apparently married one of the local trollops, and secondly, if said trollop's brother had informed her that her husband had gambled and lost "one of the finest farms between here and Cornwall" she was keeping mum about it.

The first was not his concern; he'd long ago quit judging the foolish actions of other men; the second was something he would deal with once he'd had time to take the widow's measure. He smiled to himself. This visit to Exmoor might turn out to be considerably more interesting than the simple mission of mercy he'd originally envisaged.

"Like I said," Blodgett continued, "she's turned away every young buck as come knocking at her door if her hired man, Ben Watson, is to be believed. Maybe a gentlemanly fellow like ye be what she's waiting for. Think on it, laddie, and tell her I sent ye. She'll look more kindly on yer suit knowing that."

"Thank you," Adam said, not bothering to correct the innkeeper's bizarre assumption. "And where might I find this Larkspur Farm?"

"Follow the trail that veers off to the left about five mile down the road. Ye cannot miss it. It be wide enough to take a fair-sized wagon, but ye'll find no ruts like those in the road ye've been following. No man be foolish enough to try hauling goods that far into the moors on anything but a sledge, and a fool be one thing I'd never call a Moorland farmer."

He took another swallow of his ale. "But best ye bide the night here and set out in the morning. The moors be no place for a stranger to travel with darkness coming on. There be bogs out there a man and his mount can sink into and never be seen again."

The old man set his tankard on the table and made a frank survey of Adam's worn uniform and the scar that not even a three days' growth of beard could hide. "From the looks of ye, I'd say ye're fresh from Old Hook Nose's army and in need of one bob to rub against another, as are all the lads just home from Spain."

"I can pay for my meal and lodging," Adam protested, reaching toward his pocket.

The innkeeper's snowy brows drew together in a frown. "I never said ye couldn't, laddie. I expects ye to pay fer the plate of stew and the tankard of ale; that be money out of me pocket. But no man as served his king and country will be charged so much as a brass farthing for a sleep in the loft atop me stable."

He refilled Adam's tankard for the second time. "And whilst we be about it, that be a fine-spirited mare ye rode in on— mighty fine indeed fer a fellow wearing a foot soldier's uniform."

Adam did a quick bit of thinking. "The mare belonged to the officer I served as batman," he improvised. "She was his parting gift to me for saving his life at Salamanca."

"So ye says, and so I believes. But however ye come by her, 'tis best ye leave the skitterish thing in me ostler's care and ride one of me surefooted Exmoor ponies. The beasties be born knowing how to survive on the moors—something ye cannot say for a thoroughbred."

Adam was not by nature a trusting man, especially where his favorite mare was concerned. Furthermore, he had seen a few Exmoor ponies on the rare occasions when Tattersall's had offered them for sale. He had been singularly unimpressed. The idea of exchanging the sleek thoroughbred that had seen him through four years on the Peninsula for a shaggy equine but two-thirds her size seemed too foolish to consider.

Still, there was something about the old man's warning that rang true. "I thank you for the offer," he said gravely. "I am very attached to Starfire. I'd not want her to come to harm."

Thus it was that early the next morning the second son of the powerful Duke of Bellmont rose from the hayloft bed he had shared with a hen and six newly hatched chicks, bid farewell to his blooded mare, and set out on the last lap of his journey to Larkspur Farm atop a brown, mealy-muzzled Exmoor pony.

The innkeeper saw him off. " 'Tis away with ye then, young stranger," he said, raising his hand in farewell. "Ye'll pass three other farmhouses afore ye come to Larkspur Farm, which lies at the end of the road. Ye cannot mistake it. 'Tis the only one with green shutters and flower boxes at the windows."

He waved a last farewell. "And if things works out with the widow, I'll expect ye in me taproom one of these fine summer evenings to buy a tankard or two for the local lads ye beat out."

Fiona had just put a batch of bread in the oven when she saw the dark-haired stranger ride up to her gate. Parting the sheer white curtains at her kitchen window, she took a closer look, certain he could only be calling at an out-of-the-way place like Larkspur Farm for one reason. Employment. Hiram Blodgett had lost no time in answering the request she'd sent him, by the way of Ben Watson, to keep an eye out for any stranger stopping at the inn who might want work as a farmhand.

This fellow he'd sent for her approval was a good deal taller than most of the local men—so tall in fact that he looked ungainly, even comical, astride one of the sturdy ponies that were the favorite mode of travel in Exmoor. Furthermore, the threadbare uniform he wore proclaimed him one of the many ex-servicemen wandering the countryside since the war with France ended. A wounded one at that. Even from a distance, she could see the scar slicing his sun-bronzed cheek from brow to chin.

He sat for a moment before dismounting and stared intently at the cottage, giving her a full view of his face. She felt her breath catch in her throat. Lord Almighty, he was a handsome devil—almost as handsome as her brother, Liam. And like Liam, he exuded an unmistakable air of powerful masculinity.

But where Liam was all fire and light, this man had a dark, brooding look about him. In truth, with his jet black hair and that intriguing scar, he better suited the image of a highwayman or a pirate than a farmworker. What was Hiram thinking of? This was definitely not the sort of fellow a woman alone should consider hiring.

Still, unless she was mistaken, the pony he was riding came from the Black Boar stable. The tightfisted innkeeper must have judged him trustworthy to loan him a mount. Considering that and the distance he'd come, she could scarcely turn him away without an interview simply because the look of him sent shivers down her spine.

She just wished she'd had some warning so she could have braided her fly-away hair into a neat coronet and made herself a bit more presentable. With an exasperated sigh, she whipped off her flour-dusted apron and strode toward the open door, her trusty guard dog, Caesar, close beside her. Like it or not, the stranger would have to take her as she was.

The sun was already high in the sky when Adam drew up before the pretty little thatched-roof cottage with the bright green shutters and flower-filled window boxes the innkeeper had described. The farmyard was as neat as the cottage, with none of the clutter of farm implements, sledge carts, and strolling chickens he'd seen surrounding the other farmhouses he'd passed. Still, there were ample signs the widow was at home. The door to the cottage stood open and a wisp of fragrant woodsmoke rose from the stone chimney.

Dismounting, he looped the reins over the fence and gave the pony an affectionate pat. More than once, traversing the mud-slippery trail through treacherous marshland, he'd found himself grateful for the stolid disposition and surefooted gait of his sturdy mount.

Without further ado, he unlatched the gate and stepped into the farmyard. A mistake he instantly realized when a gigantic dog, black as the hound of Satan, catapulted off the porch and charged toward him.

"What the devil!" Adam spread his legs to keep his balance, raised his hands before his face, and prepared to protect himself from the vicious attack. To no avail. The great beast rose on its hind legs, planted its massive paws on Adam's shoulders . . . and proceeded to wash his face with a tongue the size of a cricket bat.

"Down lad," he ordered, laughing in spite of his shaking knees. The dog ignored his command. Slobbering happily, it made another swipe of its wet tongue across his face.

"Down Caesar! Now!" Rich and throaty and feminine, a voice he assumed belonged to the widow, came from the porch of the cottage and to Adam's intense relief, the dog obeyed it.

"Caesar likes you," the voice said, its velvet tones wrapping Adam in a warmth that owed nothing to the bright June sun overhead. "How amazing. He never takes to strangers."

Grumbling to himself, Adam extracted a linen handkerchief bearing his family crest from the pocket of his batman's uniform and scrubbed his face from chin to forehead. The widow might find the beast's show of affection amazing; he found it damned annoying. Even now, the great sluggard had stretched its massive body across both his boot-clad feet, effectively pinning him against the widow's gate.

"You have ridden up from the Black Boar Inn, I take it. I recognize the brand on the pony's rump." The voice sounded closer and Adam gave off scrubbing, opened his eyes, and found himself staring into a pair of exotic, almond-shaped amber eyes set in an exquisite oval face that was framed by a glorious mane of red-gold hair. The widow Haines, if this be she, was without a doubt one of the most beautiful women he had ever seen.

Adam knew he was staring like a moonstruck greenling. He

couldn't help it. He'd come looking for yet another of the sturdy, plain-faced women he'd viewed in the farmyards he'd passed between here and the Black Boar Inn. Instead, he found this fey creature whose exotic beauty instantly awakened fires in his blood that were best left safely banked. No wonder the local bachelors were hammering at the widow's door.

His gaze dropped to the unsightly black gown that proclaimed her widowhood. Beautiful she might be, but the woman obviously had a deplorable sense of taste. Still, drab and ill-fitting as it was, the ugly garment could not disguise the graceful, willowy body encased within it, and Adam felt a certain part of his own body respond with an embarrassing lack of control.

"Did the owner of the Black Boar Inn direct you to me?" she asked, startling him to attention.

"What? Oh yes, if you are the Widow Haines, he did indeed."

"I am." She studied Adam with an unnerving intensity. "And did he tell you what I was prepared to offer?"

"Offer?"

"Four shillings a week. A goodly amount to be sure, but if I decide you are the man I want, you will be the only one around except Ben Watson, who is much too old to take care of my needs."

Adam felt his mouth drop open. Had he heard the cheeky little beauty correctly, or had the instant lust she'd aroused in him addled his brain?

"You are offering to pay me money for . . . for . . ." He wasn't certain exactly what it was she had in mind. But four shillings a week? What kind of offer was that?

"Well of course I intend to feed and lodge you too, if I decide to take you on," she said, with what sounded amazingly like indignation. The woman was really incredible. Who could have guessed such an angelic face could mask a nature as brazen as that of the most hardened London cyprian.

"But I feel it only fair to tell you," she continued in the same prosaic tone, "you are not at all the kind of man I had in mind."

Without stopping to analyze why, Adam felt consumed with rage that the little tart had judged him and found him wanting—something he was not accustomed to having women do. "Why not?" he demanded.

"Any number of reasons, but the most obvious one is your hands."

Adam stared at his offending appendages in dismay, one of which still clutched the square of soggy linen. "What is wrong with them?"

"There is not a callous on them. I have to wonder just how much experience you've had as a farmhand, Mr. . . ."

"Cresswell . . . Adam Cresswell," he said without thinking, as he belatedly realized what this bizarre conversation was actually about. The lovely widow was discussing hiring him as an ordinary farmhand—not as a resident stud. With the innkeeper's damning words ringing in his ears, he had automatically leaped to the wrong conclusion. Devil take it, he couldn't remember when he'd felt more a fool.

"I can tell I have embarrassed you with my blunt speaking, Mr. Cresswell. A bad habit of mine." Absentmindedly, she twisted a lock of satiny hair around her finger. "I am sorry," she continued, "but I feel I really must ask—have you ever done an honest day's work?"

Her question startled him. The widow apparently believed in getting right to the point. "No, ma'am, to be perfectly truthful I never have—at least not as a farmhand," he said, struggling to keep a straight face.

"I see. Well I appreciate your honesty." Her troubled gaze lingered on his scarred cheek. "I doubt soldiering, though an honest profession, would put many callouses on a man's hands. But tell me, Adam Cresswell, how did you make your living before you went to war?"

This was the ideal time to tell her who he was and why he'd sought her out. But some perverse streak in his nature resented her unspoken implication that he was incapable of doing the most menial work. He had gained a healthy respect for the ordinary English workingman from the many who'd served under him on the Peninsula, and he had often wondered if, like them, he could make his way in the world if he were stripped of his wealth and rank. What better opportunity to find out? But how could he convince the skeptical widow she should hire him?

Lie, a wicked little voice somewhere deep inside him whispered, and he immediately fabricated a new personality for himself so outrageous it sounded plausible, even to his own ears.

"You asked how I earned my living before the war, ma'am. I hesitate to tell you, for I am not proud of it." He stared contritely at his callous-free hands. "The truth is I was a gambler—an ivory turner—a Captain Sharp, if you will. I took the King's shilling to escape the evil lure of the London gambling hells, and now that the army no longer wants me, I've sought this remote part of England for the same reason. Addicted as I am to the green baize, I dare not return to the city of my birth."

"You are determined to reform then," she said in a voice soft as eiderdown.

Adam assumed what he hoped was a pious mien. "I most sincerely am, ma'am."

"I commend you for your good intentions, Mr. Cresswell. I have good reason to despise gambling. My husband suffered from the dreadful addiction. In a roundabout way, it was the cause of his death." She smiled, a sad little smile that sent a stab of guilt coursing through Adam. "For that reason, if no other, I am of a mind to offer you the chance to begin life anew."

She glanced down at the dog still sprawled at his feet. "Of course, Caesar's opinion carries weight as well. I have found him to be a better judge of human character than most men."

"Thank you, ma'am—and you too, Caesar," Adam said, his tongue lodged firmly in his cheek. "I shall endeavor to warrant your trust."

The dog rolled over onto its back and gazed up at him with adoring eyes. The widow, on the other hand, squared her slender shoulders and surveyed him with a look of unrelenting practicality. "But I must warn you, I shall expect you to earn every cent of your generous wage."

"I shall do my best, ma'am." Hell's bells, did anyone actually work for such a pittance? He had no idea what his family's servants were paid. But he had to believe the lowliest footman earned more than the ridiculous sum for which he had hired himself out to the widow.

Hopefully, there would be other compensations. She might

be very proper and businesslike at the moment. But the fact remained, she was an incredibly beautiful woman with a checkered past . . . and he had found ducks rarely changed the way they waddled. He'd lay odds that sooner or later the intriguing widow would revert to type.

Furthermore, staying around Larkspur Farm for a week or two would give him a chance to learn a little more about her before he made any decision concerning the handwritten deed he carried in his pocket.

"I shall not be unreasonable," she said after a moment of nerve-tingling silence. "I am aware that you will have to learn as you go along. Ben Watson will teach you anything you need to know. But if I find you are lazy or unwilling to perform the tasks assigned you, I shall have to sack you. Money is scarce on the moors; everyone must pull his weight."

She smiled, as if to soften the harshness of her warning. "In other words, I shall keep my eye on you, Adam Cresswell. Four shillings a week is a very generous wage for a man who has not yet proved his worth."

Adam smiled back. *And I shall keep my eye on you, Fiona Haines. One of the finest farms between here and Cornwall is a very generous inheritance for a pretty little widow with a questionable reputation.*

Chapter Three

Fiona shelled another of the pea pods she had picked in her garden early that morning, dropped the peas in her cooking pot and the pods in the wooden trencher she used to feed the pigs. She normally performed the pleasant task on her shady front porch. Today she chose, instead, to sit on a bench just inside the door of the stable, for the simple reason that it allowed her to observe her new farmhand hard at work splitting logs.

It was a sight well worth seeing. Adam Cresswell swung an ax with a fluid grace that was a joy to behold. A near miracle, considering his first attempt at the task had been so clumsy, she had closed her eyes and held her breath, certain he would chop off his fine leather boot, and his foot with it, before he managed to sink the ax into a log.

But Ben Watson was a patient teacher and Adam an amazingly quick learner. Now, but a fortnight later, with the blisters on his long, elegant fingers nicely calloused over, he made the task look as easy as . . . as shelling peas.

As usual, he wore one of the cream-colored linen shirts he had brought with him in his saddlebag, and beneath the thin fabric, a wealth of sinewy muscles rippled across his strong back. How a man who had spent most of his adult life with his knees beneath a card table had developed such an impressive set of muscles was a mystery—as much a mystery as where a common gambler had acquired such finely crafted shirts. But then, Fiona found everything about Adam Cresswell completely baffling.

"God willing we will make a farmer of him yet, Mistress, if the teaching of him don't wear me to a shadow first." Ben Watson looked up from the tack he was mending and regarded his pupil with weary satisfaction. "I swear the lad can learn a thing faster'n I can tell it. And him not knowing a rake from a hoe the day ye hired him."

"He is a clever one all right," Fiona agreed. She had never before dealt with a mind as quick and as sharp as Adam's. Not even her ne'er-do well half brother could hold a candle to this stranger from London. The mental challenge he offered excited her more than she cared to admit.

But Adam was much more than just clever; he was also uncommonly courteous and thoughtful—and exceedingly good company as well. She looked forward eagerly to their nightly discussions at the supper table. Just last evening she had asked him to describe London Town, then sat back and listened while the wondrous words flowed from his mouth like water over a mill wheel.

As if by magic, he had transported her to the great city she had heard so much about—his description so vivid, she could literally smell the oily black soot of a thousand smokestacks and hear the rumble of carriage wheels over cobblestone streets.

She had closed her eyes and imagined herself craning her neck to watch the flying acrobats at Astley's Circus, peeking through the doors of an elegant shop on Bond Street, strolling down a lantern-lit path in the fairyland called Vauxhall Gardens. For the first time, she had begun to understand the lure the wondrous city had held for a simple farmer like Buckley, and in some strange way her bitterness over his senseless death had lessened.

She finished shelling the last of her pea pods, and raised her head to find Adam had ceased his chopping and stood watching her with his beautiful, silvery eyes. She smiled at him and he grinned back—a curious lopsided grin that made funny little crinkles at the sides of his eyes. To her surprise, something warm and liquid pooled deep inside her, as if some intensely feminine part of her had unaccountably begun to melt.

She sucked in her breath and closed her eyes, willing the strange sensation to pass. When she opened them again, Adam had turned away, but Ben was regarding her with a look as solemn as that of the old barn owl perched on the rafter above them. "Ye like the Londoner, don't ye, Mistress?" he said in the quiet voice that warned her he found the idea worrisome.

Fiona pulled herself together. "Of course I like him," she said more curtly than she had intended. "And confess it, so do you. Who could not? My new framhand is a very charming fellow."

She knew what troubled Ben. The dear old soul was afraid she would lose her head over the fascinating stranger—afraid the Derry blood in her veins would betray her as it had every other woman in her family.

She could have told him that despite a momentary lapse, her head was safely on her shoulders. There was not a man on earth, including Adam Cresswell, who could tempt her into his bed. She was not and never would be the kind of woman to enjoy such dalliance.

Not that she thought Adam had meant to seduce her with his boyishly appealing grin. It was simply not in his nature. He was, in fact, so soft-spoken and mannerly, she couldn't believe she had ever imagined a sinister quality in his dark, male beauty.

Not once in the fortnight he had been at Larkspur Farm had she caught him looking at her with the hot, lust-filled eyes with which other men had looked at her since her body had changed from that of a child to a woman. Not once had she felt the revulsion toward him that other men aroused in her.

Instinct told her Adam Cresswell was a man with firm control over his emotions. For that reason, she trusted him. For that reason she dared hope she had finally found a friend whose keen wit and clever imagination were more than a match for her own. She had never before realized how lonely she had been for such a friend.

"Ye be two of a kind, ye and young Adam," Ben declared as if the thought had just occurred to him. "Quick and bright as two glow flies ye be—with yer fine way of talking together and yer happy laughter. In all the years I been knowing ye, Mistress, I never heard ye laugh the way ye've done since *he* come to Larkspur Farm."

Ben's eyes narrowed to slits, and the wrinkles in his leathery face seemed more pronounced than usual. "Just don't come to like him too much."

Fiona felt a sudden chill creep down her spine. "Why do

you say that, Ben?" she asked in a strangled voice, though she already halfway knew the answer to her question.

"Think on it," he said, lowering his gaze as if loath to meet hers. "Sooner or later all God's creatures seek their own kind. How long will a fellow what's used to such a grand place as London Town be content chopping wood and mending fences on a farm in Exmoor?"

Something didn't ring true. Adam felt certain he had heard the owner of the Black Boar Inn correctly. Yet, with every day that passed, he found it more difficult to picture Fiona Haines as a woman with a lurid past. Nor, for that matter, could he picture the charming, quick-witted woman with whom he'd had so many fascinating conversations in the past two weeks as the wife of a raw-boned, slow-witted farmer like Buckley Haines.

Still she played her part to perfection. With her glorious flame-colored hair tightly braided in a coronet and her graceful body encased in a shapeless black gown, she looked every inch the proper farmer's widow. Furthermore, though he often caught her watching him, as she had promised she would, he could see no hint of flirtation in her steady gaze.

She was, in fact, ridiculously straitlaced. Take this morning for instance. He had simply returned her smile with one of his own—a perfectly innocent gesture on his part. But for one brief instant, when they'd stared into each other's eyes, a breathtaking flash of awareness had leapt between them that left his heart pounding and his blood racing through his veins.

From the shock he'd seen on her face, he suspected the same bolt of lightning had struck her. Any other woman he knew would have found that sufficient reason to indulge in a bit of discreet flirtation. Fiona had instantly raised her defenses and retreated behind an impenetrable wall of shyness. But why, he asked himself, should a widow, much less one with a sordid reputation, act like a callow spinster terrified of her own sensuality?

Grimly, he drew a bucket of water from the well, washed his face and hands, and prepared to confront the annoying woman at the evening meal, knowing full well the indifferent reception he would receive. Had it really been but twenty-four hours ago she had listened with shining eyes and sweetly parted lips to his dissertation on the delights of London?

The door to the cottage stood open and he heard Fiona's and Ben's voices raised in what sounded like an argument. He stopped in his tracks, too curious to resist eavesdropping.

"Nothing you can say will dissuade me, Ben. I have made up my mind. I am leaving tomorrow morning to fetch my grandmother. And high time too. She is much too old to be living alone in one of the most isolated parts of the moors."

"Is that wise, Mistress? Think how tongues will wag if ye bring her into Buckley's house now that he be dead and gone. All as lives hereabouts knowed there was bad blood between them. I meself heard him curse her for the witch she be and warn her to never set foot on Larkspur Farm."

"I honored my husband's wishes while he lived. I owed him that much and more for marrying me in spite of the shame I brought him. But Buckley is gone; the farm is mine, and I care not a whit what the evil-tongued gossips say about me."

"But the Witch of Exmoor, Mistress! Yer neighbors will live in fear of the old woman casting a spell on them."

Adam chuckled to himself. He knew Fiona was absurdly superstitious. More than once he'd seen her toss a pinch of salt over her shoulder for good luck or go out of her way to keep from walking beneath a ladder. But to imply her grandmother was a practicing witch! That was not only ridiculous, but dangerous as well.

He fully expected Fiona to put Ben in his place. To his surprise she merely replied, "Maybe if the fools are terrified enough of my grandmother, they will stop sending their half-wit sons to court me so they can get their greedy hands on my property."

Adam shook his head in disbelief. The relationship between employer and employee was certainly different in Exmoor than it was in London or Kent, where his family's principal estate was located. He couldn't imagine any person in the employ of the Cresswells daring to speak as frankly to a member of his family as Ben Watson had just spoken to the widow.

He heard a clatter of dishes, as if Fiona were taking out her frustration over the remarkable conversation on the housewares. "And what of you, Ben?" Anger sharpened her voice. "Are you like all the others—willing to ask my grandmother for herbs to cure what ails you, then skittering away like a scared rabbit for fear she will give you the evil eye?"

"I'll not say nay, Mistress. For I fear her same as any other proper Christian. But I be trusting ye'll put in a good word fer me."

Something rubbed against Adam's leg, and he glanced down into the worshipful eyes of his ever-present shadow. "Shhh, Caesar," he whispered, patting the dog's mammoth black head. "I'll be sorely embarrassed if you call attention to my unconscionable snooping."

"But how will ye fetch the witch, Mistress?" he heard Ben continue, sounding very much like a man resigned to his fate. "Ye cannot ride that far into the moors alone, and me bones is too old to fit comfortable in a saddle nowadays."

"I shall take Caesar with me."

"Will ye now? And the first time ye turned yer head, the silly bugger would hie himself back here to drool at the Londoner's feet. 'Tis a fact, and well ye know it, the fickle hound has abandoned ye for another. So, Mistress, if ye must do this thing, ye'll have to take young Adam with ye."

"And spend all my time worrying about keeping the useless townee from sinking into one of the bogs that lie between here and Blackrock Tor? No thank you."

Adam had heard enough. A "useless townee" was he! He had spent enough time around these two provincials to recognize he had just been dealt the supreme insult. Flexing fingers still stiff from hours of grasping an ax handle, he vowed that one way or another he would see Fiona Haines eat her words before he took his leave of her . . . and Exmoor.

He scraped the mud off his boots on the burlap sacking she kept on her porch for that purpose. Then poking his head in the door, he greeted the two squabblers with an affability he was far from feeling. "Good evening, Mistress Haines. And a pleasant evening to you too, Ben."

He paused, chuckling to himself at the furtive glance exchanged between them. "By any chance," he asked innocently, "was that my name I just heard mentioned?"

Adam was awakened from a sound sleep by the touch of a hand on his shoulder. Momentarily disoriented, he thought the figure bending over him was his trusty batman. "What's wrong?" he demanded. "Are we under attack?"

"Nay, laddie. Never fear, ye're not back to warring in some foreign land, but safe here in Exmoor."

"Ben? What the devil are you doing prowling about in the dark of night?"

"It so happens 'tis near dawn, and there's things I needs to say to ye afore ye go riding off with the mistress."

Adam sat up in bed, instantly awake. "What sort of 'things'?" he asked warily. Fiona had made it clear she did not want him to accompany her, which was understandable. No proper lady of his acquaintance would consider traveling alone with a man not of her family. She had only given in to Ben because he had insisted the trip was too dangerous for her to attempt alone.

"Things as needs be said by an old man to a young one regards a woman," Ben declared in the same obstinate tone of voice with which he had addressed Fiona the previous evening. "My eyes may be a bit dimmer than they once was, but not so dim I can't see the way ye looks at Mistress when ye thinks she don't notice."

Adam felt his hackles rise. "Devil take it, you old coot, if you are inferring what I think you are, I'll have you know I have never taken liberties with any woman unless she invited me to do so. I am not about to make an exception of your precious mistress."

"Never said ye was, Londoner. But a smart city fellow such as ye be must look mighty tempting to a country innocent what's never known but one man—and him, God bless him, a bit of a slow top."

"The Widow Haines? A country innocent?" Adam heard the skepticism in his own voice.

"Aye. I can see ye've been told the shame of her past. Probably by that scurvy old talebearer, Hiram Blodgett. 'Tis the sort of thing he'd enjoy telling. But she be a good, kindhearted woman, for all she be a Derry."

The first gray light of dawn had crept through the window of Adam's attic bedchamber, and he could see the genuine worry etched on Ben's face. "Perhaps you had better tell me your version of Mistress Fiona's past," he said, rising from his bed to pull on the breeches he had tossed across a chair the night before. "For I admit the innkeeper's words aroused my curiosity. To begin with what, pray tell, is a 'Derry'?"

"The name she carried afore she married—and a name black with shame it was, with every Derry woman as far back as any could remember dangling after one scoundrel or another and left to raise her baseborn babe alone."

Adam stared dumbfounded at the frail old man hovering in the shadows beside his bed. "Are you saying this 'shame' the innkeeper referred to is none of Mistress Fiona's own making, but simply that she was born on the wrong side of the blanket."

"Aye." Ben nodded solemnly. " 'Tis said, and I believe it, the ring young Buckley put on her finger were the first wedding ring any Derry woman had ever worn. 'Twas her sixteenth birthday the day she stood up with him at the altar—and a wild, half-starved moorland creature she were too.

"Not a soul hereabouts, meself included, but thought the lad had lost his buttons for sure. But she turned out to be as fine a wife as any man ever had. Truth be, the poor little mite were so grateful to Buckley for marrying her, he could do no wrong in her eyes. Never once in the six years they was married did I hear her complain when the foolish lad drank too much ale or lost her egg money in a card game at the Black Boar Inn."

Adam wrestled briefly with the idea that something this simple could not possibly explain the mystery of the Widow Haines's lurid past. But Ben Watson's telling of it was much too matter-of-fact to be anything but the truth.

He thought of Fiona as he had first seen her. With her glorious mane of hair and her luminous gold-flecked eyes, she had seemed more like one of the fey creatures in an Irish folk tale than a living, breathing woman. For one brief moment, a part of him rejoiced that such exquisite beauty was not simply a mask that hid a coarse and common nature, as he had so often discovered in other women he'd known.

But another baser, more selfish part felt a keen disappointment that he would never taste the sensual pleasures her lithe young body promised. For his code of honor forbade his seducing a virtuous woman—particularly one who had survived the shame and ostracism Fiona must have known before the farmer came to her rescue.

Ben Watson shifted from one foot to the other, obviously uneasy with the task he had set himself. Adam pulled on his socks and boots, then stood up, to tower over the older man. "The point of all this is, I take it, that you want me to promise I shall do nothing to tempt your mistress to abandon the respectability that means so much to her."

"Aye, Londoner. 'Twould be a cruel thing to do when chances are ye'll soon tire of Exmoor and all that be in it."

If any other man had demanded such a promise from him, Adam would have promptly willed him to perdition. But there was something very touching about Ben's unswerving loyalty to his beloved mistress. That, combined with a new wave of guilt over his part in Buckley Haines's death made Adam decide to humor the old fellow.

"Very well," he said solemnly. "If it will ease your mind, I promise I will make no effort to seduce the lovely Widow Haines."

"I know'd ye would, lad." Ben smiled. "Ye be a stranger to me and a Londoner to boot. But there be a look about ye told me ye're not the kind of fellow needs to prove his manhood by bedding every woman comes his way, as some I knows does."

Before Adam could comment on this amazing analysis of his character, a noise from the kitchen below warned that Fiona was up and busy preparing breakfast. Ben instantly sprang into action. "I'll be on me way," he declared, shuffling toward the door as fast as his legs could carry him. "I'd not want Mistress to know about our little talk."

He stopped in midshuffle and turned to face Adam. "One more thing ye should know, laddie. Mistress told ye she planned to fetch her gram to come live here at Larkspur Farm. What she didn't tell ye is Creenagh Derry be a witch. Could turn ye into a toad or a hooty owl quicker'n ye could blink if she took a mind to. Whatever ye do, don't look the evil old besom in the eye. She can't cast a spell on ye less ye do."

With that astonishing bit of information duly imparted, Ben Watson removed himself from the chamber and closed the door behind him.

* * *

They set off across the open moors shortly after dawn, Fiona in the lead, Adam behind her on the pony he had ridden up from the Black Boar Inn, Caesar loping along beside him.

Fiona was dressed in men's breeches, a homespun shirt, a short linsey-woolsey jacket, and sturdy boots. With her hair tucked up beneath a soft-brimmed cap, she could have passed for a young boy until one took a closer look at how the jacket curved over her softly rounded breasts and the breeches molded her womanly hips. Adam had never before seen a woman dressed in such a fashion, nor one who rode astride. He found it oddly provocative.

· But then everything Fiona had done in the last hour had set his senses reeling. He'd watched her move about the kitchen in that graceful way of hers, setting out the usual bowls of porridge, slicing thick slabs of bread and cheese to carry with them on their journey—and felt his body tighten with desire. It was as if the very act of promising he would never lay hands on her had sharpened his sensual awareness of the lady tenfold.

He had never been a man to let his emotions rule him, and he told himself that once they were under way, he would find things to fill his thoughts other than a frustrating longing for a woman he could never have. He lied. With every mile that carried the two of them farther onto the vast, lonely moor where seemingly no other living being existed, the ache inside him intensified. All nature seemed dedicated to tempt him beyond his limits.

Now, with the sky above them a bright, cloudless blue, and a soft breeze carrying the tantalizing scent of the heather blooming around them, he faced the fact that his desire for Fiona went much deeper than a mere fascination with a beautiful woman. Everything he had learned about her difficult past and the courage with which she had endured it had only strengthened his admiration for her.

It was plain to see the only solution to his dilemma was to settle his affairs with the widow and return to London before the temptation she offered made him forget his promise and betray his honor. Part of him would be relieved to put such temptation behind him; another part would miss the challenge of Fiona's quick mind and the undeniable satisfaction he derived from the hard physical labor that working as her farmhand entailed. For the first time since returning from Spain, he had fallen in bed each night so exhausted he had slept deeply and peacefully without the nightmares that had plagued him in London.

They had ridden at a slow trot for close to an hour on a barely discernible trail when Fiona raised her hand to call a halt. "Stay directly behind me from here on," she called over her shoulder. "There is a boggy patch of moor up ahead and only one way through it. Stray a few feet to the right or left and you will find yourself in serious trouble."

She tucked a stray lock of flame-colored hair behind her ear. "Give your mount his head," she continued. "Exmoor ponies have an uncanny sense of self-survival on the moors."

Alert to the danger she described, Adam reined in his wandering thoughts and concentrated on following her instructions. The heather was sparser now, and here and there he spied tufts of brown, yellow-tipped grass standing in shallow pools of slate-colored water. He suspected these marked the treacherous moorland bogs of which she spoke.

Another mile or two and she raised her hand, again signaling him to ride close behind her. "That is the Devil's Bog ahead," she said, pointing to a great black hole off to their right.

An evil, sulphurous odor assaulted Adam's nostrils and as they drew nearer to the dark morass, he could see it bubbled like a gigantic witches' cauldron. Surrounding it, like a hideous parody of a garden, was a collection of gray malformed plants that only the denizens of Hell would seek to propagate.

A buzzard circled overhead as if its intended victim had just disappeared beneath the seething mass, and Adam shuddered, remembering the birds of prey that had circled above the body-strewn battlefields of the Spanish Plain.

Once again the moors had surprised him. In the midst of wild, breathtaking beauty lay this macabre obscenity of nature. For no reason he could name, Ben's warning about Creenagh Derry flashed through his mind. Why, he wondered, would any human being choose to live in this godforsaken part of the moors? And how could it be possible that such a one was grandmother to the lovely woman riding ahead of him? He shuddered, at once dreading his meeting with the woman Ben had called the Witch of Exmoor, yet for some inexplicable reason, strangely fascinated by the idea.

"There are bogs ahead, but none so dreadful as this," Fiona said. She had watched the look of horror cross Adam's face at the sight of the Devil's Bog, and remembering her own reaction the first time she had visited the evil place, gave him what she hoped was a reassuring smile. "Just a mile or two more of this treacherous lowland, then we shall come to higher, safer ground."

The quicker, the better, as far as she was concerned. She disliked the look of the sky; the vivid blue of a few moments ago had subtly faded to a dusky pewter, and ominous clouds rimmed the horizon. The breeze had changed too, its warmth suddenly chilled by moisture. The weather on the moors could deteriorate without warning, and the last thing she wanted was to be fog-bound in some lonely spot with a man who made every rational thought in her head scatter like leaves in a high wind.

Less than a quarter mile away, she could see the gentle hills she sought and urged her pony forward more recklessly than she would normally do in this boggy area. He snorted in protest at her heavy hand, and she eased off, bowing to the moorland animal's instinctive wisdom in this land his ancestors had roamed millenniums before the first human had set foot on it.

Her own instincts dulled by her acute awareness of the man riding close behind her, she was unprepared for the Exmoor sheep and lamb that suddenly rose up from where they lay in a stand of gorse to bolt across the trail almost beneath her pony's feet. Caesar barked his indignation and she struggled to keep her startled mount from straying off the narrow trail. Behind her, Adam cursed as he brought his own animal under control.

Then without warning, she found herself living her own worst nightmare. As she watched, a dense shroud of swirling mist rose from the marshy fens surrounding the moorland track, blotting out everything in sight and trapping Adam and her in a chilly white cocoon from which they dare not venture.

Chapter Four

Adam couldn't believe his eyes. One minute Fiona and he were riding beneath a clear sky with an unobstructed view of the distant horizon; the next, they were enveloped in an eerie white mist, as thick and opaque as custard pudding, and could see no farther than the tips of their ponies' noses.

Fiona raised her hand in warning, and brought her mount to an abrupt halt. "I am afraid we must stop here. I cannot see the trail and there are treacherous bogs ahead."

Adam reined in his pony close behind her. "Incredible! I have never seen anything like it. There was no warning whatsoever. Does the fog always rise so rapidly off the moors?"

"Always." Frustration sharpened her voice. "The hills where my grandmother lives are so close, but I dare not try to reach them until the fog lifts."

Adam found no reason to dispute her judgment. He had made his way through fogs as dense as this in the Scottish Highlands. But there the trails had been clearly marked and bordered by rocks and trees and fragrant blooming heather— not putrid quagmires capable of sucking a rider and his mount into their evil, glutinous depths.

He noted the rigid set of Fiona's slender shoulders, and wondered why she should find this delay in her plans so disturbing. Surely they were safe enough as long as they stayed where they were. "Have you any idea how long it will be before the fog lifts?" he asked, thinking she must be afraid they could be trapped here indefinitely.

"If it were winter, it could last for days. This time of year it is more a matter of hours, even minutes—whenever a breeze comes up or the sun grows a trifle warmer."

So, it wasn't the length of the delay that worried her. Then what? A sudden thought occurred to him. Surely she didn't imagine he would try to ravish her simply because they were temporarily fogbound. His curiosity piqued, he urged his pony forward a step or two and watched her flinch when his leg brushed hers. By God, that was it! The little prude feared for her virtue. This was even more insulting than the grilling he had been subjected to by Ben. Did these provincials automatically assume all men from London were unconscionable rakes?

Out of sheer orneriness he leaned forward in the saddle and brought his face close to hers. "As long as fate has offered us this opportunity to be alone together, I, for one, think we should make good use of it. What say you, Mistress Haines?"

Her amber eyes widened like those of a doe startled by a hunter's rifle. "Wha . . . what do you mean by that, Mr. Cresswell?"

"Why simply that from what I have seen of your relationship with Ben, the usual barriers between employer and employee don't exist here in Exmoor—at least not on Larkspur Farm. If I too am to become part of your little family we should get to know each other better. What more propitious time to do so than now?"

He bestowed his most seductive smile on the silly chit—the one his mistress had once claimed turned her into "a helpless mass of seething passion" and sidled even closer.

She held her ground, but even in the mist he could see the color blanch from her face. "H . . . how do you propose we should go about this getting to know each other, Mr. Cresswell?"

Devil take it, she was terrified. Much as she deserved it, he couldn't bring himself to tease her further. He cocked his head as if contemplating her question. "To begin with, ma'am, it occurs to me that while you have asked me questions about my life before the war, I have never had an opportunity to ask you the questions that puzzle me."

"What could a man like you find puzzling about me?"

"Any number of things, ma'am. For one, your manner of speech. Surely you realize how different it is from that of Ben Watson or the owner of the Black Boar Inn—the only other residents of Exmoor with whom I have spoken. How is it that

you, alone, speak the refined English one might expect of a
student of the classics."

She visibly relaxed, as if greatly relieved by his question.
He'd lay odds she had expected him to start prying into her
past. He gritted his teeth; now she'd judged him a busybody as
well as a defiler of women.

"I suppose I am a 'student of the classics' in a manner of
speaking," she said with the first smile he had glimpsed in the
two hours they had ridden together. "I had no education whatsoever until I reached sixteen." Adam remembered Ben's description of her as a "wild, half-starved moorland creature"
when Buckley Haines married her—a pcture he found impossible to equate with the beautiful, soft-spoken woman who was
currently his employer.

"Then," she continued, "a new vicar came to the village—a
wonderfully kind old man who took pity on me and offered to
teach me to read and write. The previous vicar had taught my
half brother, Liam, but he didn't believe in educating women.

"All my life I'd had so many thoughts and feelings inside
me and no way of expressing myself. In truth, I could barely
make myself understood." She stared into the fog, as if envi-
sioning the young girl she had been then. "But once I heard the
fine way Vicar Edelson had of telling a thing, I vowed I'd
learn everything he could teach me so that one day I could say
all the things I longed to say."

"And so you did, and in an unbelievably short time," Adam
said, filled with admiration for her courage and determination.

"Aye, I did, but only because Vicar Edelson was as patient
as Job. I shall never know how he put up with me that first
year. He had only four books, you see: the Holy Bible, the
Iliad and the *Odyssey*, and the complete works of Mr Shakespeare. They were very difficult primers for a young girl as ignorant as I was. But each time we came to a word I had never
heard before, the vicar would explain what it meant and make
me repeat it over and over until it was lodged in my brain. Little by little, between the reading and listening to him talk, I
learned what you call my 'refined English.' "

Her smile held a tinge of sadness. "The only trouble was,
except for the vicar, and Liam on the rare occasions when he
was about, there was no one on whom I could practice my

wonderful new vocabulary. Everyone else thought it a ridiculous waste of time—my husband included. Not that Buckley ridiculed me like the others did for trying to talk above myself. There was not a mean bone in his body, and he could see it was important to me."

She shook her head, as if dispelling a painful memory. "There were times when even I wondered if the goal I had set myself was worth the effort it took to reach it. But eventually I managed to read all four books from cover to cover."

Adam stared at her in amazement. "Never say those are the only books you have ever read."

"The only ones, and I treasure them because Vicar Edelson gave them into my keeping when his eyesight became so dim he could no longer read. But I am hoping one day soon the farm will yield enough money so I can travel to Plymouth Town to buy other books. Ben has already put up a shelf in my bedchamber to hold them when I do."

Adam thought of the magnificent family library he had always had at his disposal, and the tutors his father had hired to prepare Ethan and him to study at Eton and Oxford—all of which he had merely taken for granted.

He consoled himself with the knowledge that he hadn't wasted his opportunities, as Ethan had. He had been a conscientious student; one of his professors had even gone so far as to call him a brilliant one. But he found himself wondering just how brilliant he would have been if he'd had to overcome the kind of handicaps Fiona had faced.

"I wish I could show you Hatchard's Bookstore in London with its floor-to-ceiling shelves of every kind of book ever written," he said. "Or better yet, Hookum's Library or The Leadenhall where but for a few pence you could borrow any book your heart desired."

Fiona searched his face with obvious skepticism. "Surely you exaggerate. I find it difficult to believe such places really exist."

"They exist all right."

"Anyone in London can buy books or take them out on loan as they choose?"

"Anyone at all," Adam said, though he knew he was stretching the truth. "Anyone" was necessarily limited to the aristocracy or members of the wealthy merchant class, most of whom dwelt in the city's fashionable West End. Had the great un-washed multitudes living out their miserable lives in such places as St. Giles or Shoreditch or Seven Dials developed a taste for literature, they would never have been allowed past the doors of such renowned establishments.

"Then London must truly be the most marvelous city in all the world," Fiona declared fervently. "How on earth could you bear to leave it?"

No sooner had the words left her mouth, than her eyes widened in horror. "Good heavens, what a cruel thing to say." She leaned toward him, her face a picture of contrition. "Please forgive me for my thoughtlessness."

Forgive her? For what, Adam wondered, too mesmerized by her nearness to think logically. Then he remembered the bouncer he had told her about having to leave London be-cause of his addiction to gambling. He stared into the swirling white mist surrounding them, too stricken with guilt to look her in the face.

"Please, Mr. Cresswell . . . Adam. I am so very sorry to have caused you pain. I never, till this moment, realized all that you had sacrificed to regain your self-esteem. I think you are the most courageous man I have ever known."

Courageous? Adam groaned. Despicable would be a more apt description of his present conduct. Out of the corner of his eye he saw a tear slip down her cheek. Good Lord, she was crying for him. Crying for a lying bastard who deserved her disgust, not her sympathy.

He turned his head and faced her squarely, determined to confess his sins then and there. But one look into her beautiful tear-misted eyes and he was lost.

He didn't intend to kiss her; it was the farthest thing from his mind. But her mouth looked so soft and warm and sweetly vulnerable, he promptly forgot his vow to resist the temptation she offered.

Yet, oddly enough, though he ached to feel the touch of her lips on his, it was not an ache born of the lust he had harbored for her the past fortnight—but rather a compelling need to pay homage to her compassion and courage and incredible opti-mism in the face of almost unbelievable odds. Twisting in the saddle, he reached across the narrow space between them to cup her chin in his fingers, while his lips sought hers with a gentleness bordering on reverence.

The last thing Fiona expected Adam to do at that moment was kiss her. He was, after all, a very gentlemanly fellow and she a recent widow. It was most improper. Furthermore, she had just made a remark so stupidly thoughtless he should, by rights, be very angry with her. Instead, his brief, feather-light kiss had been so profoundly tender, it had shaken her to the very core of her being.

"Forgive me, Mistress Haines, I should never have done that," he said, looking every bit as shocked as she felt. "I swear I do not know what came over me. I assure you I meant no disrespect, and I promise it will never happen again. I was just so moved by your tears, I momentarily forgot myself. No woman has ever cried for me before."

"I accept your apology; we shall forget it ever happened," Fiona lied. For, in truth, she felt certain she would remember till the day she died how it felt to be kissed by Adam Cresswell. Brief as the touch of his lips had been, it had brought home a bewildering truth. She might be immune to the raging passions that had led her mother and grandmother to lose their virtue to ne'er-do-well libertines, but tenderness was another thing entirely—and Adam Cresswell was a tender man. A lonely, deeply troubled man who had bravely faced his own weakness and exiled himself from all he held dear to overcome it. She could very easily make a fool of herself over such a man.

As if the Good Lord she had read about in Vicar Edelson's Bible sensed her dilemma and offered his heavenly assistance, she felt a breeze like the flutter of angel's wings fan her heated cheeks. As she watched, the dense, white mist around them eddied and swirled as if some giant celestial hand had reached down to give it a stir. Then, as quickly as it had descended upon them, the fog disappeared, revealing the rolling hills to be even closer than she had realized before the mist had obscured them.

"It appears our delay is over," she said, deeply thankful that the enforced intimacy she had shared with the handsome gambler had ended just in the nick of time.

Beside her, Adam shaded his eyes against the sudden brilliance of the sun and scanned the gradually rising slopes ahead of them. "Look! Do you see it?" He pointed toward a rocky promontory jutting out below the crest of the first hill. "A pony," he said with a smile. "An Exmoor."

Fiona looked where he directed. "But it cannot be," she gasped. "It is white. A strange silvery white."

"But an Exmoor nevertheless," Adam insisted, remembering the distinctive features of the Larkspur ponies that Ben had pointed out to him. "Even from a distance I recognize its wide forehead and the way its tail lies flat and low against its rear. Except for its color, it is identical to the ones we are riding."

He glanced at Fiona to find her gaze fixed on the pony, her eyes huge and startled. "But what do you suppose our sighting it signifies?" she asked.

He frowned. "Why should sighting an Exmoor pony on the moors signify anything unusual? From what Ben said, this has been home to herds of the beasties, as he calls them, since time began."

"But you don't understand. Everyone knows there is no such thing as a white Exmoor pony—except in ancient Celtic myths."

Adam couldn't help but smile at the idiocy of Fiona's statement. She may have managed to acquire a more cultured manner of speaking than the uneducated folk around her, but deep down inside she was still a simple country woman steeped in the age-old superstitions of the moors. "It appears 'everyone' is wrong, as we have living proof," he pointed out with irrefutable logic.

Fiona looked unconvinced.

"Think about it. If just one of us had seen it, I might agree the pony could be a figment of the imagination; it is admittedly an unusual color for an Exmoor. But I seriously doubt it is possible for two people to share the same hallucination."

He glanced again toward the hill and even as he watched, the white pony disappeared—but not in the usual manner one would expect of such a creature. For it neither galloped over the crest of the hill nor picked its way down off the promontory toward the patch of lush green grass below it. One second it was there, its silvery white coat glistening in the bright June sunshine; the next it was gone—disappearing as swiftly and mysteriously as the moorland mist had before it.

Adam blinked. "What the devil!"

Fiona shook her head. "I doubt the devil has a hand in this. I sensed no evil in the mystic pony." She studied Adam with solemn eyes. "Did you?"

He refused to dignify her ridiculous question with an answer. A mystic pony, for God's sake! Was Exmoor and its inhabitants still living in the Dark Ages?

"I shall describe what we have seen to my grandmother. If anyone can know its portent, she will," Fiona said, urging her pony forward on the narrow track.

Ah yes, her grandmother, the Witch of Exmoor. The old crone would undoubtedly have an interesting interpretation of the sighting and subsequent disappearance of the "mystic pony." Not that Adam had the slightest doubt but that the animal's strange vanishing act was merely a trick of light. It was a well-known fact that simultaneous sun and rain created a rainbow; who could tell what kind of phenomenon a combination of sun and mist might produce.

With greater misgivings than ever, he followed Fiona toward the hills where the witch had her lonely cottage—eager to get this tedious journey over and done with. Then, before he got any more involved with such bizarre things as witches and mystic ponies, he would settle affairs with the widow and return to London, where he belonged, with never a backward glance at this antediluvian land and all who dwelt within it.

As it turned out, the Witch of Exmoor didn't live in a cottage, but in a cave, the entrance of which opened off a grassy plateau perched halfway up a rock-strewn hill that Fiona identified as Black Rock Tor. A sledge cart, similar to the one in the Larkspur Farm stable, stood beside the entrance to the cave and beyond it, a pony grazed on the lush grass covering the plateau. But the old woman was nowhere in sight.

"My grandmother is out gathering herbs, no doubt. Spring is the best time of year for it," Fiona said, after she had searched the cave and found it empty.

She settled herself on one of the flat rocks that stood near the entrance and folded her hands in her lap. "But she will soon return. I would not be the least bit surprised if she has been expecting me. She has an uncanny sense where I am concerned. She often knows what I am going to do even before I am certain of it myself. I found her ability to read my thoughts most disconcerting when I was a young girl."

"I should imagine so." Adam smiled, remembering how he had hated it when his Aunt Tansy had found him out when he was up to his usual mischief as a lad.

"Did you live with your grandmother when you were a child?" Adam asked, dismounting and looping his pony's reins around a small bush. Fiona had left hers untethered. Apparently she trusted the animal to stay nearby.

She raised an eyebrow, as if to imply he was being a little too inquisitive. "Yes. My mother died giving me birth."

"Did you live in this cave then?"

Up went the eyebrow again. "No," she said stiffly, "though I would have preferred it over the cottage where we did live. The roof of the cave doesn't leak and except in a winter as cold as this last one, it is relatively warm and dry.

"My grandmother has lived here for four years. She enjoys the beauty and the solitude." Fiona gave a sweep of her arm to encompass the magnificent view of the moors below and the hills above. "But she is no longer young, and it is rumored we are in for another winter as severe as this last one. I am determined to take her back to the farm, no matter how much she may protest."

"Are ye now, me girl? And how will ye go about it if I say ye nay." Adam gave a start at the sound of the female voice behind him and the low, menacing growl emanating from the dog at his feet. The speaker had approached so silently, he had been unaware of her presence. But Caesar had seen her and apparently didn't like what he saw.

"Down lad," Adam commanded and wheeled around, expecting to find a toothless old hag, sister to those portrayed in William Shakespeare's play, *Macbeth*.

Creenagh Derry was a far cry from Shakespeare's, or Adam's idea of a witch. She was tall—a good three or four inches taller than Fiona, but every bit as slender. Her hair was a rich sable brown with but one streak of white over her left temple, and hung in lustrous waves to her waist, as Fiona's had the first day he had seen her.

But it was her amazingly youthful face that surprised him most. Her skin was as clear and unlined as that of a young girl, her eyes the same exotic almond shape as Fiona's, but darker and more inscrutable. Logic told him the woman had to have fifty or more years on her plate, but in her own way, Creenagh Derry was every bit as beautiful as her granddaughter and could easily pass as Fiona's older sister.

He watched Fiona rise from the boulder on which she had been sitting and regard her grandmother with a look that plainly said she would suffer no opposition to her plan. "It will do you no good to be difficult, Creenagh. I have come to fetch you to Larkspur Farm, and fetch you I will. You are long past the age when you should be living alone on the moors."

"Ha! That is for me to decide, missy, and the day's not yet come when I take orders from ye or anyone else."

"Now, Creenagh, you know it is for the best." Fiona cast a desperate glance in Adam's direction. "I have brought my new farmhand to help move you and your possessions."

"Have ye now." The Witch of Exmoor raked Adam from head to toe with a fulminating look he assumed was designed to reduce him to a state of absolute terror. He had to hand it to the old girl; she could teach Edmund Kean a thing or two about drama. He found this eccentric cave dweller almost as fascinating as her lovely granddaughter.

Fiona cringed as her grandmother turned her infamous "evil eye" on Adam. Any other man she knew would have cowered in terror. To her surprise, Adam responded with that same lopsided grin that had had such a devastating effect on her.

It obviously took Creenagh by surprise as well. "Does this cheeky farmhand have a name?" she sputtered, an odd light in her tawny eyes.

Adam's grin widened and he bowed from the waist. "Adam Cresswell at your service, ma'am."

"He has the sound of a Londoner and the manner as well." Creenagh's eyes narrowed. "I be wondering what ye had in mind, hiring such a one as this for yer farmhand, missy."

Fiona felt a flush of heat flood her cheeks when she realized what her grandmother was intimating. "I hired Adam for a good day's work, which so far he has provided, thanks to Ben Watson's teachings."

"Ben Watson! That old fool couldn't teach a duck to quack."

"On the contrary, ma'am, Ben has proved an excellent instructor on the rudiments of farming," Adam protested. "You may judge how apt a student I am when we return to Larkspur Farm. Which, by the way, is something I suggest we do while the day is yet young. It is a good two-hour trip at best and could be considerably longer if we are caught in another moorland mist."

Just like that, her "cheeky farmhand" took control of the situation. The next thing Fiona knew, he had Creenagh by the arm and was urging her toward the cave with the admonition that she had best begin packing what she planned to take with her so he could load it in the sledge cart.

As Fiona expected, her grandmother took umbrage at his high-handed ways. "How dare ye lay a hand on me without me leave, ye young rascal."

Adam's laugh echoed through the hills. "What will you do, ma'am? Turn me into a toad or a hooty owl as Ben warned?"

"I told ye the man were a fool," Creenagh snapped. But the sparkle in her eyes belied her sharp tone of voice—and with a meekness Fiona found it hard to credit, her irascible grandmother submitted to the handsome Londoner's will.

Chapter Five

Fiona had spent the entire morning scrubbing out the former tackroom to make it ready for Creenagh's precious dried herbs. Ben had let her know in no-uncertain terms what he thought of turning what had heretofore been his private domain into a place for "the witch to mix her evil brews." But Fiona had remained firm and finally convinced him there was no other suitable place to store the yarrow and the mugwort, the betony and verbena, selago and nettles and dozens of other herbs Creenagh had brought with her in the sledge cart.

Though to be perfectly honest, it had been Adam who had done the final convincing by simply transferring the bridles and saddles, as well as Ben's workbench to an empty stall at the back of the stable. In no time at all, he had driven pegs into the wall to hold the bridles, draped the saddles over sawhorses, and spread the strips of leather with which Ben was creating new reins onto the newly placed workbench.

Once again, he had taken things out of her hands and quietly and efficiently accomplished what she had set out to do. This "taking over" was getting to be a habit with her new farmhand—one she knew she should curtail—and so she would if he ever seriously overstepped his bounds. But right now it was rather pleasant to let someone else handle things for a change.

Buckley had been a hard worker, but the only decision he had made in his entire life was to marry her. From then on, he had happily relinquished all responsibility, including the management of Larkspur Farm.

"Ye've a bossy rascal on yer hands, me girl," Creenagh remarked as Fiona and she sat outside in the sun enjoying a cup of tea once the herb room was in order.

Fiona didn't need to ask to whom her grandmother was referring. "Adam is a great help to both Ben and me," she declared, though why she should feel the need to defend him, she couldn't say.

Creenagh smiled enigmatically. "Could be he's the one. He be a handsome-enough devil."

"What one?" Fiona asked impatiently. She was in no mood for one of her grandmother's obtuse observations.

"The man ye'll give yer heart to, o' course. Ye be a Derry, for all ye married that thickwit farmer. Sooner or later ye're bound to find yer grand passion, same as every Derry woman."

"Ah yes, but you have told me time and again the Derry women only fall in love with men of noble blood—and conscienceless rogues as well, if the men who seduced you and my mother are examples. But Adam Cresswell fails to fit that description on either count. He is not titled; he is, or was, a common gambler and a common foot soldier, and he is not the lest bit rakish. So, I am afraid he cannot be 'the one' you have been predicting would one day sweep me off my feet."

Fiona lifted her skirt an inch or two. "You will note my feet are firmly planted on the ground."

"Odd that. I could swear that handsome face with the devil-marked scar on one cheek were the one I seen in me dream the day ye turned twelve-year-old. But how could it be? No Derry woman has ever given her heart to a commoner—and surely ye would have seen a sign by now if he were the one meant for ye."

"A sign?" Fiona's heart skipped a beat. "What kind of sign?" she asked warily.

"Ye'll know it when ye see it, missy. For 'twill be a magical thing ye'd never thought to see and likely'll never see again."

An odd tension vibrated through Fiona. "Magical?" she repeated in a strangled voice.

"Aye, magical." Creenagh sighed deeply. "And likely 'twill be the same sign as were showed me when me own true love come riding up to me door on his fine white stallion. And the same sign as were shown every Derry woman before me as long as our kin have lived on the moors. Tell me true, girl, did ye see nothing as struck ye peculiar when ye and the Londoner crossed the moors yesterday?"

"Who, me? Good heavens no. Nothing the least bit peculiar. Nothing at all." Fiona sipped her tea in silence, careful to avoid looking her perceptive grandmother in the eye. But her hand shook when she placed the cup in its saucer, and a plethora of confusing thoughts raced through her mind.

For she could not ignore the fact that sighting a mystic white pony qualified as peculiar—much too peculiar to deny it could very well be the magical "sign" her grandmother spoke of.

But there was no possibility that a common gambler could boast of noble blood—unless Adam had some long-forgotten ancestor who had laid claim to a title.

But suppose he had such a long-lost relative, and suppose he proved to be as good and as honorable as he appeared. Did she really want to give her heart to the handsome Londoner?

Never, she told herself firmly. For as Ben had pointed out, a man like Adam Cresswell would never be content to call a farm in Exmoor his home or a woman of Exmoor his wife. And had she not lived all her life with the consequences of foolishly giving one's heart away? But a small voice deep inside her whispered it might not be her choice to make. For like it or not, the wild, tempestuous blood of the Derry women flowed in her veins—and as everyone knew, sooner or later blood would tell.

"Well, what do ye think now, laddie?" Ben Watson laid down the knife he was sharpening to watch Adam hard at work currying the pony he'd ridden across the moors the previous day.

"About what, Ben?"

"About sleepin' under the same roof as that Friday-faced witch, that be what. Don't know about ye, but it fair puts me back up, it does. I've half a mind to tell Mistress Fiona I be going to hire meself out to another farmer."

Adam paused, brush in hand. "Come now, Ben, you know you could never bring yourself to leave Larkspur Farm."

"Maybe not, but that don't mean I'll ever have a day's peace or a night's sleep long as that she-cat bides here. Didn't I tell ye she were a witch? Ye can see I told ye true now that ye've eyed her firsthand."

"On the contrary, I find Creenagh Derry an extraordinarily beautiful woman, especially considering her age. She is a little eccentric to be sure, but then I suppose anyone would be who had lived alone on the moors as long as she has."

"Lord luv us, have ye no more sense than God give a flea? O' course she be comely. O' course she looks to be twenty years, when all hereabouts knows she be older than sin. Be that the natural way of things? Can ye say that of any other woman ye knows? O' course ye can't. But Creenagh Derry be a witch and everyone knows witches and such don't grow old same as the rest of us."

The same "everyone" Adam assumed who had decreed there was no such animal as a white Exmoor pony.

Ben picked up the lethal-looking knife he had been sharpening and ran the edge across the whetstone yet again. "I just be hoping that spawn o' the devil don't put a hex on the hog we're about to butcher. 'Twould taint the meat for certain."

"We? You want me to help you butcher a hog?" Adam shook his head. "You have the wrong man in mind, Ben. I know nothing about butchering."

"Ye knew nothin' about splitting logs a sennight ago neither. But I'll stack ye up against the best in Devon County now. It all be a matter of learnin' and I'm an old hand at killing a hog and dressing it out."

Killing. After the carnage he had witnessed at Ciudad Rodrigo and Salamanca, the very word made Adam's knees go weak. Riding to the hunt had been his favorite pastime before the war; now he abhorred the idea of trapping and killing a helpless fox. But how could he explain such a sensitivity to a man who had never known the horrors of war—a man to whom butchering a hog was as normal a part of farming as planting a seed?

Because he could think of nothing else to say, he simply said, "I am sorry, Ben. I cannot do it."

"Sure ye can, lad. I'll not expect ye to do any of the butchering itself. Buckley never did. Just held the porker down whilst I tied his hooves together. Then after I'd slit his throat, Buckley hung him from a tree limb so's the blood could drain. I'll need no more from ye than that."

Blood. Adam had seen the soil of Spain run red with it. The blood of men and horses, dead and dying, had turned the sweltering plain into an earthly hell more horrendous than any sinner's afterlife he had heard described by a preacher. He had hoped to live the rest of his life without seeing another drop of blood. But now, as he watched Ben shuffle through the open door of the stable, knife in hand, he realized that unless he could come up with a good reason not to, he had no choice but to follow.

After five minutes or so of scrambling about in the muddy pen, while the pig squealed, Caesar barked and Ben shouted encouragement, Adam came to the conclusion that pig wrestling would never be one of his favorite pastimes.

But once he managed to get the chosen porker onto its back, the worst was over. Tying the hooves presented little problem, mainly because Ben had chosen one of the smaller pigs in the pen. As he had explained it, only the legs and haunches would be smoked, which meant the balance of the meat would have to be consumed in a relatively short time.

Adam stepped back and looked the other way when Ben slit the animal's throat. But the acrid, rusty smell he remembered so well from the battlefield instantly filled his nostrils and it was all he could do to keep from gagging.

"Come, lad, lift the blighter up," Ben commanded a few minutes later. Adam turned his head to find the ground around the dead hog awash in blood. Choking back the bile rising in his throat, he tossed the rope attached to the animal's hind legs over the tree limb, yanked the carcass off the ground, and tied off the rope. Quickly, he stepped back, but not quickly enough to keep the blood from dripping onto his boots.

He stared at the crimson splotches staining the black leather—remembering other boots in like condition. Remembering the bodies of his men scattered around him like so many wooden soldiers tossed to the nurseryroom floor by a careless child. Remembering the ghastly pallor of his second-in-command's face as his lifeblood drained from the hole in his chest.

A swirling black mist blinded his eyes and clouded his mind. With a groan, he lurched to brace himself against the wall of the barn before his legs gave out beneath him.

"Lord amighty, lad, what be wrong with ye. Ye're white as Mistress Fiona's window curtain." Ben's voice sounded faint and far away.

"Blood," Adam gasped, too benumbed to stop the words that tumbled from his mouth. "Hog or human, it all looks the same splattered on a man's boots. My lieutenant died in my arms at Salamanca. It was his blood on my boots that day."

He slid down the wall to sit with his back against it, his head on his knees. Ben squatted down beside him. "Lord luv us, ye should have told me. What an old fool I be, not to remember ye're fresh from the killing in that foreign land."

He patted Adams's arm. "Rest, lad, and gather yer wits. I'll draw ye a dipper of cool water from the well and fetch Mistress Fiona to look after ye."

"Good God no! The last thing I want is for *her* to see me like this."

"Ye've naught to be ashamed of, lad. I'll wager there's many a man what's seen the killing ye have would feel the same. Let me fetch the mistress; she'll know just what to do to bring ye round."

"No!" Adam struggled against the wave of nausea engulfing him. "Keep her away from me, you damned fool. There is nothing she can do—nothing anyone can do to convince me I should be alive while so many brave men I soldiered with are dead."

With her candle lighting the way, Fiona trudged down the shadowy hall to her bedchamber, pondering the unusual evening just past. To begin with, Adam had neither said a word nor eaten a morsel of the delicious fresh pork she had cooked for supper. He had just stared at his plate with something akin to horror, then excused himself and retired to his room in the attic.

Ben hadn't been himself either. She had never seen him look so hangdog. She had not wanted to embarrass him by questioning him in front of Creenagh, since it was no secret there was no love lost between them. But later in the evening, she had followed him onto the porch when, as usual, he sat on the steps and smoked his pipe.

"What is wrong, Ben? Did you and Adam quarrel?" she had asked when it became apparent he was not about to offer any explanation for the odd goings-on.

"No, Mistress."

"Then what is it? The two of you are acting very strange."

"It be my fault, Mistress, mine alone. Like he said, I'm an old fool."

"Adam called you that? But how unlike him. He is always so polite. Whatever did you do to anger him?"

"He weren't angry. Just sad. I never should've made him help me with the hog butchering." Ben took a puff on his pipe, and the bowl glowed red in the evening dusk. "His lieutenant died in his arms at a place called Sala . . ."

"Salamanca," Fiona prompted, remembering reading about the battle in the copy of the *London Times* delivered by the coach that came once a week to the Black Boar Inn.

"Aye, and the poor bloke bled on his boots, same as the porker."

"I see," Fiona said, though she was not at all certain she did. But she hadn't the heart to question Ben further.

Now, as she made her way to bed, she thought about her strange conversation with her elderly farmhand, and the pieces began to fall into place. Apparently Adam had been in the thick of the terrible battles she had read about—probably lost a good many of his comrades.

She remembered the description of the Peninsular War in the *Times* written by someone just returned from Spain. "A slaughter of men and beasts, the magnitude of which is beyond description." No wonder the bloody business of butchering a hog had brought it all back to a man who had been part of that slaughter.

Long after she had blown out her candle and settled into her bed, she lay staring into the dark, thinking of the man sleeping in the attic above her. She might not want to give him her heart, but she ached to comfort him. Still, how could anyone who had never known such horrors find the words to give peace of mind to someone who had?

She was just dozing off when the sound of someone crying out in anguish shattered the silence of the night. She sat up, heart pounding, ears alert, knowing instinctively who it was.

There it was again, this time unmistakably Adam's voice. "Take cover," he shouted. "The rifle fire is coming from that ridge ahead."

Dear God, he must be dreaming—reliving the horror of the battlefield. Without bothering with slippers or wrapper, she bolted out her chamber door and groped her way up the narrow stairwell to the attic room where he slept.

Ben was there before her, candle in hand, looking older and more withered than ever with nothing covering his skinny body but his woolen underdrawers. "The lad be having a bad time of it," he said, the candlelight reflecting the anxiety stamped on his weathered face.

Fiona nodded. "There is nothing for it but to wake him."

"Aye," a voice behind her agreed, and she suddenly realized Creenagh had followed her up the stairs. "But be careful how ye go about it, missy. A man's soul will fly out of his body fast as a bird on the wing ifen he be waked too suddenlike from a dream."

With Ben leading the way with the candle, the three of them tiptoed into the room where the man they sought thrashed about on his narrow bed, obviously in the throes of a hellish nightmare. Ben raised the lighted taper, and Fiona could see beads of moisture on Adam's brow. She touched his bare shoulder and found it, too, was slick with perspiration—and the thin sheet covering him was soaking wet.

"He will need fresh bedding," she declared. "You will find it in the bottom drawer of the chest in my bedchamber, Ben."

"Aye, Mistress. I'll just light the bedside candle for ye afore I go."

"I'll go with ye, old man," Creenagh said. "The Londoner will need more than dry bedclothes to cure what ails him. I'll make him a tea of maythen and rosemary. 'Twill bring him deep sleep the rest of the night and guard against evil dreams."

The look on Ben's face plainly said he didn't like the idea of the witch accompanying him, but with a great deal of muttering under his breath, he finally left the room with Creenagh trailing after him.

Fiona immediately returned to her efforts to wake the sleeper from his nightmare. Seating herself beside him on the bed, she again laid her hand on his shoulder. "Wake up, Adam," she said softly. "You are having a bad dream."

He rolled his head from side to side and mumbled something under his breath, but his eyes remained tightly closed. She watched him for a moment, struck by how much younger and more vulnerable he looked when asleep. With his hair a tousled black mop and his brow puckered in a frown, he looked more like a beautiful, troubled boy than the strong, take-command kind of man she had come to know.

She imagined his mother coming to him when he cried out in his sleep as a child—imagined her brushing that errant blue-black curl off his forehead and gently kissing the spot where it had lain. Something soft and infinitely tender stirred within the hidden places of her heart—a longing for the child she would now never hold in her arms nor suckle at her breast, a longing that for some unknown reason this troubled, sleeping man brought to life.

And this was the man her grandmother had suggested could be the one with whom she would share the "grand passion" that had been the legacy and the curse of all the Derry women who had preceded her. How ridiculous. A man who aroused such motherly instincts in her could scarcely be the object of a "grand passion."

Adam did his best to obey the voice that called to him. It was a lovely voice, soft and melodic, and he sensed it was trying to help him escape the terror that held him in its grip. But his eyelids felt locked shut and he could find no way to unlock them.

"I cannot open my eyes," he moaned.

"Of course you can." Soft fingers brushed the hair off his brow and soft lips replaced it with an airy kiss. Those same soft lips feathered delicate kisses across his eyelids, and as if that were the magic key that unlocked them, they immediately popped open.

With his mind not yet fully awakened from his troubled sleep, his first thought was that the beautiful creature bending over him was a visiting angel. Then he realized it was Fiona. In her voluminous white nightrail, and with her hair hanging loose about her shoulders, she could have been the model for any of the heavenly beings painted by the sixteenth century masters.

He couldn't imagine what had brought her to his bedchamber in the middle of the night unless, God forbid, he'd had one of his nightmares and cried out in his sleep like some raving Bedlamite. But surely if that were the case, Ben would have heard him as well, and Ben was nowhere in sight.

But Fiona was here. Alone, in the dark of night. And he was not such a fool as to question her motives.

"Kiss me again," he entreated softly, "and this time on the lips, if you please."

How could she refuse when he asked in such a sweetly boyish manner? How could she resist his funny, lopsided smile or the note of humble entreaty in his voice? Without another thought, she leaned forward and gave him a brief, motherly kiss—or at least that was what she intended it to be.

But the minute her lips touched his, something flashed between them—something unbelievably tantalizing and frighteningly erotic. Bewitched by such intimate contact with his blatant masculinity, she instinctively imitated the accommodating angle of his head, the provocative curve of his mouth as it fit hers. Instantly, a dizzying rush of warmth spread through her, weakening her limbs and sending her senses reeling.

Adam caught her shoulders in his long, elegant fingers and drew her closer, deepening the kiss. It had never before occurred to her that the touch of a man's lips could evoke such profoundly exquisite pleasure. Buckley's certainly hadn't.

She gasped from sheer delight and instantly Adam's tongue slipped past her lips to explore her mouth with an intimacy that left her trembling and breathless. In all the years they'd lived together as man and wife, Buckley had never kissed her *that* way.

It was too much. Once again Adam Cresswell had taken control and this time in a way that both frightened and fascinated her. She pushed away from him. "Wh . . . what are you doing, Mr. Cresswell?" she stammered.

"What does it look like?" Adam frowned. "I am kissing you, of course. Am I so out of practice you couldn't tell?"

"I am not a green girl, Mr. Cresswell. Of course I could tell you were kissing me, but I never expected . . . you surprised me. I had thought you a man of honor."

Adam sat up, and Fiona stifled a gasp as the sheet fell to his waist, plainly revealing that he slept without a stitch of clothing. Something that should have occurred to her when she had touched his bare shoulder. It was her first glimpse of so much bare male flesh. Buckley had always worn a nightshirt to bed and had dressed and undressed in the dark.

"I am as honorable as the next man," Adam said, brushing

back the lock of hair that had again tumbled onto his forehead. "But I do have my limits." The cheeky fellow actually had the gall to appear affronted. "Devil take it, madam, if you were not looking to be kissed, why did you come to my bedchamber at this hour, dressed only in your nightrail?"

"Why you insufferable . . . How dare you infer . . ." Fiona had no chance to finish her denunciation of him. At that moment Ben marched through the door with an armful of fresh bedlinens and behind him, carrying a steaming cup of foul-smelling tea, marched her grandmother.

"My, my, and ain't ye looking fine as fivepence, lad." Ben grinned broadly, obviously happy to see that Adam had suffered no ill effects from his nightmare. "But ye'll have to get out of that bed if ye want it made up with dry linens."

"That would not be advisable with ladies present, Ben, for as you know, I sleep as the good Lord made me."

To Fiona's embarrassment, she saw a glint of something that looked very much like approval in her grandmother's eyes. The woman really was the outside of enough.

"We will leave the minute you finish your tea," she said sweetly. She had been subjected to some of Creenagh's herbal teas in the past. While they were unarguably effective in curing whatever ailed one, the cure sometimes seemed worse than the ailment. At the moment, she could think of no one on earth she would rather watch choke down the evil brew than Adam Cresswell.

"Here it be, Londoner." Creenagh held out the cup of greenish brown liquid. "Ye'll not much care for the taste of it, but I promise ye'll sleep with nary an evil dream."

Adam took the cup in hand and set it on the table that held his bedside candle. "Why thank you, ma'am. I sincerely appreciate your going to the trouble to prepare me such a fine cup of tea. But I find I have no need of it now."

"And how say ye that, Londoner? Ye were raving like a madman, so wicked were yer dream but a few minutes past."

"Why it is like this, ma'am." Adam turned silver eyes gleaming with pure mischief in Fiona's direction. "Thanks to the tender ministrations of your lovely granddaughter, I do believe I shall be able to sleep like a newborn babe the balance of this night."

Chapter Six

Fiona was still bristling with anger. Adam could see it in the rigid set of her shoulders, the militant tilt of her chin. She had avoided him all day and now, sitting opposite him at the supper table, she stared right through him as if he didn't exist.

He couldn't really blame her. He should never have teased her about her "tender ministrations" in front of Ben and Creenagh. It had made the kiss they had shared seem like a moment of illicit passion, when in truth it had been nothing more than two lonely people reaching out to each other for momentary comfort . . . or so he chose to tell himself.

But when the older members of the household marched through his doorway bearing fresh bedding and mind-soothing tea, he had known instantly that he'd had another of his cursed nightmares and wakened the entire household with his ravings.

He had been mortified—doubly so since he had made an even greater fool of himself by leaping to the conclusion that Fiona had come to his chamber with seduction in mind. He had hidden his discomfiture behind a flippant remark aimed at retaliating for the censure she had heaped on him a few moments earlier—as boorish a thing as he could ever remember doing and one of which he was deeply ashamed. Even in the dim light of the candle, he had seen the look of disgust in her eyes and the flush of embarrassment that flooded her cheeks.

Much as he might wish it, there was no taking the stupid remark back and ironically, though he'd uttered it in jest, it had proved to be profoundly true. For amazingly enough, the kiss they had shared had exorcised the demons that had haunted him earlier. He had spent the remainder of the night dreaming of a red-haired angel in a white homespun nightrail—though what transpired between him and that angel could not by any stretch of imagination be called heavenly business.

He had awakened with the dawn, his mind clear from a pleasant night's sleep and his resolve to leave Exmoor firmer than ever. He lay for a few minutes staring at the ceiling of his tiny attic room and made two momentous decisions.

Firstly, while he would give Fiona the money he had won from her husband, he would never show her the handwritten deed to Larkspur Farm that Buckley Haines had forfeited to him. He had gathered from what little she had said about her marriage, that she had been deeply grateful for the respectability and relief from the grinding poverty it had provided her, but she'd had few illusions about the man she had married. Destroying yet another of those illusions would be beyond cruel.

Secondly, that kiss they had shared had added a whole new dimension to the desire he felt for the lovely widow. Her passionate response told him she was not nearly as prudish as she appeared, nor as indifferent to him as she pretended. Still he suspected she placed too high a value on her own worth to find gratification in a casual coupling with a near stranger—which was all he had to offer her.

For that reason, he must forget Fiona Haines and return to London before he found the temptation she offered too great to resist. The last thing he wanted to do was cause her more grief than she had already suffered because of that blasted card game he had played with her husband.

But first he must make his peace with her. With that in mind, he cleared his throat and made a stab at starting a congenial conversation. Fiona would have none of it; the lady was offended and she let him know it in every toss of her head and flash of her eyes.

So be it; he would simply have to introduce a topic that would capture the attention of the other two people at the table—something that would be certain to draw Fiona into the discussion.

He tried again, this time directing his remarks to Creenagh. "Tell me, ma'am, what conclusion did you come to about the white Exmoor pony Mistress Fiona and I spied on the moors?

She seemed to think our sighting it might have some significance."

A shocked silence followed his question. But he was successful in one respect; Fiona quit ignoring him. In truth, she raked him with a look of such fiery anger he fully expected the flesh to melt off his bones.

Creenagh, on the other hand, abandoned her usual dour expression for a smile so smugly triumphant, Adam instantly sensed he had inadvertently dealt her the winning card in whatever game she was currently playing with her granddaughter.

"A white pony did ye say, Londoner? Now don't that curl the cat's whisker. Such a wondrous thing as that, and me granddaughter never mentioning a word about it. Could it be a sign of some kind, do ye think?"

"A sign?" Adam frowned, remembering Fiona's odd reaction to what she had called a "mystic pony." "But of what, ma'am?"

"Of nonsense, nothing more," Fiona interjected before Creenagh could answer his question. Adam watched her rise and clear the dishes from the table, but not before she gave her grandmother a warning frown.

"More'n likely 'twere a sheep as wandered from some shepherd's flock," Ben remarked. "Everyone knows there be no such thing as a white Exmoor pony—except in tales as told of the ancients what lived on these moors before ever a God-fearing Christian set foot on them."

The ancients. The term echoed in Adam's head, evoking images of the mysterious Celts who had once roamed the very land Fiona and he had traveled. A people so closely tied to the earth on which they trod, their souls still seemed to haunt every rock and tree and blade of grass.

He remembered his first impression of Fiona. With her glorious flame-colored hair and her unique almond-shaped eyes, she had struck him as a fey creature, too exquisite to belong to the ordinary world around her. He knew now there was nothing whimsical or otherworldly about her.

She might give an appearance of ethereal beauty, but in actuality she was a woman of the earth—as strong and courageous and resilient as the sturdy moorland ponies she rode on the moors. And like them, she seemed more in harmony with that ancient race of people lost in the mists of time than the simple farmfolk who were currently her neighbors.

The sound of Creenagh's voice interrupted his musings and snapped him back to attention. "More'n likely ye're right, old man," she said in a rare show of affability toward Ben. "The 'white pony' me granddaughter and the Londoner thought they seen were probably naught but a stray ram."

But an enigmatic smile lifted the corners of her mouth and the dark, inscrutable gaze she leveled first on Fiona and then on him made a mockery of her words. Adam felt the hair rise up the back of his neck. It was obvious the Witch of Exmoor attached some mystical portent to the sighting of the white pony. But why was Fiona so determined to keep her from voicing it?

He could see there was no point in pursuing the subject further. He would get no answer to his question this night. Not that it mattered. In a day or two, he would be on his way back to London, and these provincials and their bizarre superstitions would be nothing more than an intriguing memory.

He watched Ben pull his pipe from his pocket and pack it with the precious tobacco he had confessed was the only luxury he supported from his meager wage. "Were that Dooley Twigg I seen ride into the farmyard this afternoon, Mistress?" he asked as he rose from the table.

"It was, as I intended to tell you before I was diverted by . . . other things. He came to let me know the gathering of the ponies will begin tomorrow. Everyone is meeting at his farm shortly after dawn."

Ben shook his head sadly. " 'Twill be the first time ye've rode to gathering without Buckley at yer side, Mistress. 'Tis thankful I be ye've Adam to ride with ye. Else ye'd have to hire one of the local lads to help ye claim the foals as belongs to Larkspur Farm."

Adam stared from Ben to Fiona, wondering if he had heard what he thought he had. "Are you saying the moorland ponies are not the wild creatures they appear to be, but actually belong to you and the other farmers of Exmoor?"

Fiona took a deep breath, put her anger aside, and pondered his question. Ben was right; like it or not she needed the cocky

Londoner to support her tomorrow and it behooved her to mend her fences with him.

"I think of us more as the ponies' keepers than their owners," she said. "They roam free except for the once-a-year gathering, when the foals are claimed and given the same brand as their mothers."

Ben stopped in the doorway. "And the yearlings is culled out and sold fer a fair bit of profit at Plimpton Fair if they catches the eye of a buyer."

"Well yes, I suppose in that respect, we do treat them as livestock. The truth is not a farm in Exmoor could survive without the ponies and the revenue they bring. There is little call for our sheep these days, what with half the counties in England raising larger, fatter sheep on pasture that is far richer than any found on the moors."

Ben nodded in agreement. "Aye, Adam me lad, ye've come to Exmoor when times be bad and fixing to get worse if them crazies in the King's government has their say."

Fiona had had no intention of divulging her problems to her new farmhand, but the look of genuine concern on Adam's face prompted her to explain Ben's impassioned remark. "There are two main herds of Exmoors—one on Withypool Common and the other, which includes the Larkspur Farm ponies, on Royal Forest land."

Adam's eyes widened. "There is a forest here in Exmoor?"

Ben laughed. "Nay, Londoner. Not the kind of forest as grows in the Midlands where me cousin Guthrie bides. Just a great stretch of moor with a few streams and such, and black tors so tall they fair reach the sky."

"It is called a Royal Forest because it was the favorite hunting ground of the English kings when the Tudors still sat on the throne," Fiona said. "Since the time of King John, in the year 1200, it has been leased to a series of Forest Wardens, who have administered it with the help of Free Suitors."

Adam raised an eyebrow. "Free Suitors?"

"The men who patrolled the forest to keep it safe from poachers of the red deer and ponies, and who counted and recorded the ponies each farmer owned, and the sheep he turned out to graze every March. As payment for collecting the grazing fees due the warden, they were allowed to graze their own sheep and ponies free of charge on forest land.

"My husband was one of those suitors, as were his father and grandfather before him. But the lease ran out this year and the King's administrators refused to renew it—or to sell the land to Sir Thomas Acland, the last warden."

Ben snorted. "Would ye believe it? Some dimwit's come up with the idea of planting trees on it so's it'll be a 'real forest.' As if aught but scrub oaks and heather could get a toe-hold in such barren, rocky soil." Muttering to himself, he stomped onto the porch and slammed the door behind him.

Adam searched Fiona's face with worried eyes. "What will become of the Larkspur Farm ponies if the King's administrators go ahead with their plan?"

"I cannot know." Fiona squared her shoulders. "But whatever happens, they will survive and so will I. If there is one thing we moorland creatures excel at, it is survival."

She shrugged. "But I shall deal with that problem when it happens. In the meantime, Ben is right. I shall need you with me tomorrow." She smiled, unable to resist the urge to get back some of her own. "It will be a long day and a hard one, Londoner. We leave at dawn and we will be in the saddle until nightfall. I hope it will not be too much for you."

Adam hesitated and for one heart-stopping moment, she thought he was going to refuse to accompany her. Then he returned her smile. "Never worry about me, Mistress Haines. In my time I have spent longer and harder days in the saddle than any you could show me." He stood up and in his usual polite way, thanked her for a fine meal, excused himself, and retired to his attic chamber for an early night.

Fiona wheeled around to face her grandmother the minute he was out of sight. "I will not listen to a single word out of you, Creenagh. I am in no mood for your soothsaying tonight—and I warn you, I will not take it kindly if you ever again intimate to my new farmhand that the pony we saw was a 'sign' from those blasted pagan gods you worship."

"Foolish girl, do ye think that silencing me tongue will change the way of things?" Creenagh's smile was infuriatingly complacent. "I fancied he be the one first time I laid eyes on him, and now that ye've admitted to seeing the 'sign,' I knows it for certain. Rant and rave all ye wish; there be naught ye can do about a thing once the gods has laid their plans."

The first rosy fingers of dawn had just crept over the eastern horizon when Adam rode through the gate of Larkspur Farm the next morning and headed back down the same trail he had traveled three weeks earlier. Only this time Fiona rode ahead of him and Ben brought up the rear in a pony-drawn sledge cart.

They rode in silence—the only sounds the clip-clop of the ponies' hooves on the rock-strewn trail and the chirping of the moorland birds greeting a new day. Early morning had always been Adam's favorite time, but the beauty of this particular sunrise was lost on him. He had too much on his mind.

It was frustrating enough that Fiona's admission that she needed him had forced him to put off his departure from Exmoor; he was bedeviled by an inexplicable riddle as well. Over and over he repeated to himself the words he had heard Creenagh say when he had stood in the hall outside the main room of the farmhouse the night before. *He be the one . . . and there be naught ye can do about it once the gods has laid their plans.*

The witch of Exmoor had been speaking of him; of that he was certain. And while he never had, and never would, believe in witchcraft, he was admittedly curious as to the meaning of her strange declaration. He was also curious as to why it had upset Fiona so much she had issued her grandmother a thinly veiled threat.

So engrossed was he in his thoughts, he was unaware of anything around him until Fiona brought her mount to a sudden stop directly in front of him. "What is the matter?" he asked, as he reined in his startled pony and raised his hand to signal Ben to bring the sledge cart to a halt a short distance behind him.

Fiona put her finger to her lips. "Shhhh. Listen."

At first the only sound was the plaintive sighing of the wind through the branches of a small stand of scrub oaks bordering the trail. Then he heard it—a low, rhythmic creaking like the moaning timbers of a ship at anchor. He frowned. "What is it?"

Fiona's eyes were dark with horror, her face ghostly pale. "You can see it up ahead. There, at the crossroads, just beyond the last oak."

Adam pulled up beside her and looked where she pointed. A crudely constructed gibbet, with a body dangling from the cross bar, stood beside the trail. He had seen men hanged before. It was a common occurrence at Newgate Prison. But something about the macabre sight in this lonely location lent an additional horror to the scene.

"Who is it?" Fiona asked as Ben shuffled up to stand beside her.

"It be nobody ye need fret about, Mistress. A young lad from t'other side o' the moor, come looking to steal a pony from the Royal Forest now there be no warden or Free Suitors about. The local beadles stopped by the farm with the foolish fellow in chains two days ago while you rode the moors."

"And hanged him without a trial apparently." Adam's stomach clenched. From the mottled skin and bulging eyes of the corpse, he could see the poor sod had died of slow strangulation, not of a broken neck as would be the case if the hanging had been properly executed.

Ben shrugged. "Didn't need no trial. He were riding the pony when they come upon him, and anyone with eyes could see the brand of Larkspur Farm on the beastie's rump."

"Stealing is a hanging offense in Exmoor," Fiona said, her expression guarded. "Anyone who steals knows the risk." She averted her face from the grisly sight and urged her pony forward, giving Adam the impression it was a risk that she herself had taken on occasion—probably when hunger had driven her to it. Once again she had shocked him with a glimpse into her bleak past.

He wondered what the future held for this remarkable woman. How would she survive if the Larkspur sheep and ponies were driven from the Royal Forest by a decree made by men as ignorant about life on the moors as he had been less than a month before?

The thought was too depressing to contemplate. He almost wished he had taken his father's advice and never become involved in the lovely widow's affairs. For he suspected he could never put enough miles between him and Exmoor to eliminate Fiona Haines from his thoughts.

They had ridden another ten minutes or so when the sound of men's voices and the occasional whinny of a horse told him they were near their destination. Fiona slowed her pony to a walk. "Here we are," she announced, "and it looks as if most of the others have arrived before us." She was still unusually pale and the haunted look lingered in her eyes, but her resolute expression defied him to question her ability to perform her part of the work they were slated to do together in the next few hours.

Adam glanced ahead to find they were approaching one of the farmhouses he remembered passing the day he had ridden up from the Black Boar Inn. A dozen or more men, mounted on Exmoor ponies identical to the ones Fiona and he rode, were gathered just outside the farmyard fence. To a man, they stared in open-mouthed astonishment at Fiona's provocative breeches and mannish shirt.

One of the men, a stocky fellow with small, bloodshot eyes and a shock of straw-colored hair, broke loose from the group and approached them. "So, ye've brought yer new farmhand with ye, Fiona." He raked Adam with a disdainful glance. "A woman dressed in her husband's breeches and a muddleheaded townie—what kind of crew be that to do the gathering for Larkspur Farm? 'Tis glad I be me friend Buckley cannot see how low the name o' Haines has sunk this day."

Fiona stared down her nose at the rude fellow. "Adam and I will do our part, never fear, Dooley Twig. Which is more than I have ever seen you do at previous gatherings."

Angry color flooded the farmer's face. "Mind yer tongue when ye speak to yer betters, ye red-haired trollop. Buckley may have been moonstruck by ye, but I've not forgotten what ye were afore he made a decent woman of ye."

Adam had heard enough. He urged his pony forward until he sat alongside Fiona, facing the loud-mouthed bully. "Is this fat toad bothering you, Mistress Haines?" he asked in the quietly ominous voice he had used to bring the brash young officers in his command into line.

It had worked then; it worked now. The color leached from the farmer's face and with a parting expletive that would have put a London dockworker to shame, he quickly returned to his circle of friends.

"Thank you for coming to my aid Adam. It was very gallant." Fiona sounded more amused than grateful. "But I take no more notice of pests like Dooley Twig than I do a fly buzzing round my head, and I assure you I am quite capable of swatting my own flies."

"Are you really, Mistress Haines? I wonder." Didn't the foolish woman see how these men stared at her with hot, hungry eyes? He would lay odds that, like Dooley Twig, every one of them thought her fair game now that her husband was no longer around to protect her.

As usual, he felt swamped with guilt at the thought of the part he had played in Buckley Haines's death. But this time the guilt was compounded by the knowledge that once he left Exmoor, there would be only a frail old man to stand between Fiona and this collection of country jackals.

Grimly, he acknowledged this gave him a whole new perspective on his responsibilty toward the lovely widow. He couldn't leave the little fool to her own devices when she hadn't the sense to see the danger she was in. He would simply have to reveal his true identity and offer her his protection; if need be, insist she return to London with him.

He smiled to himself. Yes, of course, that was the perfect solution to the problem. He would begin a subtle campaign this very day to win her over to his way of thinking— a campaign he felt certain would succeed. For what woman in her circumstances wouldn't jump at the chance to be kept in style by the son of a duke?

Fiona couldn't help but notice the assembled farmers were a little less blatant in their ogling of her scandalous breeches after Adam's challenge to Dooley Twig. Much as she hated to admit it, there were times when it was very comforting to have a man at her side—expecially a man as forceful as her new farmhand.

Ben had advised her to wear the heavy skirt Buckley had insisted on when she had assisted him at the gatherings in past years, but she had decided it was much too cumbersome. This year she would be heading the Larkspur Farm team with an assistant who knew nothing about how to round up the wild ponies; she couldn't afford the luxury of feminine modesty.

A good half hour passed while Dooley Twig decided in which sections of the Royal Forest the various teams should search for the herds. Buckley had always been assigned one of the grassy areas particularly favored by the ponies. As she expected, Adam and she were given the least desirable section in the entire forest. A land chiefly composed of black tors and rocky hillocks, it was so devoid of vegetation she doubted the ponies ever grazed there.

"This may be an exercise in futility," she said bitterly as she bid Ben farewell before riding out. "We have been assigned the corner of the forest beyond Mole's Chamber and the Old Hoar Oak."

"Lord luv us, ye'll be lucky if ye see so much as a hungry buzzard in that hellish spot." Ben's eyes twinkled. "Dooley Twig be a sore loser, Mistress. He'll not soon forgive ye for turning him down when he come a' courting."

Ben patted the branding iron that lay on the seat beside him. "But never ye mind. However the ponies be brought in, I'll be here waiting for 'em, and I'll see to it the suckers as was foaled by Larkspur mares be properly branded."

Fiona sighed. "Bless you, Ben. I have a feeling we will sorely need any income we can get from the yearlings next summer."

With Adam close behind her, she guided her pony back onto the trail and followed the string of riders heading toward the Royal Forest. The trail was narrow here, just wide enough for two riders abreast, and for close to a mile lay wedged between steep, rocky banks.

It was this unique formation of the land that made the Twig farm the ideal place for the terminal point of the gathering. For once the ponies were herded into the far end of the natural chute, they had no place to go but into the series of holding pens that had been constructed to receive them.

With Adam beside her, she emerged from the chute and crossed the boundary of the Royal Forest. Here the riders separated into two-man teams which fanned out across the vast territory in search of the elusive herds.

Fiona waited until Adam and she were alone before she explained what was entailed in the gathering of the ponies. "The area we have been assigned to search is north of here beyond the two black tors you see in the distance. If we sight the herd—which all things considered, will be a miracle—I will blow this ram's horn hanging from my saddle to alert other teams that we need help in driving the ponies toward the chute.

"Remember, they are wild animals, for all they bear the brands of human owners, and they will not go willingly. The trick is to keep them all together. If one or two manage to break loose, the whole herd will soon scatter in every direction."

"I have had no experience at herding horses, but my lieutenant and I once chased a dozen or so French Dragoons and cornered them in an area much like this chute of yours. I suspect the process was very similar to what you described."

Adam leaned forward in the saddle, his face alight with anticipation. "Never worry, love, we will find the herd and when we do, I promise you I will not disgrace you."

Fiona's heart fluttered so wildly, it felt as if a bird had been trapped within her breast. But for the life of her she couldn't decide if the erratic rhythm was due to the infectious optimism she heard in Adam's voice or the shock of being called his "love."

Chapter Seven

Fiona's reaction to his calling her "love" was all Adam could have hoped for. She turned ten shades of red, but miraculously, she failed to give him the tongue lashing he had expected. She simply acted as if she hadn't heard the endearment.

"There are no trails leading to the area we have been assigned," she informed him in a brisk voice. "It is so desolate no one ever goes there." Though she didn't say so, Adam gathered there was little chance the ponies went there either.

Then without further ado, she set off across the moors toward the two black tors that like ancient, sleeping gods sprawled across the northern horizon.

He felt too exhilarated by his decision to take her under his protection to be pessimistic about something that would, in the long run, matter little to her future. "If no one ever goes there, how can you be sure what it is actually like?" he called after her. "There may be a lush green valley that only the ponies know about."

She glanced over her shoulder. "Now you sound like the muddleheaded townie Dooley Twig called you."

He caught up with her, but she stared straight ahead, never looking at him though they rode side-by-side at a slow trot. "I never remember any team being assigned the black tor area in a past gathering," she said. "It was, as Ben said, just Dooley's way of getting even with me. Everyone knows there is nothing beyond those hills but rocks and gorse and maybe a few stands of scraggly heather."

"Ah yes, the ubiquitous 'everyone.' The same 'everyone' I assume who decreed there was no such thing as a white Exmoor pony." Adam expected to get a rise out of her with that remark and he wasn't disappointed. She stiffened instantly and the pinched look on her face told him that particular subject was not open for discussion.

A streak of devilment in him made him pursue it anyway. "By the way, what *did* your grandmother conclude about our sighting of the pony?"

Fiona remained stubbornly silent.

"I think I have the right to know since it obviously involved me."

"It is just a silly bit of folklore she maintains has been part of our family for generations. I would not put it past her to have invented it to suit her purposes. She is not above doing such a thing."

"Then why are you so loath to let me hear it?"

"Because it is . . . embarrassing—and nothing that would make the least bit of sense to someone like you."

"Try me."

Fiona reined in her mount and faced him. "Oh for heaven's sake, stop badgering me. Suffice it to say my grandmother is a hopeless romantic."

Adam brought his pony to a halt and gave it a reassuring pat. So the Witch of Exmoor's interpretation of the "sign" somehow tied Fiona and him together romantically. God bless the wicked old besom. He hid his elation behind a thoughtful frown. "And you, I take it, are not . . . a romantic?"

"Most certainly not."

"Hmmmn. Interesting. Your husband won your hand with the promise of security then."

"And respectability. He offered that too."

Adam chuckled. "Oh I doubt that respectability is all that important to you, love. Else you would be dressed in a proper skirt and be waiting back at the farmyard with the rest of the women—not be out here doing a man's work."

"Respectability is not a matter of clothing, but of deportment," she declared primly.

"But it is based on others' opinions. I doubt you care that much what your neighbors think of you." Leaning forward, he placed his hand atop hers. "I understand you were but sixteen when you married. People change with time. Tell me, what would a man have to offer you nowadays to win your favor?"

Fiona whipped her hand out from under his as if his touch scorched her. "Nothing any man could offer would induce me to give myself into his control. Thanks to Buckley, I have the means to make my own security and so I intend to do for the balance of my life."

This discussion was not going precisely as Adam had planned. Frustrated, he countered her declaration with, "There is more to life than security." Bookstores and libraries came to mind, as did evenings at the theatre and any number of more intimate pleasures he could think of that he would teach her to enjoy once she was under his protection. He refrained from mentioning them, lest he tip his hand before he had determined the most diplomatic way of offering her carte blanche.

"I know there is more to life than security," she said. "But I lived so long without it, it has become my primary goal."

"But surely you'll concede there are more ways than one of achieving it." Devil take it, if it was security the woman craved, he would have his man of affairs draw up a contract deeding her the charming little house on the outskirts of London that was presently occupied by his current mistress—and a generous yearly competence as well.

He told himself it was the least he could do for the widow of a man whose death was partly his fault. He almost convinced himself that the fact that he would thoroughly enjoy visiting that little house and take great pleasure in showing Fiona the wonders of London played little part in his decision.

He couldn't help but smile. This discussion had been worthwhile after all. He knew now what arguments he would use to persuade her to put the drudgery of Larkspur Farm behind her and seek the kind of life a beautiful woman was meant to live.

They rode in silence for nearly an hour across an increasingly bleak landscape, Caesar loping along beside Adam's pony. The first thing Adam noticed when they finally drew close to their destination was that the two massive tors were separated by a narrow ravine.

He pointed this out to Fiona. "We are in luck. I was afraid we would have to circle around these cliffs to reach the other side."

Fiona drew a square of linen from her pocket and wiped the

dust and grime from her face. "Do you still think there is a lush green valley beyond?"

"Quoting Pope," Adam said, mopping his own face with one of the monogrammed handkerchiefs he had brought with him from London, " 'Hope springs eternal within the human breast.' "

Fiona's face went blank with shock. "You are a papist? I had no idea."

Adam laughed. "No, I am not a papist, and I was not quoting the Roman Pope. The line is from the works of Alexander Pope, an English poet and satirist of the last century. You will discover many such fascinating writers once you have access to books other than the four you now possess."

He felt riddled with guilt at the look of longing his words evoked, but he told himself such jibes were necessary if he hoped to convince her that her future happiness lay in London.

A sudden gust of wind whipped the grimy handkerchief from his hand and drove grit into his eyes. Swearing under his breath, he grabbed his pony's reins and headed toward the entrance to the ravine. "Shall we see where this leads? If nothing else, we should be protected from the wind once we are off the open moor.

"I will go first; you follow," he said, urging his reluctant pony forward. "We have no way of knowing what we might encounter."

Now that he'd made his decision, he was anxious to get things settled between them—something he couldn't hope to do until this business of the gathering was behind them.

Fiona shook her head in dismay. Adam had taken charge again. It seemed to come as easily to him as breathing. If she hadn't seen the uniform he had worn when he first arrived at Larkspur Farm, she would never believe he had been a common soldier in General Wellington's army. He was obviously a natural born leader.

Very well, she would let him assume control in this instance—so long as it didn't become a habit. In truth, she had always hated feeling confined and the idea of riding into that crevice that separated the two tors made her blood run cold. If she panicked and needed to get out in a hurry, she would rather have him ahead of her than behind her.

With Adam in the lead, Caesar following close behind him, and Fiona bringing up the rear, they inched forward into the narrow opening that hopefully led to whatever lay beyond the two great piles of black rock. The usual chilling, irrational fear gripped her. She fought it by gritting her teeth and concentrating on the broad shoulders and gleaming black hair of the man who rode in front of her—never looking to right nor left at the rock walls towering above her.

Cold sweat trickled down her back and between her breasts and her stomach roiled with nausea. She had just decided to give it up and turn around when she heard Adam call out, "The end is in sight though I cannot yet see what lies beyond . . . beyond . . . beyond." His voice echoed back and forth between the confining walls, but his words gave her the courage to press on.

Caesar chose that moment to dash ahead, and Fiona promptly urged her pony closer to Adam's, desperate to reach the safety he promised. Unexpectedly the track widened to where they could ride abreast. Together they emerged from the narrow ravine onto a shallow plateau to find Caesar crouched at the edge, his ears flattened against his head, his tail tucked beneath him.

"What is wrong, Caesar? What is it that makes you so wary?" Fiona dismounted, shielded her eyes against the sudden glare of the sun, and stared dumbfounded at the miraculous sight laid out before her.

A meadow carpeted in rich emerald-hued grass stretched between rolling hills of purple heather and golden-flamed gorse. Through it meandered a sparkling stream, its mossy banks lined with blue bells and silvery bracken and bushes of the luscious black whortleberries prized by both humans and ponies.

The drowsy hum of bees filled the air and somewhere a thrush warbled its lilting song. Fiona took a deep breath and inhaled the rich, tangy scent of wild thyme.

Adam dismounted and stood beside her. "I was joking when I suggested there might be such a valley in this desolate part of the moors," he said in an awestruck voice. "It never occurred to me it might really exist. This rivals anything I have seen in Kent or even the Cotswolds for sheer beauty."

Fiona released the breath she hadn't realized she was holding. "It truly is an enchanted valley. But for lack of an apple tree, it might be the Garden of Eden I read about in Vicar Edelson's Bible." She frowned. "But I cannot understand how it is that no one else has ever discovered this treasure."

"I believe someone has." Adam grinned from ear to ear. "Unless I am hallucinating, there are ponies grazing off to my left—a great many ponies—and by all that's holy, one of them is white." He chuckled. "It appears this 'everyone' in whom you place such great store is wrong on all counts."

Fiona looked where he pointed and felt a shiver creep up her spine. Common sense told her that she couldn't be seeing what she thought she saw. Yet there in all his kingly glory stood the white Exmoor stallion that had appeared out of the mist not three days past, his sleek silvery coat gleaming in the morning sun.

Close to two dozen dun-colored mares, each with a foal at her side, made up the immediate court that surrounded him. Beyond them stood a wider circle of yearlings and a few young stallions who had yet to claim mares of their own.

"This has to be about a quarter of the Royal Forest herd," Fiona exclaimed. "The white stallion must have lured the mares away from old Tengo, who has been the herd leader for as long as I can remember. The yearlings and young stallions would follow them."

Adam surveyed the scene with narrowed eyes. "You must admit he is a handsome fellow, but I suspect he may have helped things along by hinting he knew the whereabouts of a pasture, the likes of which these ladies had never before seen. I know I would have were I in his place."

He frowned. "But now that we have found the ponies, how the devil are the two of us and Caesar going to control twenty-five or thirty of them long enough to get them across the stretch of moor between here and the Twig farm? I assume the other teams are all within hailing distance of each other and can call for help when they need it. Thanks to your friend, Dooley Twig, that is not true in our case."

"It is obvious two riders and a dog cannot bend an entire herd to their will. But there has to be a way to get them into the holding pens." Fiona pondered the problem, trying to think as Buckley would have. If there was one thing her husband had been good at, it was herding wild ponies.

"The lead stallion is the key to our success," she said finally. "We just have to cut him out of the herd and drive him in the direction we want him to go; the mares and foals will follow, and hopefully the others as well."

"In that case I will ride down and discuss it with him beforehand—see if I can make him understand we mean him no harm." Adam mounted his pony and before Fiona could stop him, started down the gradual incline at one end of the plateau.

"Wait, you crazy Londoner. You cannot have a discussion with a wild pony. You are just going to frighten the mares if you try to ride amongst them, and once they scatter, all is lost." Fiona might as well have saved her breath for all the good it did her. Frantically, she mounted her own pony and followed him.

Adam knew he was taking a risk. If he stampeded the herd, Fiona would never forgive him. But his gut instinct told him the white stallion was a unique animal and as such, would respond to unique methods. He remembered watching a famous horse handler at Tattersall's bring a temperamental thoroughbred under control and eat out of his hand by simply talking to it in a low, soothing tone of voice. If it worked for one stallion, why not another?

As Fiona had predicted, the mares and their foals shied away from him the minute he drew near them. But since the white stallion stood his ground, they didn't go far. Adam stopped some thirty feet from the magnificent animal to let it get used to him, and heard Fiona ride up behind him. A low growl told him Caesar was with her.

He glanced over his shoulder. "Don't worry, love, I've not lost my mind," he whispered. "I am merely gaining the old boy's confidence."

Fiona rolled her eyes toward the heavens. "Your success with Caesar has gone to your head. A wild pony is a different animal entirely. Surely you do not expect the stallion to become so enamored of you he will follow you docilely across the moors."

"Of course not. But the less he fears us, the better chance we have of getting him to do as we want."

She gave a sigh of resignation. "You are right, of course. Do what you can. Maybe your indisputable charm will work on a pony as well as a dog. But sooner or later, we will have to cut him out of the herd and drive him before us."

"Let me try winning his trust first. No animal can be expected to act rationally when he is terrified." He turned back to the stallion and found it even more breathtaking close-up than it had been when viewed from the plateau. Its silver-white coat had a strangely diaphanous quality to it that gave him the eerie sensation he was not only looking at it, but through it as well.

He thought of asking Fiona if she found anything odd about the animal's appearance, but quickly discarded the idea. She already looked askance at his conversing with a pony; she would be convinced he had attics to let if he posed such a question.

Fiona waited to see what Adam would do next. He was certainly handling the situation differently than Buckley would have. But she couldn't fault him for trying to win the stallion's trust, and she had to admit that so far it showed none of the uneasiness around humans she had come to expect of a wild pony. But then this could hardly be termed the typical Exmoor.

She looked closer at the animal facing them with such equanimity and realized the color of its coat was not the only thing that was unusual about it. With the sun glistening off its sleek white flanks, it looked almost translucent—or was she guilty of letting her imagination get the best of her? She blinked and the picture before her eyes came back into focus.

"Look here, fellow, I have a proposition to make you." Adam spoke in the same silky tone of voice she had heard him use on Caesar. There was something terribly seductive about it—something that made her understand why a dog, or a pony, might willingly do his bidding. In his own way, Adam was as adept at using sorcery as Creenagh.

The pony pricked up its ears and regarded him with hooded eyes that sparked with intelligence. "Toad eyes" was the commonly used term for that distinctive feature of the Exmoors. It seemed a sadly inadequate description in the case of this superb animal.

Patiently and in a consistently low and soothing voice, Adam explained that the branding of foals born to Larkspur

Farm mares was as much for their protection as for that of their keepers. She smiled, grateful he had remembered to use the term she had coined to describe her relationship with the ponies. For though she knew it to be impossible, she could swear the stallion understood every word he said.

As if to confirm the fact, the animal suddenly rose on its hind legs, pawed the air, and gave a loud, commanding whinny that raised the head of every mare grazing within a hundred feet of it. Then as if dismissing the humans confronting it, it made a wide circle around them, trotted up the shallow incline to the plateau, and disappeared into the crevice separating the two tors.

One by one the mares, with their foals beside them, followed suit, as did the yearlings, and young stallions. Good herd dog that he was, Caesar chased after them.

"Well I'll be damned!" With a bewildered glance in her direction, Adam took off after them. Too stunned to feel her usual fear of enclosure, Fiona followed him.

Moments later they emerged from the ravine to see the herd stretched out across the moor like a great serpentine. With the white stallion at its head and running at full gallop, it was a breathtaking sight. Fiona had seen the herd on the move many times, but the spectacle never failed to thrill her. She glanced at Adam and saw, from the rapt expression on his face, that he found it every bit as fascinating as she. As one, they urged their mounts forward and galloped after the ponies.

Bent low in the saddle, Adam coaxed his pony to literally fly over the ground that lay beneath its hooves. He couldn't remember when he had enjoyed anything as much as this mad dash across the moors. It had all the elements of the chase he had loved in the hunt, with none of the blood lust he had come to despise.

With Caesar yapping at its heels, the white stallion galloped unerringly toward the planned destination. Behind it streamed the mares and the stouthearted little foals who were striving valiantly to keep up with their mothers. Adam found himself oddly moved by the sight. Something about the game little fellows made him think of Fiona as she must have been as a young girl, battling to rise above the limitations a cruel fate had imposed on her.

He glanced at the woman racing hell-for-leather beside him. Her hair had come loose from its neat braid and streamed behind her like a mantle of fire, and her eyes shone with the thrill of the chase. As he watched, she proudly raised the ram's horn to her lips and sounded the signal that proclaimed hers was a team that had located ponies.

In another time, another place she could have been one of the legendary Valkyries of Scandinavian myth or the Roman goddess Diana riding to the hunt. She was magnificent, and the desire she stirred in him was as fierce and primitive as the moors they raced across together.

He threw back his head and laughed from the sheer joy of the moment—and the certain knowledge that come what may, he would one day take this incredible woman as his lover.

As Fiona had known they would, the mares eventually tired of their wild run and slowed to a more reasonable pace. Indeed, even the white stallion appeared ready to take it a bit easier. But past experience had taught her this was the most difficult time of all to control the herd. "Watch for strays," she warned Adam, and the words were scarcely out of her mouth when one of the mares panicked and veered off across the moor with her foal close behind her.

Fiona watched in amazement as Adam quickly rode the high-strung mare to ground and forced it back into line with a competence that was amazing for someone new to the business of herding. Not for the first time, it occurred to her that this reformed gambler she had hired had the makings of a fine farmer. Her heart skipped a beat as somewhere in the deepest recesses of her mind a tantalizing thought began to take shape.

"We have company," Adam announced as he dropped back beside her. Fiona turned her head and glimpsed a group of riders who had crested a low hill off to their right and were galloping toward them. "Oliver Pinchert and his three sons," she said, instantly recognizing them. "Good herdsmen all and just in time. We will have no more trouble keeping the strays in line with the four of them riding flank."

The men gave congratulatory salutes as they passed Adam and her, then fanned out to take their places, two on each side of the line of ponies. With Caesar as guide, the white stallion and the ponies that followed it soon crossed the border of the Royal Forest and headed unerringly toward the Twig farm.

Just before they reached it, two of the Pinchert brothers galloped forward to ride abreast at the head of the line as the ponies were shepherded into the natural chute that led to the holding pens. Adam and another brother brought up the rear.

Fiona reined in her pony next to the patriarch of the family. "Well done. I thank you and your sons for your help."

" 'Tis ye and the townie has done well, Fiona Haines. In all the gatherings I've rode to, I've not seen the like of it."

Fiona nodded. "Nor have I. The minute I saw it, I knew I was witnessing a miracle."

"Aye, a miracle it be all right." He shook his grizzled head in obvious disbelief. "For who'll there be to believe me when I claims I seen the two of ye driving thirty or more mares and suckers and yearlings across the wildest stretch o' heath in Exmoor with naught but that ugly black dog o' yourn to lead 'em."

Chapter Eight

Devil take it, what kind of flimflam were these yokels trying to pull off?

Adam was certain he had seen the white stallion enter the far end of the so-called chute directly behind two of the Pinchert brothers. Yet by the time he had helped drive the last of the herd to its final destination, there was no sign of it in any of the holding pens in Dooley Twig's farmyard.

There could only be one explanation for its absence. Since not even the strongest of stallions could have scaled the steep banks that hemmed in the mile-long trail, someone had to have secreted it away the minute it entered the first pen—and right under Ben's nose from the look of it.

He felt consumed with rage. If the animal was as rare as Fiona claimed, it would be very valuable—and she should have finder's rights to it. He intended to see she got them, even if it meant rearranging the features of every farmer in Exmoor to do so. Grimly he dismounted, secured his pony's reins to a nearby fence post, and strode toward the men gathered around the pens.

"Wait, Adam. We need to talk." The note of urgency in Fiona's voice stopped him in his tracks. He turned back to find her hurrying across the yard toward him, her face pale, her expression guarded.

He waited until she caught up with him. "I cannot talk now, love," he said in a quiet voice meant only for her ears. "The white stallion has mysteriously disappeared and I intend to find out why."

"I know why. That is what we need to talk about. But not here. Someplace where we cannot be overheard." She glanced to her right. "Over there, by the barn."

Together they worked their way through the crowded yard to the tall, slope-roofed, wooden structure. "There is no way to say it other than right out," she declared, once they were out of earshot of the others. "Oliver Pinchert just congratulated me on accomplishing the nearly impossible task of driving a herd of wild ponies across the moors with no stallion to lead them."

Adam shook his head in disbelief. "Is the fellow daft?"

"No. On the contrary, he is one of the most levelheaded men I know. He simply could not see the . . . the mystic pony; nor could any of his sons."

"Mystic pony! Are we back to that nonsense? I would be more apt to believe the entire Pinchert family suffers from myopia. Damn it, Fiona, you know as well as I do that stallion was as real as any of those mares and yearlings we are looking at right now."

"Was it? Can you honestly say there was nothing about it that seemed a trifle . . . odd?"

Adam opened his mouth to deny her preposterous suggestion, but the words stuck in his throat. There had been that moment in the valley when it had appeared strangely insubstantial. But no, that had to have been a trick of the sunlight on its silvery coat.

Fiona fixed him with a grave gaze that reminded him she had witnessed the same mystifying sight he had. "Then why is it that only you and I could see it?" she asked bluntly. "And where is it now? Do you honestly think that if such a rare animal had been seen by anyone else there would be no talk of it amongst the men in this yard?"

"I cannot answer your questions, as well you know." Adam struggled to control his rising temper. "But I will tell you this: there has to be an explanation other than that we saw some mystical creature visible only to the two of us. I am as certain of that as I am that I am a Christian by faith and a logical-thinking man of the nineteenth century by nature.

"Nothing on earth could induce me to subscribe to this pagan mumbo jumbo you prattle. You may have the blood of witches in your veins; I do not. And quite frankly, this talk of a mystic pony makes my skin crawl. Damn it, madam, the rest of England left the Dark Ages behind some eight hundred years ago; I suggest you do the same."

Fiona flinched as if he had struck her, and Adam immediately regretted his outburst. As always, when he found himself in a situation he could not control, he vented his frustration in anger. He hadn't felt this angry since Salamanca.

"If you come up with a logical explanation for the white pony, I shall be happy to hear it," Fiona said quietly when she recovered from the shock of his vitriolic attack. "In the meantime, may I remind you that I am your employer, and as such I forbid you to discuss this with any of my neighbors."

"Have no fear on that score, madam. I have no desire to be carted off to the Exmoor equivalent of Bedlam Hospital. But I warn you, I do not like unsolved mysteries, and sooner or later I intend to get to the bottom of this bizarre business. Is that understood?"

Fiona nodded. "You could not be more explicit. Very well. We will speak of this later, after we help Ben with the branding of the Larkspur foals." Though what she could find to say to this enraged skeptic from London was beyond her.

How could she explain to a man with his roots firmly planted in the nineteenth century that she had come to the conclusion that the white pony was, as her grandmother claimed, a sign from the ancient Celtic gods. That like it or not, forces that had figured in the destinies of Derry women since the beginning of time had apparently chosen him as her soul mate. She could just imagine what he would say to that!

She herself had wholeheartedly accepted the benevolent Christian God she had read about in Vicar Edelson's Holy Bible—especially as he was depicted by his son in the New Testament. She found him to be a much wiser and more comforting God than the warlike gods of the ancient Celts. But she was still a Derry and had lived too long under her grandmother's influence to categorically deny the existence of the old gods.

In truth, she sometimes felt like a pony caught straddling a deep, rushing stream. With its front hooves on one bank and its hind hooves on the other, it dare not commit itself fully to either direction without courting disaster.

She gnashed her teeth. A pox on the old gods! Could they not see how they were complicating her life?

With her sullen-faced farmhand stalking along beside her, she hurried to where Ben was heating his branding iron in a fire pit outside the first holding pen. "I know nothing about this part of the gathering," she told the old man. "Buckley always handled it without me. You will have to tell Adam and me exactly what you want us to do."

" 'Tain't nothing much to it," he shouted over the voices of the other men conducting the branding and the whinnies of the terrified ponies. "Just one of ye needs to hold the wee beasties' heads, the other their hind ends whilst I brand the herd number on their rumps and the Larkspur brand on their withers."

He tested the iron by splashing a few drops of water on it. Apparently the resulting sizzle told him it was not yet hot enough because he instantly thrust it back into the bed of glowing coals.

The thrashing hooves of the restless, penned animals raised a thick cloud of dust that swirled around Fiona, filling her eyes and nose and mouth with the gritty substance. From a nearby pen there rose a sickening stench of burning hair and flesh, and she saw Adam scowl as he watched a farmer hot-brand a foal he had claimed from a lot that had been rounded up earlier.

She knew instantly what he was thinking. "It does not really hurt the little fellows all that much if it is done right, and Ben is very skillful," she ventured.

Adam's scowl only deepened. It was plain to see that he found nothing connected with Larkspur Farm or its owner to his liking at the moment. Indeed, she would be surprised if he were not laying plans to quit Exmoor for good as soon as he returned to the farmhouse and packed his few belongings in his saddlebag.

The thought was too depressing to contemplate. Only now, when she faced the prospect of his leaving did she admit to herself how much the clever Londoner had come to mean to her in the short time she had known him, and how empty her life would be without his challenging presence.

She pulled herself up short when she realized where her thoughts were leading. The very idea was ridiculous. It was Creenagh, with her fanatic belief in the "sign" and its portent, who saw him as the one and only man for her granddaughter. Fiona herself entertained no such illusion. Adam Cresswell was simply a charming stranger whose funny, crooked grin made her pulse beat a little faster and whose kisses . . . but she had rather not think what his kisses did to her.

She reminded herself that kisses, no matter how pleasant, were not an end in themselves. If allowed to continue, they invariably led to something far more intimate than the mere pressing together of lips—and she already knew she was not the kind of woman who enjoyed such intimacy.

With grim determination she forced herself to abandon her troublesome thoughts and return to the problem at hand. "How many of our foals are in this lot, Ben?" she asked the faithful old man, who had waited patiently while she woolgathered.

"Fourteen in all, Mistress, which far as I can tell, is every one due us. Leastwise, that's what I figured we could expect when I took into account the mares we turned onto the moors last spring."

His brow knitted in a perplexed frown. "Odd thing that. The Larkspur ponies is usually scattered all over the Royal Forest—not running in a single pack like this. It be almost like someone had searched out the beasties belonging to us and banded them together aforetime to make it easier fer ye to bring 'em in."

Adam raised an eyebrow at that thought-provoking comment, but to Fiona's relief, he kept his counsel. If Ben were to hear about the sightings of the mystic pony, he would undoubtedly jump to the conclusion that Creenagh had been dabbling in the witchcraft of which he was always accusing her. Ben was not one to keep his opinion to himself, and such talk could be dangerous. Though she understood the custom had long ago been abandoned in the rest of England, an old woman accused of practicing witchcraft had been burned at the stake as recently as ten years ago in Exmoor.

Ben gestured toward a pen on his left. "There they be, Mistress, the Larkspur mares and their foals. The Pinchert brothers helped me weed them from the herd as they come into the yard. We put the ten yearlings ye'll be wanting to take to Plimpton Fair in the next pen over, and a fine, healthy lot they be. Should bring a good price at auction."

He tested the iron again and finding it to his liking, shuffled forward and opened the gate to the first pen. "Let's get on with it, then. There be nothing I'd like better than to get home in time fer supper. I'll say one thing fer the witch; she do have a way o' seasoning the mutton with them herbs o' hers that makes it slide down a man's throat easy like."

The branding was accomplished in record time, and Fiona had to admit it was chiefly because of Adam. While she performed the ignominious task of holding the foals' hind ends steady and staying out of the way of their sharp little hooves, he held their heads and talked to them in the same low, soothing voice he had used on Caesar and the white stallion. The results were miraculous. The terrified foals immediately calmed down and submitted to the branding without so much as a whinny.

Ben made no attempt to hide his astonishment at how docile the young animals were under Adam's manipulation. "The townie has the gift," he bragged to anyone who would listen. "In all me years o' branding the wild beasties, I never seen 'em take to it as easy as they does with the Londoner whispering in their ears."

"And he be a drover to reckon with as well, as me sons and me can tell ye," Oliver Pinchert added in a booming voice that carried over the noise of the busy farmyard. He held out his great ham of a hand to Adam. "Fiona's found herself a good man and I, fer one, welcomes him to Exmoor."

Oliver Pinchert was a tough, hardworking farmer who was one of the most respected men on the moors. Such praise from him was a rare thing and not to be taken lightly.

As Fiona watched, the assembled men came forward one-by-one to shake Adam's hand. The only exception was Dooley Twig, who stood alone, a scowl black as a thundercloud on his beefy face.

Adam appeared both pleased and embarrassed by his unexpected welcome into the farming community. Fiona suspected his embarrassment stemmed from the fact that he had no intention of remaining in Exmoor—a suspicion that grew by the minute since he had not once looked her in the eyes since he had accused her of dealing in pagan mumbo jumbo.

With aching heart, she helped herd the mares and their newly branded foals into the large holding pen reserved for the animals to be counted, recorded, and turned back onto the moor. Then under Ben's direction, Adam and she roped the ten yearlings together and with the line securely attached to the sledge cart, began the ride back to Larkspur Farm.

This time Fiona rode alone at the head of the little procession, Ben and the string of yearlings followed and Adam and Caesar took up the rear. The trip of necessity was a slow one, and Adam had ample time for reflection on the bizarre happenings of the day and the bewildering turmoil that raged in his mind.

He had been deeply touched by the offers of friendship he received from Oliver Pinchert and his fellow farmers. Like the foot soldiers who had served under him on the Spanish Peninsula, they were plain, gruff-spoken men who judged him on his own merits, not his family's wealth and position. For the first time since leaving Spain, he had experienced the same sense of belonging that he had enjoyed with his comrades-at-arms.

Nor could he discount the feeling of satisfaction he had gained from the part he had played in the gathering of the ponies. If nothing else this sojourn in Exmoor had convinced him he could never return to the life of idle pleasure-seeking he had led in the months he had been back in London. He found himself wishing he truly was the simple fellow he purported to be—a man free to build a life for himself here on the west country moors.

It was, of course, an impossible dream for the son of the Duke of Bellmont. The closest he could ever hope to come to farming the land would be to reside on one of his father's country estates in the same token capacity as his uncles and the husbands of his two sisters. Much as he loved working with animals, this could never be a satisfying lifestyle, for the estates were all managed by highly capable stewards who took their orders directly from the duke.

Nor could he hope to find work as a steward for another titled landowner. The Duke of Bellmont expected his son to act like an aristocrat, and there was not a man in England foolish enough to risk the duke's displeasure by hiring his rebellious offspring.

No, better to accept Lord Castlereagh's offer of a diplomatic post than to spend his life as a puppet whose strings were pulled first by his father and then by his brother, Ethan, when he came into the title.

And what about the preternatural granddaughter of the

Witch of Exmoor? How will you fit such a pagan one as her into the civilized life of a diplomat? the annoying little voice of his conscience inquired.

He stared ahead at the object of his painful ruminations. As usual Fiona rode with her head high and her back straight as a ramrod. His gaze slid to her softly rounded hips, swaying to the gait of the pony beneath her. He groaned, imagining all too vividly how that lithe womanly body would feel beneath his on a feather bed.

The temperature of his blood instantly shot upward and he felt himself harden with desire. Devil take it, Fiona was as much a witch as her grandmother. She had cast a spell over him and he doubted any other woman would ever satisfy him.

He cursed himself for a fool. Witch she might be, but he had to have her as his lover. It was as simple as that. Somehow he would find the words to persuade her that she was destined to belong to him.

But first, for the sake of his sanity, he must solve the mystery of that blasted white stallion. Nothing could convince him it had been an illusion. It had been as real as the herd that had followed it across the moors. The ponies had obviously seen it. But why had Fiona and he been the only humans to whom it was visible? He felt certain she knew the answer to that question, and just as certain she would never tell him the whole truth—especially now that he had as much as called her a raving lunatic.

The only course left to him was to corner Creenagh and demand an explanation. Nay, not demand—cajole. He had charmed the irascible old woman into cooperating with him once before; with any luck, he could do it again. Then once he had the facts at hand, he could put the perplexing problem behind him and get on with his plans for the future.

Adam waited until after the evening meal before seeking out Creenagh. A full moon bathed the farmyard in a bright, silvery light, and the minute he stepped onto the porch he saw her sitting on a stump beside the barn. He drew near and realized she was smoking an odd-shaped little pipe that looked as if it had been carved from a root of the local heather. The wisp of smoke curling upward from its bowl smelled strangely sweet and the old woman's eyes had a faraway look to them.

Hunkering down beside her, he got straight to the point before whatever she had concocted from those herbs of hers made her so mellow he couldn't wring a sensible answer out of her. "Did Fiona tell you we saw the white pony again—this time leading the herd across the moors?"

"No, but 'tis not surprising. She be doing her best to pretend she never seen the beastie."

"Why?"

"'Cause she knows 'tis the 'sign' and she's afeared, that's why. Afeared if she allows the meaning of it she will be tempted to throw her precious respectability to the winds."

Adam felt a twinge of apprehension. Respectability was the one thing he could not offer Fiona. "I was not aware she attached such importance to social convention."

"Me granddaughter were the first Derry woman ever to choose a proper churchified marriage over real love." Creenagh took a puff of her pipe. "And a fine lot of happiness it brung her! I ain't saying Buckley Haines were a bad fellow, 'cause he weren't. But his thinking were slow as a ewe lamb mired in a bog, and he were no kind of man fer a smart woman like Fiona."

Remembering the raw-boned farmer who had foolishly challenged him to a game of hazard, Adam had to agree with her. In truth, he found it impossible to imagine two more diverse personalities than Fiona and her husband.

"I warned her the marriage were doomed," Creenagh said, "but she closed her mind to what I said, just like she be closing her mind to the sign now."

"I take it the sighting of this mysterious white pony is the sign to which you refer," Adam said, determined to get to the bottom of the perplexing puzzle in which he found himself involved.

"Aye. The same sign as were given to every Derry woman since the days when the ancients walked the moors."

"Given by whom?"

"By the gods o' course, ye thickhead."

"And for what purpose?"

"Why to tell her she's met up with the one nobleman what were created just for her. What else?"

Adam cleared his throat, suddenly self-conscious beneath the old woman's critical gaze. "Are you saying I am that man for Fiona?"

"Do ye doubt it, Londoner?"

Adam stared at her, as taken aback by her blunt question as by the fact that she had somehow guessed his aristocratic bloodlines. "No," he said finally, and knew in his heart he told the truth. "No, I don't. Not for one minute."

So, Fiona was destined to be his lover. If Creenagh were to be believed, her gods had ordained it. He wanted to shout for joy, or dance a jig or better yet, find Fiona and kiss her the way he had been longing to do ever since that fateful night when she had kissed away his nightmare.

Not that he believed in this crazy old woman's gods—or even in mystic ponies, despite the fact that he had seen one with his own eyes. He had always had a horror of anything connected with the black arts. Still, he had to admit that at the moment, this particular bit of mysticism appeared more helpful than ominous.

He stood up, anxious to find someplace where he could be alone to think about what Creenagh had told him, but he realized she had more to say. Curiosity kept him rooted to the spot.

She took another puff of her pipe and stared dreamy-eyed at the starlit sky above her. "I remember well the day I seen the white pony. 'Twere but a fortnight after word come of the fighting at Culloden. I looked out the window o' me mam's cottage and there it be grazing on the only patch o' grass in that stretch o' the moors. 'Twern't a minute later I heard a lad from the village shouting that the Stuart hisself had landed on the coast of Exmoor and were riding our way."

She sighed. "What a grand fellow he were, with his eyes as blue as a summer sky and his hair the color of a winter sunset—and the words rolling off his tongue in that fine way the Scotsmen have. Every girl in the village were begging to lift her petticoats for the handsome devil, but I could see he had eyes only fer me."

Adam frowned, wondering what the old woman was smoking to have produced that particular pipe dream. The epic battle of Culloden had been fought some sixty-eight years ago, which would mean Creenagh Derry had to be in her eighties. That in itself was too much for him to accept without asking him to believe she had consorted with the man known as Bonny Prince Charlie.

"Charles Stuart, the Young Pretender, was here in Exmoor?

Now that's a story I have never heard before," he said, tongue in cheek.

"Charles Stuart? That hen-hearted snake what run off to Gaul and left them as followed him to be slaughtered like dogs? Ye insult me, Londoner, to think I'd give me virtue to such a one as that. The Stuart I took fer me lover were his cousin Jamie—and a braver man never lived, nor one more true to the men he fought with. If 'twere my Jamie what rode at the head of the clans at Culloden, there'd be a Scotsman on the throne of England this day."

Creenagh's eyes turned dreamy again. "Jamie bided with me but three days before the King's soldiers come and dragged him from me bed. I never seen him again. But I tell ye this, Londoner, I'd not trade one minute of that three days fer a hundred lifetimes of Fiona's fine respectability."

"And you bore Jamie Stuart's child?"

"That I did. Nine months from the day last I saw him."

"Fiona's mother, I take it."

"Fiona's mam? Be ye daft, Londoner? Or do ye know so little o' history it slips yer mind the battle o' Culloden were fought near seventy years ago? 'Twere not Fiona's mam I bore, but her grandmam, Shana Derry."

"Are you saying you are Fiona's great-grandmother?"

"Don't recall ever saying it, but it be what I am, all right."

Adam stared at her in disbelief. "Good God! Then you must be in your eighties."

Creenagh nodded. "Two-and-eighty to the best o' me recollections, though I'll thank ye to keep that interesting bit o' news to yerself. I were fourteen years old the day Jamie Stuart rode into me life."

She tamped out her pipe on the side of the log and put it in her pocket. "Two-and-eighty be too long to live. Buried both me daughter and granddaughter in me day. Pretty as spring flowers they was, but not half a brain between the two of 'em. But Fiona now—I swear the gods saved up all the brains the Derry women had coming and give 'em all to her."

Creenagh rose to stand beside Adam, as slim and straight as a young girl. "I wishes ye luck, Londoner. 'Tis for certain ye'll need it if ye hopes to talk me stubborn granddaughter into sharing yer bed."

Adam flicked an annoyed glance at Creenagh's striking moon-lit profile. "You are changing your story, old woman. I distinctly remember your saying our sighting the white pony indicated those gods of yours approved of Fiona's becoming my lover."

"The gods can approve all they wants; it be Fiona ye have to get round. And ye might as well know the worst o' the problems ye're facing. Not only be she bound and determined to be respectable, she be fair muddled in the head about other things as well."

"What other things?"

"Thanks to what she learned in that proper marriage bed o' hers, she's got it in her mind she wants no more to do with what goes on betwixt a man and woman."

"The devil you say." Adam groaned. No wonder the lovely widow acted like a frightened spinster. Her husband may have been a decent, kindhearted fellow, but he apparently had been the worst kind of bumbling clod when it came to making love to a woman.

Creenagh shrugged. "I told her Buckley Haines were the wrong kind of man fer her to take up with the first time I ever laid eyes on him, but she were too stubborn and full of herself to listen to ought I had to say." The old woman studied Adam, a thoughtful expression on her youthful face. "But I can see ye be cut of a different cloth, Londoner."

Moonlight gleamed in Creenagh's lustrous black hair and a bewitching smile tilted the corners of her generous mouth. Seeing her like this, Adam found it easy to understand how a lusty young Scotsman who was running for his life could have lost his head and tarried too long in the arms of the enchanting coquette.

" 'Twill not be easy to change Fiona's mind, fer she be the most mule stubborn female ye'd ever care to meet." Creenagh's strange cat eyes glittered mischievously. "But ye be a handsome young devil fer all the black, thatchgallows look o' ye, Londoner."

With an enigmatic smile, she took her leave of Adam, but not before she purred, "If ye knows half as much about pleasuring a woman as I think ye does, ye'll find a way to convince the silly chit there be Derry blood in her veins after all."

Chapter Nine

Fiona was aware that Adam and Creenagh had had a long talk the night of the gathering. From the way her grandmother avoided her eyes the next morning, she felt certain they had discussed the white pony and its significance in the lives of Derry women.

A pox on the troublesome old woman. Whatever it was she had said to Adam, it had made him exchange his angry frown for a complacent grin. Furthermore, the devilish look in his eyes every time they met made her feel as if he were about to challenge her to a game of wits she had no hope of winning.

She found this new attitude on the part of her handsome farmhand even more disturbing than his anger. Not for the first time, she wished she had never thought to bring her grandmother to Larkspur Farm. She had not had a moment's peace since the day Adam and she had made that fateful trip across the moors to Creenagh's cave.

As it turned out, she had little time to worry about what Adam was plotting, or even if and when he planned to leave Exmoor. A runner arrived two days after the gathering to announce that Plimpton Fair would be held a full fortnight earlier than usual to accommodate the Plymouth buyers, and from that moment on her every waking minute was devoted to preparing for it.

The annual event was always important to the Exmoor farming community. This year the very survival of Larkspur Farm hinged on whether or not Fiona bargained successfully with the shrewd sheep and pony buyers. Buckley had seriously depleted her savings to make his ill-fated trip to London, and unless she came home from the fair with a goodly sum of money in her pocket, it would matter little whether or not

Adam chose to stay on for the balance of the summer, for she would be unable to pay his weekly stipend.

She halfway expected him to use the extra work suddenly thrust upon him as his excuse to make an early departure. But after Ben launched into an enthusiastic discourse on the wonders of Plimpton Fair, she could see Adam was intrigued by the idea. In fact, he threw himself so wholeheartedly into learning how to shear the Larkspur sheep and bale the wool, how to cull out the lambs to be sold at the fair, even to packaging the medicinal herbs that would earn Creenagh her yearly spending money, that everything was in readiness two days earlier than Fiona had hoped. All that was left was a last-minute currying of the yearlings to insure their attracting the eyes of the pony buyers.

"Thank you for your help, Adam. I could not have done it without you," Fiona said as the two of them caught a breath of fresh air on the porch the night before they left for the fair.

"I was glad to be able to pull my weight when the need arose."

Fiona felt a flush suffuse her cheeks at his reminder of the warning she had given when she hired him. "Your work has been more than satisfactory, as I am certain you know."

"Then perhaps you could see your way clear to adding a little something extra to my usual four shillings a week, ma'am."

"Something extra?" Fiona searched his face to see if he was serious in his request or still teasing her. It was hard to tell with Adam, especially when the porch was so deep in shadows. Unfortunately, from what she could see of him, he appeared to be in earnest.

"I wish I could," she said gravely. "But the wages I paid you and Ben this morning took everything I had except the fees for the two holding pens I have reserved for Larkspur stock. But perhaps if we are successful in selling the yearlings and lambs, I will be able to see my way clear to pay you a few extra shillings."

Adam sucked in his breath, as if shocked by her confession. Apparently it had never occurred to him that the owner of one of the finest farms in Exmoor could be short of money. She wondered if all gamblers had so little concept of the reality of the world outside the London gambling hells.

"Money is not my prime concern," he said, moving a step closer to her. "I have little use for what I already have while I am here in Exmoor."

Fiona could attest to the truth of that statement. Just this morning, when she'd swept his attic room, she'd noticed all the shillings she had paid him so far tossed carelessly onto his bedside table, as if they were of so little value to him, he could not be bothered to put them safely away, as any prudent person would. For all his cleverness, the man was a fool where money was concerned.

"What is it you need then?" she asked. "Is your bed not satisfactory? Are your meals not adequate?"

"My bed is narrow put perfectly satisfactory since I sleep alone, and while I have never before cared for mutton, I find I am beginning to acquire a taste for it as your grandmother seasons it. My material needs are quite adequately met, thank you ma'am."

He paused. "I fear it is my soul that is suffering."

"Your soul!" Fiona gasped, remembering his violent reaction to her mention of the Mystic Pony and his taunt about her pagan mumbo jumbo. "I assure you that despite what recent events may have led you to believe, your soul is in no danger here at Larkspur Farm."

"Is it not? I imagine you find it hard to comprehend how an aimless wanderer such as I could feel starved for human warmth."

"St . . . starved?"

"Starved." He moved another step closer. "There are times when I literally ache to touch another human being just to prove to myself I am really alive."

She could readily understand his problem, considering all he had endured in the war. The poor man. Her heart went out to him. "You are not alone, Adam," she said softly. "Both Ben and I have grown very fond of you in the short time you have been with us. You need only tell us when such a feeling comes upon you and we will do everything in our power to help you."

"You are very kind, ma'am—as is Ben, though I doubt he is endowed with the same nurturing instincts I sense in you." He gazed up at the heavens. "I think it must be that full moon that has done me in tonight. Have you never noticed how lonely

such a moon looks hanging there in the sky like the great silver orb of some long-forgotten king?"

As a matter of fact she had. More than once she had stood
alone at her window on a moonlit night and felt a terrible longing well up within her for something or someone she could not
begin to name. Her compassion for the lonely, troubled man
standing before her robbed her of her usual caution. Without
further thought, she reached out her hand to a fellow being
whose plaintive admission of need forged a unique bond between them.

He clasped her fingers in his and before she realized what
he was doing, drew her into his arms. "Ahhhh," he murmured,
resting his chin atop her head, "how comforting this is. I feel
better already."

His arms tightened about her and she found her body
pressed against the hard, muscular length of him, her hands
resting against his chest. He had not exaggerated his need for
human warmth; she felt a shiver ripple through him. In truth,
she felt a little shivery herself. Human warmth might be comforting for the one in need, but it could certainly arouse
strange feelings in the comforter.

She raised her head. "Adam?" she whispered, wondering
why this man's touch should make her breath catch in her
throat from sheer wonder, when all Buckley's had aroused in
her was a feeling of profound indifference.

"Yes, love." Adam bent his head and captured her lips in a
kiss so tender and fraught with need it nearly broke her heart.
She couldn't help herself; she kissed him back and a wave of
pure, joyous pleasure washed through her, so profound it left
her dazed and trembling—and shocked by the strength of her
own emotions.

Frantically, she pushed against Adam's chest and he instantly released her. "What is it, love? What is wrong?"

"Nothing, really. You just surprised me. I didn't expect you
to . . . well, you know . . . kiss me." She stepped back, putting
distance between them while she sorted out her jumbled emotions. While she had acknowledged the mystic pony could be a
sign that Adam was the man the gods had chosen for her, she
had never, until this moment, felt her heart was involved in
that acknowledgment. It was certainly involved now. The silly

thing was pounding so wildly she was amazed it hadn't leapt from her breast.

She pressed her fingers to her trembling lips. Could this incredible sensation she had just experienced be the passion Creenagh spoke of in such glowing terms? If so, the bright, breathtaking beauty of Adam's kiss was nothing like she had expected passion to be.

She had always thought of it as a dark, primitive urge that had trapped the women of her family into falling prey to unconscionable rakes bent on seduction. She felt anything but trapped at the moment. For the first time in her life, she felt like a beautiful, desirable woman and—God forgive her for the vain creature she was—she loved it.

"I am so sorry if I startled you." Adam sounded deeply contrite. "I can offer no excuse for my behavior other than that you felt so good in my arms, it just seemed natural to kiss you." He held out his hand. "Are we still friends?"

Fiona smiled to herself. Those were hardly the words of an "unconscionable rake bent on seduction." Maybe losing her heart to a man of such noble spirit would not be so terrible after all. She slipped her hand into his and felt his strong fingers once again close around hers. "Of course we are friends, and there is nothing to forgive. I believe we are both victims of that lonely moon of yours."

Gently, she withdrew her hand. "But I shall say good night now, Adam. We have a long day ahead of us tomorrow and I have a feeling we will both need every minute of sleep we can get."

She stopped in the doorway and turned back toward him, her brow knitted in a frown. "One more thing. I really must ask that in the future you refrain from calling me 'love.' It may be a common form of address in London; it is not in Exmoor. It is, in fact, considered a term of endearment. If someone should hear you addressing me thus, they might get the wrong impression."

"Well, we certainly would not want that to happen. I shall make certain I only use the term when we are alone."

That was not precisely the promise she had hoped to get from him. Was he being purposely obtuse or was his manner of thinking so different from her own, they found it difficult to communicate with each other. Why, she wondered as she made her way down the narrow hall to her bedchamber, was nothing ever simple where Adam was concerned?

With mixed feelings, Adam watched Fiona disappear through the doorway of the cottage. She had responded to the loneliness he had expressed with a compassion that had both humbled and shamed him. What had started as a less-than-honorable effort on his part to win a forbidden kiss had quickly changed into honest, heartfelt need.

In the end, he had kissed her because he was powerless to resist the temptation she offered. She, on her part, had returned his kiss with a sweet, uninhibited eagerness that intrigued him far more than the practiced sensuality of the skilled London courtesan who was currently his mistress.

But once again the pesky little voice of his conscience reminded him he had no business kissing a woman so recently widowed. Had he become so enthralled with Creenagh's claim about the significance of the white pony that he had lost all sense of propriety?

Or had he rushed his fences because he sensed time was his enemy? He knew his father too well to believe he would wait much longer before issuing a summons to his rebellious son. Any day now a messenger from the Duke of Bellmont would arrive at Larkspur Farm and expose his charade. Before that happened he must make certain Fiona was committed to returning to London with him.

To accomplish that, he must lay his plans carefully. As Creenagh had warned, Fiona was stubbornly independent. She would not be easy to bring round to his way of thinking. Somehow he must make her see the advantages of the life of wealth and leisure he could offer her in London as opposed to the drudgery of scraping a barely adequate living out of a farm in Exmoor—and he must do so without delay.

He would wait until Plimpton Fair and all it entailed was behind her. Then he would launch an all-out campaign to woo and win her.

He groaned, as the dull ache in his groin reminded him how Fiona's soft womanly curves had felt nestled against him. His was a deeply sensual nature and he did not live easily with abstinence—especially around a woman who tempted him as much as Fiona did.

On a spur-of-the-moment decision, he hied himself down to the small lake that lay at the southeast corner of Larkspur Farm. Stripping off his clothes, he plunged into the icy water and swam back and forth until he was so thoroughly chilled he had reason to hope his traitorous body might allow him a few hours of sleep before Ben woke him at dawn.

With Adam and Fiona astride their ponies, three bales of wool and a dozen bleating lambs crowded into the oversized sledge cart driven by Ben, as well as ten Exmoor yearlings strung out behind, it was an odd little cavalcade that departed Larkspur Farm early the next morning. Only Creenagh and Caesar were missing—and they could hear the dog howling his protest at being locked in the barn long after they pulled out of the farmyard.

The slow, tedious journey took the entire day. The sun was setting when they finally rode down the main street of the village where Plimpton Fair was to be held, and a number of the local farmers had already arrived—among them some of the men Adam had met at the gathering. But if the holding pen they had passed on the way into town was any indication, Fiona was one of the few to reserve separate pens for her ponies.

A herd of thirty or more Exmoors, along with a dozen sleek thoroughbreds and a like number of mammoth draft horses milled about inside the small, muddy enclosure. Adam breathed a sigh of relief that the yearlings with whom he had made friends during the past few days would be spared such miserable accommodations.

Some of the men of the village were busy building stalls to accommodate the merchants who would provide the food and drink for those attending the fair, others were erecting barricades along the fronts of the houses lining the main street. "To protect them from rampaging livestock," Fiona explained. "Things sometimes get a bit out-of-hand when the selling begins, which is why I felt it worthwhile to reserve space next to the arena where the pony auctions will be held."

She led the way to two small, empty pens at the far end of

the street and dismounted beside the first one. "We will feed the livestock and bed them down for the night. Then we can look to our own supper and sleeping arrangements."

Adam had seen but one inn as they passed through the village and while it was a fair size, the number of carriages in the innyard made him think there would be little chance that three bedchambers were still available. He said as much and found himself surveyed by two pairs of eyes wide with amazement.

"The inn is reserved for the stock buyers from Plymouth and Ilfracombe, and the wealthy landowners from Dartmoor and Cornwall who come up each year to find ponies suitable for crossbreeding. It is not for Exmoor farmers," Fiona explained.

"If it is a matter of money, I brought the shillings I have earned this past month with me."

Ben shook his head. "Save your money, lad. There'll be plenty of places to spend it tomorrow when the fair be under way. Farmers eats their own bread and cheese and sleeps under their carts, as we'll do this night on the quilts mistress brought."

The old man shuffled to the back of the sledge cart. "Now, give me a hand coaxing these lambs and ponies into their pens afore I drops in me tracks from hunger."

Embarrassed by his obvious faux pas, Adam did as he was asked without further comment. It would not be the first time he had slept on the ground. He had spent more nights than he cared to remember with nothing but a British army blanket between him and the rocky soil of the Spanish plain. But there, a beautiful young widow had not numbered among his sleeping companions. He had found it difficult enough these past few nights sleeping with Fiona in the same cottage; he doubted he would so much as close his eyes with her lying next to him.

As it turned out, he was spared that particular torture. Fiona slept on the bales of wool in the cart and only Ben and he slept on the ground beneath. Still, even with his eyes closed, he could picture her above him as clearly as if he could see through the floorboards of the cart. What little sleep he managed to get was so riddled with erotic dreams, he rose at dawn with a pounding head and eyes as gritty as if he had spent the night riding across a windy moor.

Fiona and he spent a good two hours giving the yearlings a final currying, while all around them tents were raised, hurdles installed, and all was made ready for the great event. The currying completed, Fiona availed herself of one of the tents to change from her breeches and shirt into her ugly, but proper, widow's weeds, for by then it was eight o'clock and the fair was in full swing.

People thronged the main street of the village, sampling the various foods offered at the hastily constructed stalls, or seeking a place at the edge of the arena where the pony auctions were due to begin in a little over an hour.

Farmers and their wives in simple homespun garments rubbed shoulders with nattily dressed buyers and the painted and powdered lightskirts they had brought with them from Plymouth, and the even more elegantly attired landowners from nearby counties. To Adam's surprise, no one seemed to find the blend of humanity any odder than the mixture of horseflesh in the main holding pen.

He was left to guard the Larkspur yearlings while Fiona negotiated the sale of the lambs with an interested buyer and Ben visited the stall where the owner of the Black Boar Inn sold tankards of his famous ale. Lounging against the end of the sledge cart, he surveyed his first farmers' fair with mixed feelings.

On the one hand, he was intrigued by the striking contrast between the holiday atmosphere of the swelling crowds and the serious demeanor of the local farmers who had come to offer their livestock to the highest bidder.

On the other hand, the pungent aroma of fresh animal droppings and stale human sweat made him slightly nauseated, and his ears rang from the sound of the honking geese and gobbling turkeys waiting in wooden crates for the farmers' wives to buy them for their Sunday dinners.

Behind him, the Larkspur lambs bleated their disapproval at being torn from their mother's sides and transported to this strange location, and some of the yearling ponies showed signs of raising a ruckus of their own. He suddenly had visions of putting in a long, hard day on top of an interminable, sleepless night.

His stomach rumbled, and he decided that what he needed

more than anything else at the moment was some nourishing food. He hailed a scrubby-looking lad weaving through the crowd with a tray of hot pastries and sausages, or "bangers," as Ben called them. He purchased one of each and promptly devoured them.

He had just taken his last bite of the steaming pastie when a male voice close to his right ear remarked, "I had heard my sister found herself a strapping young farmhand. I see the rumor was true."

Adam wheeled around and found himself face-to-face with the tall, red-haired man who had been Buckley Haines's companion in London. He swallowed hard, but the bite of pastie refused to go down. Now that he had met Fiona, he realized the likeness between the two was unmistakable. This had to be her estranged half brother of whom Ben had spoken.

The smile faded from the redhead's face and his amber eyes, so like Fiona's, widened in obvious shock. "What the devil? You are the last person I expected to see at Plimpton Fair," he exclaimed in a strangled voice.

He turned abruptly to the pretty, apple-cheeked brunette clinging to his arm. "Run along, Molly my love. I want a word alone with this fellow."

The brunette gave an angry toss of her head. "I will not, for how would ye be finding me again in this crowd, Liam Campbell?"

"Wait by your father's stall and I'll come for you as soon as I finish here." With a playful swat on her plump backside, he sent her on her way with the admonition, "Draw me a tankard of the old man's ale, love, and not too much foam if you please."

He watched his lady friend until she was out of earshot, then turned to Adam. "Now tell me, what is a high-and-mighty-milord doing in Exmoor?" he demanded. "And why is he posing as a farmhand?"

Adam didn't particularly like the fellow's tone of voice, but all things considered, he was in no position to quarrel with him. "I have my reasons."

"The same reasons, I suppose, that led you to tell Molly's father you were a lowly foot soldier recently home from Spain."

"I take it Molly's father is Hiram Blodgett, owner of the Black Boar Inn," Adam said, stalling for time while he gathered his wits.

"He is indeed and knowing Hiram, he is keeping an accounting of every bucket of oats he feeds that elegant thoroughbred 'your grateful officer gave you for saving his life in battle.'" Liam Campbell raked Adam with a look of disgust. "Did you even serve in Wellington's army, milord, or was it all a bouncer?"

"I was a major in the First Hussars. The uniform I wore en route to Exmoor belonged to my former batman. It seemed a wise precaution considering the brigands prowling England's highways these days."

Campbell nodded in agreement. "I will give you that, but I would still like to know why you are posing as my sister's farmhand."

Adam could see he had no recourse but to tell this brother of Fiona's the truth—well, most of it anyway. He took a deep breath. "It all started because of the unwitting part I played in Buckley Haines's death. I came to Exmoor to return the deed I won in that blasted card game to his widow—"

"You are not here to claim the farm?" Liam Campbell interjected, searching Adam's face with unbelieving eyes.

"Of course not. What would I want with a farm in Exmoor?"

Campbell relaxed noticeably. He even managed a weak smile. "What indeed?"

"As for my posing as a farmhand, that came about when your sister mistook me for an ex-soldier applying for work. On a sudden whim, I accepted her offer because . . ." Adam shrugged. "Damned if I can remember exactly why I did it. But now I cannot think of a tactful way to tell her the truth—"

"Without spoiling your chances with her." A knowing smile crossed Campbell's handsome face. "I am Fiona's brother and as such, immune to her charms. But I can understand why the little minx intrigues you."

He laughed softly. "Good luck, milord. I cannot think of anything that would do my starchy sister more good than a flaming affair with the likes of you. But you will need a miracle to pull it off. She is prickly as a hedgehog where men are concerned."

"So your grandmother warned me."

"My grandmother? If you mean Creenagh Derry—that crazy old soothsayer is no kin of mine. The only relative Fiona and I share is our father, and while the old boy has his faults, there is no taint of witchcraft in his bloodline."

Liam Campbell glanced toward the town square and drew a sharp breath. "Speaking of hedgehogs . . . I believe I see my sister heading this way. In which case, I had best be making myself scarce. The last time we spoke, she made it very clear she never wanted to lay eyes on me again."

His amber eyes clouded with some indefinable emotion. "It was I, you see, who talked Buckley into going to London, and Fiona blames me for his death."

He frowned. "But one thing more before I leave—you appear to be a man who respects honesty, if your intentions concerning the deed to Larkspur Farm are to be believed."

Adam stiffened. "My present situation notwithstanding, I normally make it a point to deal with my fellow men—and women—with complete honesty."

"A word of warning then, milord. Were I you, I would not be too scrupulously honest with Fiona about what transpired in that London gaming hell. She is not entirely rational where her husband is concerned. I strongly suspect it stems from the fact that while she was grateful for all he did for her, she could barely tolerate the poor dimwit.

"But be that as it may, if she ever learns you had a hand in the sorry string of events that led to Buckley Haines's death, she will undoubtedly hate you the same way she hates me."

Chapter Ten

Fiona's spirits were higher than they had been in a long time. Early that morning she had talked Hiram Blodgett into allotting a corner of his stall where he sold his ale to Creenagh's healing herbs. He had even agreed to put one of his daughters in charge of selling them.

Then she had engaged in an hour of energetic bargaining with a sheep buyer from Ilfracombe, which resulted in an excellent price for her lambs. She had even managed to sell her bales of wool to the owner of a small mill in Dawlish. Now if she had any kind of luck auctioning off her yearlings, she would return to Larkspur Farm with enough money in her pocket to survive another year—maybe even persuade Adam to stay on.

But she dare not let herself think of the tantalizing idea that was beginning to take shape in her mind regarding her handsome farmhand—not until the auction was over and she knew exactly what she had to offer him.

She pushed her way through the crowd of people thronging the village common and headed toward the pens which held the Larkspur sheep and ponies. Then she saw him! Her half brother, Liam, lounging against the sledge cart, engaged in what appeared to be a serious conversation with Adam. He looked up, met her gaze for a brief instant, then immediately disappeared into the crowd.

But the damage was done. One look at the man who had lured Buckley to his untimely death with his tales of the wonders of London, and her lovely daydream evaporated like a puff of smoke. Riddled with guilt, she reminded herself that the small triumphs she had just enjoyed should have been ones she shared with her husband—not a handsome stranger whose dulcet voice had the power to charm wild animals, and whose tender kisses turned her into a starry-eyed idiot.

"What did Liam want?" she demanded the minute she reached Adam's side.

"Your brother had heard about your new farmhand and came to introduce himself," Adam said. But his gloomy expression told her that more than a simple introduction had transpired between them.

What could Liam have said to make Adam look as if he had just had the wind knocked out of him? She laid her hand on his sleeve. "I feel I should warn you, Liam Campbell is an unscrupulous rogue. Never take anything he says to heart."

"On the contrary, I found him to be a very well-spoken fellow with a good head on his shoulders. Would that my own brother were more like him. For reasons I shall never understand, we have grown apart, and I miss the closeness we once shared." Adam leveled a look on Fiona that made her squirm uncomfortably. "A quarrel between siblings is a sad thing, as is a quarrel between friends."

Fiona stiffened. "I see Liam mentioned our recent falling-out. Since it is nothing that concerns you, I see no point in discussing it."

Adam's expression darkened even more, but before he could comment further a shout of, "Here they come!" rose from the square behind him.

"What the devil?" he exclaimed as down the street leading to the sales arenas surged a seemingly endless stream of men on foot, men on horseback, herds of cattle, flocks of sheep, and droves of wild ponies, all mixed together in a noisy, chaotic hodgepodge that threatened to burst through the hastily erected barricades.

Fiona had to laugh at the look of shock on Adam's face. "Can you see why I thought it advisable to reserve a pen adjoining the pony arena?"

"Good Lord yes. How do the farmers know which of the livestock is theirs?"

"I am not sure they do, which is why I felt we should keep the Larkspur ponies separate from the common drove. Furthermore, the fee I paid for the pens for my lambs and ponies provided an added benefit as well. Because of it, I was given my choice of spots at the pony auction. Ours will be the fifth lot offered."

"That is advantageous?"

"In my opinion it is the perfect spot." She raised her voice to be heard above the noise of shouting men and pounding hooves. "The auctioneer told me there were twelve lots of ponies scheduled to be shown today. I reasoned the buyers would hesitate bidding on the first few lots for fear something better would come along— and they would have already made their purchases before the last few lots were offered. Therefore, it seemed logical they would be most ready to part with their money when the fifth and sixth lots were shown. Oliver Pinchert agreed with my thinking, so he took lot six. What do you think?"

Adam chuckled. "I think, love, that the war in Spain would have ended a year sooner had Wellington been able to consult you concerning his battle strategy."

Fiona felt her cheeks flush with pleasure and embarrassment at Adam's words of praise. She was not accustomed to compliments. Buckley had been unswervingly loyal; as far as she knew he had never looked at another woman. But words had not come easily to him. She turned Adam's words over and over in her mind, treasuring the sound of them—wondering if he really meant them or if such clever turns of phrase were commonplace in the world from which he came.

To cover her own confusion, she made a pretense of watching the confusion that reigned in the main street of the village for the next hour. Buckley had always considered this period of pandemonium before the pony auction the most exciting part of the fair. She hated every minute of it.

This year it seemed particularly out of control. With Adam beside her, she sat on the end of the Larkspur sledge cart and watched the farmers who had drawn lots one through four in the pony auction attempt to separate their animals from the frantic muddle. By the time some semblance of order was achieved, the ponies were crazed with fear.

One pony in the first lot broke loose from its drover and bolted into the arena to race willy-nilly around the circle with the handlers chasing after it. Fiona's heart went out to the wild-eyed creature. Once the handlers managed to subdue it, it stood stock-still in the center of the spectator-ringed arena, too terrified to move another inch.

At this point the auctioneer's assistant, a beefy fellow with a bulbous nose and bald pate, took over, cracking his blacksnake whip again and again above the pony's head to prod it into going through its paces. To no avail, the animal was frozen with fear.

When it became apparent there would be no bids offered on the first pony, it was dragged off by the handlers and another was herded through the gate with much shouting and waving of sticks. This one appeared every bit as terrified as the first and in addition to the assistant and his whip, one handler grasped the animal around the neck and another pushed it from behind to get it under way. The same procedure was repeated with every pony in the first lot. But as far as Fiona could see, the only response this elicited from the poor creatures was a growing pile of smelly, steaming manure.

She glanced at Adam sitting beside her. The grim set to his jaw told her he found this method of showing the wild ponies as distasteful as she did. "Barbaric," he muttered as once again the whip sliced the air within inches of an animal's nose.

"The pony auction at Plimpton Fair has been conducted in this same manner since the time of Kind Henry VIII," Fiona explained. "When I voiced my objection to my husband two years ago, he assured me I would accomplish nothing except to humiliate him if I spoke out." She sighed. "It is very difficult to go against tradition in Exmoor."

Adam's only reply was a noncommittal grunt. But Fiona could see his anger building as the ponies in lots two and three were put through the same nerve-racking ordeal. Bidding was sporadic and those ponies that sold went for prices far lower than what Fiona had hoped to get for her yearlings. Her spirits sank. Unless something sparked the bidders' interest, Larkspur Farm would be in serious financial trouble.

The ponies in Dooley Twig's string made up the fourth round. His animals started out somewhat calmer than those that had gone before them, since he too had reserved a pen for them. But the whip-cracking auctioneer's assistant and the two handlers managed to properly terrify them once they entered the arena.

Still, for all his faults, Dooley was a conscientious farmer. He and his brothers had curried their yearlings until their sleek summer coats gleamed in the bright June sun. As a result, the bidding grew a little more enthusiastic. All but three of the Twig ponies were claimed by the buyers, but the prices paid for the fifteen which sold were still far below what they should have been.

Bitter disappointment was etched on Dooley's florid face as he pushed his way through the crowd to collect the money due him from the two Plymouth buyers who had bid on his livestock. He was one of the more affluent Exmoor farmers, but even he depended heavily on the revenue gleaned from the sale of the wild ponies.

He stopped in front of Fiona, who had moved to stand in the owner's spot by the gate of the arena while Ben and Adam brought the Larkspur ponies forward from their pen. "If ye're thinking to fill the empty pockets me friend Buckley left ye with, ye'll not be doing it this year at Plimpton Fair, Fiona Haines."

He jerked a thumb toward Adam. "And how long will yer fancy townie stay with ye when ye've no money to pay his wages and naught but yer oldest mutton to fill his belly?"

Fiona drew herself up to her full height. "Save your worrying for your own problems, Dooley Twig. It appears to me you have plenty of them."

"Ye've a sassy mouth on ye, woman. Ye always have had. But fer the sake of me friendship with Buckley, I were willing to take ye to wife when yer fields had just been plowed by one man. But don't look to me fer another offer when the last o' yer luck runs out. "I've no use fer the leavings of a London footpad."

Fiona tossed her head. "As if I would consider wedding a man with the mind of a snake and a mouth as foul as the Devil's Bog." With a look of disgust, she turned her back on her closest neighbor, whom Buckley had once declared "the best friend any fellow could ever have."

Dooley Twig moved on, but not before he uttered an invective so obscene it singed her ears. She was still quivering with anger when a few minutes later Adam and Ben arrived with the string of Larkspur ponies.

By means of a halter Adam led the lead pony, a young stallion, to the entrance of the arena. Instantly the two handlers converged on it, bent on driving it to the center of the ring as they had those shown in the other four lots. Adam raised his hand and stopped them cold. "I will put these animals through their paces myself," he said in a loud, clear voice. He glanced toward Fiona. "With your permission, of course, Mistress Haines."

Fiona registered the sudden hush that fell on the watching spectators and the looks of astonishment on the faces of the auctioneer's assistant, the handlers, even the auctioneer himself. She felt her heart drum a nervous tattoo against her rib cage. To the best of her knowledge, no one had ever before challenged the established procedure of the Plimpton Fair pony auction.

She knew why Adam was doing it. He couldn't bear to see any animal terrorized. Nor could she, but with so much at stake, did she dare risk the auctioneer's censure for the sake of a principle?

Beside her, Ben hopped first on one foot, then the other like a flea on a hot rock. "Don't listen to the Londoner, Mistress," he begged in a hoarse whisper. "He means well, but he don't know our ways. He'll get us throwed out on our arses with his foolish talk."

Fiona swallowed hard, conscious of Adam's angry silver eyes, daring her to support him. For one brief instant her conscience warred with her sense of self-preservation. Her conscience won. With an apologetic glance toward Ben, she stepped forward and faced the auctioneer—a tall, distinguished-looking man with a wealth of snowy hair and a hawkish nose. "If you please, sir, I ask that you allow my . . . my associate, Mr. Cresswell, to show the Larkspur Farm ponies without the aid of your assistant or handlers."

A cumulative gasp spread through the ring of buyers and spectators, followed by a silence broken only by the sounds of the restless animals still waiting their turn in the melee outside the arena.

The auctioneer removed a pair of spectacles from his pocket, slipped them onto the bridge of his prominent nose and studied Fiona with an intensity that nearly buckled her knees.

"Your request is out of keeping, madam. Why, pray tell, should I countenance a change in a procedure that has proved successful for the past three centuries?"

Fiona racked her brain to come up with an answer that would satisfy him. But before she could speak, Adam handed the pony's halter to Ben and stepped forward. "I am new to Exmoor, sir, but in the short time I have observed the moorland ponies I have come to the conclusion they are blessed with a great deal of native intelligence, as well as an inherent sense of self-worth. This is probably why they do not respond favorably to being controlled by fear."

Another audible gasp rose from the gathered spectators. Adam carried on as if he hadn't heard it. "I believe the ponies will show to the best advantage when treated with the courtesy and respect due all God's creatures. I should like the chance to prove it."

A ripple of laughter spread through the crowd at such an outrageous statement, but the auctioneer perused Adam with narrowed eyes and a solemn demeanor. "An interesting theory, young man. I believe I shall grant your request out of curiosity, if nothing else. But I warn you, if even one of those ponies of yours get seriously out of hand and disrupts my auction, I shall ban the entire lot from the bidding. Is that understood?"

"It is, sir." Adam turned to Fiona. "Trust me. I have made friends with the yearlings these past two days. We understand each other."

Fiona gulped and nodded her agreement, instinctively winging a silent prayer to Vicar Edelson's kindly Christian God for forbearance on the part of the auctioneer.

As she watched, Adam took the halter from Ben and led the yearling stallion to the center of the arena. She could see his lips moving and knew he was speaking to the animal in his usual soothing manner—probably explaining the procedure he was about to put it through.

For a long nerve-racking moment the pony stood quietly, ears pricked, as if it truly were listening to every word that was said to it. Then with Adam holding the end of the halter, it circled him, first in a slow walk, then a gentle trot.

Its gait was smooth and its strong hooves pounded neatly and rhythmically on the hard-packed dirt. With its head at a haughty angle, the yearling went through its paces with an energy and aplomb that proclaimed its proud heritage to all who watched. Fiona felt her heart swell with pride for the sturdy young pony and for the man who had won its confidence with his gentle ways.

Finally, when the animal had sufficiently demonstrated both its physical fitness and its keen intelligence, Adam brought it to a halt and brushed his hand lovingly along its sleekly curried back—much like he rewarded Caesar whenever the dog particularly pleased him.

The auctioneer made no comment, but Fiona felt certain she saw a twinkle in his eyes when he opened the bidding on the first of the Larkspur yearlings.

"I will take every animal this fellow has worked with and save you the trouble of auctioning them off one-by-one," a buyer from Plymouth called out, and named a price that was everything Fiona could have hoped for.

A buyer from Ilfracombe leapt to his feet. "The devil you will. I want my chance at three of them. I demand the auction proceed as usual."

"As do I. I have two young brothers in need of mounts, and ponies gentled in such a manner would suit them admirably," declared an elegant fellow who Ben whispered was the eldest son of a wealthy landowner from Cornwall.

The auctioneer pounded his gavel to bring order to the noisy crowd. "The auction will proceed as usual. I, for one, am interested to see if Mr. Cresswell can work his magic on all ten of the Larkspur ponies with his 'courtesy and respect.'" The elderly man's eyes definitely twinkled now. "It is a revolutionary theory to be sure, but one that apparently has a certain merit."

"The Londoner has done ye proud," Oliver Pinchert declared, stepping up to stand beside Ben and Fiona. "Fer certain, ye'll get a fine price fer all yer beasties this day."

"Aye," Ben agreed. "I should've knowed better than to doubt the lad." He licked his lips in glee as the fiercely competitive bidding for the first yearling came to a close at a figure beyond Fiona's wildest dreams.

The same was true of the other nine after Adam patiently put each one through its paces. In less than an hour and a half, the Larkspur yearlings had yielded enough revenue to see

Fiona through the year ahead. She might even be able to put a few pounds by for an emergency.

She heard murmurs of, "Did you see that?" and, "Can you believe it?" all around her as the auctioneer pounded his gavel to signify the end of the bidding on lot five. As she made her way to the tent where the buyers' men-of-affairs waited to pay her the money due her, she saw Adam turn the last yearling over to the stockmen employed by its new owner. He talked to them briefly, a sober expression on his face—no doubt giving them the same lecture on the proper care and handling of the animal he had given to all the others.

When a short while later the auctioneer declared a two-hour recess for the noonday meal, Adam strode toward the spot where Ben waited at the gate with Oliver Pinchert and his three sons.

Ben greeted him with, "Well done lad." The old man beamed from ear to ear. "It's proud I be of ye fer what ye've done fer Larkspur Farm this day."

"And for the ponies," Fiona added as she joined them. The happy glow in her amber eyes lent an even more breathtaking beauty than usual to her expressive face, and Adam felt an instant surge of desire so intense he felt as if he'd been struck by a bolt of lightning.

Fiona's lips curved in an admiring smile. "You have done the ponies a great service, Adam. The buyers' stockmen are not fools; they have to see your method of handling animals is much more successful than any they have been following. I feel certain they will treat the animals in their care far more gently from now on."

Adam felt a foolish grin spread across his face at her words of praise. Fiona knew him well. He was glad he had helped her earn the money she needed, but in truth he cared much more about the fate of the ponies at the hands of the men who had purchased them.

"What Fiona says be true. Ye've taught us all a lesson this day, Londoner." Oliver Pinchert stepped forward, his hand outstretched. "Me beasties is next to be auctioned and I'll take it kindly if ye'll agree to show 'em for me."

Adam groaned. He liked Oliver Pinchert and he was grateful to him and his sons for their help at the gathering. But the persistent throbbing in this temples could only grow worse if he agreed to spend another hour or two in the sun-drenched arena.

Fiona stepped forward to stand between him and Oliver Pinchert. "He cannot do it," she declared in a tone of voice that brooked no argument. "Surely you can see Adam is exhausted. Putting ten frisky yearlings through their paces with the auctioneer's threat hanging over his head was no easy task."

Adam smiled in spite of himself. She looked for all the world like a banty hen protecting her chick. Normally he would resent anyone's speaking for him, but between a sleepless night and the tension of the past two hours, he was too tired to object.

Oliver Pinchert's hangdog look was pitiful to behold. "I knows I asks a lot, Fiona, but I only does so because I've as sore a need as yerself fer the extra fees his wondrous way with the ponies will bring. 'Tis been hard year fer the farmers of Exmoor."

Fiona glanced at the bulging reticule she clutched in her hands and her cheeks flamed. "I am all too aware of that fact, Mr. Pinchert. But we have a long ride ahead of us this afternoon and if Adam agrees to your request, we will not reach home until well after dark."

"A long ride and most of it on a lonely road," Pinchert agreed. "And even if ye leave this very minute, darkness will be upon ye the last few miles of yer journey. Why don't ye wait till tomorrow morning to leave the fair? 'Twould be much safer, since then me lads and me could offer ye our protection in return fer the favor I be asking of yer man."

"Tomorrow?" Fiona frowned. "Oh, I think not, Mr. Pinchert. My grandmother is alone at the farm, with the cow to milk and the chickens and hogs to feed and a dozen other chores I cannot think of at the moment. We really should return home today."

"Foolish thinking if ye asks me." Pinchert made a sweeping gesture with his hand. "Look about ye lass. Plimpton Fair draws the dregs of the Plymouth docks as well as livestock buyers and simple farmers—and 'tis no secret the cache of pound notes ye'll be carrying with ye when ye heads back to Larkspur Farm.

"Ye'll be easy pickings fer the blackhearted rogues what preys on honest travelers if ye've just one outrider and an old man to guard ye. But even the boldest of 'em will think twice afore they try robbing a woman guarded by five armed outriders."

He turned to Adam. "Ye do carry a firearm, do ye not, lad?"

"I do, sir." Adam opened his jacket to show the pepperbox pistol he'd stuck in the waistband of his breeches. "But you make a good point. One man alone would be hard put to protect Mistress Haines if we were attacked by a band of cutthroats. If you are saying that you and your sons would be willing to escort us all the way to Larkspur Farm if I put your ponies through their paces, we might well be able to strike a bargain."

"We would, lad, and gladly."

"And how many ponies did you bring to the fair?"

"Only eight this year I be sorry to say."

Adam turned to Fiona. "If you can see your way clear to staying over, I think it would be wise. I confess I am not too comfortable with the idea of the three of us traveling alone— particularly on that last lonely stretch between the Twig farm and Larkspur."

"The Londoner be right, Mistress." Ben's faded eyes sparked with sudden excitement. " 'Tis the foolishest of ideas, now that I think on it. Ye'll recall Buckley always stayed over the night of the fair."

"Buckley could afford to hire one of the local lads to do the chores while he was gone."

"The witch be not so old or helpless she cannot do what chores needs doing fer a couple o' days," Ben said sourly. His gaze darted from one to another of the group surrounding him as if to gage the way the wind blew. "I fer one would be more'n willing to wait till the morning if it meant traveling with enough outriders to discourage any rascal with mischief on 'is mind."

Adam did his best to hide his smile. Ben was not only willing to stay over; he was literally dancing a jig at the thought of spending the evening with his cronies at the stall where Hiram Blodgett dispensed his fine, dark ale.

Fiona sighed. "What can I say? The argument in favor of accepting Mr. Pinchert's offer makes good sense, but I will leave the final decision up to you, Adam. You are the one on whom the extra work will fall."

"It is agreed then," Adam said quickly before Fiona could change her mind. "If the auctioneer will allow it, I will show your ponies right after the nooning, Mr. Pinchert."

"The stiff-necked fellow had best allow it if he knows what be good for 'im. I'll not take no for an answer. I promises ye that."

"Very well, sir." Adam pulled his watch from his pocket and checked the time. "It is exactly twenty minutes after the hour of twelve. I shall plan on meeting you at this same spot at ten minutes before the hour of two."

He stifled a yawn as he watched Ben and Oliver Pinchert hurry off in the direction of Hiram Blodgett's stall. A month ago he would have been tempted to go with them. All that tempted him today was the thought of exploring the more pleasurable features of a rollicking country fair with Fiona.

What fun they would have! And what better way to launch a campaign to win the heart of a woman who had led as bleak a life as the lovely widow Haines than to give her a taste of the good times the two of them could have together? For win her heart he must before she learned who he really was and what part he had inadvertently played in her husband's death. Only then would she be likely to listen to reason when he pled his case.

He smiled tenderly at the object of his affections. "I feel much easier in my mind now that it is settled we will be traveling with the four Pincherts," he said softly. "I would never forgive myself if any harm came to you because I had not made adequate preparations for your protection."

She blushed prettily. "I am not your responsibility, Adam."

"My ears hear what you are saying, love, but my heart knows better." Catching her hand in his, he slipped it through the crook of his arm. "But we will speak of such serious things some other time. Right now I am hungry, as I am certain you must be too."

"We still have some bread and cheese."

"Which might possibly excite me if I were a mouse. I am thinking more of a nice hot pastie dripping with gravy. I had one this morning; it was delicious. I would not recommend the sausage, however. It was nowhere near as good as what you make."

No sooner had he spoken than he spied the same young boy who had sold him his breakfast crossing the square with his tray balanced on one shoulder. "Ho, lad," he called, "two pasties if you please." He pulled his clean handkerchief from his pocket, wrapped the steaming hot pies in it and tossed the boy a shilling with a careless, "Spend what is left yourself. You've earned it."

Fiona's eyes were as round as the proverbial saucers. "You are very careless with your money, Adam. One might almost say foolish."

"Might one, indeed? Wait until I have put the Pinchert ponies through their paces; then I will show you just how foolish I can be. I have my entire hoard of shillings burning a hole in my pocket. I cannot wait to see what fascinating ways we can find to spend them."

Fiona frowned disapprovingly. "Has it never occurred to you that you should save your hard-earned shillings for a rainy day?"

"And miss the fun of spending them with a beautiful woman on a sunny day?" Adam laughed softly . . . provocatively. "Never, love. For to my way of thinking, that would be the greatest foolishness of all."

Chapter Eleven

For lack of a better place to hold their impromptu picnic, Adam and Fiona sat on the back of the Larkspur sledge cart while they devoured their pasties and shared a pitcher of buttermilk Adam had purchased at one of the stalls adjoining the arena. Fiona couldn't remember when anything had tasted as delicious as the chunks of hot beef and the flaky crust oozing with rich brown gravy—and the nicest thing about it was someone else had cooked it.

She glanced up to find that funny, lopsided grin on Adam's face—the one that made her insides go all topsy-turvy. "Why are you looking at me like that?" she demanded.

"I am thinking how enormously pleased I am that I got my money's worth out of that shilling I spent. For what could I have bought with it that would be more fun than watching you eat that pastie?"

Fiona felt her cheeks flame. "Beef is a rare treat. The cow we keep at the farm is for milking." She licked her lips. "Thank you very much. I may deplore your spendthrift ways, but I must admit I enjoyed every bite."

Adam removed his jacket, folded it into a pillow for his head, and stretched out beside her. "Life is meant to be enjoyed, Fiona. You should let yourself do so more often."

"Now you sound like Liam."

"As I have mentioned before, I found your brother to be a very astute fellow." He gazed at her with sleepy eyes. "You have gravy on your chin." He reached up, drew his forefinger across a spot beneath her lower lip, then sucked the drop of rich brown liquid from the tip. Fiona's pulse pounded dizzily in her ears. For some reason she couldn't explain, the simple act seemed unbearably intimate.

Adam obviously didn't find it so. He yawned mightily and let his eyes drift shut—the picture of peaceful contentment. Fiona sighed. Were all men basically the same under the skin? Buckley had been prone to nap whenever his stomach was full.

Tentatively, she touched Adam's arm. "You are not going to fall asleep, are you? Oliver Pinchert will be expecting you in a little less than an hour."

"No, of course not. I am just resting my eyes. The sun is devilishly bright in the arena. But just to make certain, you had best hold my watch." He rolled onto his side, withdrew the watch from his jacket pocket, and handed it to her.

Fiona stared at the elegant timepiece that reposed in the palm of her hand. It was a rich burnished gold with an ornate engraving of a coat of arms, similar to the ones she had seen on the doors of the carriages belonging to the noblemen who came to Exmoor to hunt the red deer every October.

She shook her head in disapproval. Adam must have won it in a card game with some unlucky aristocrat. It most certainly was not the sort of watch one would expect a common gambler to own.

Adam yawned again. "I guess I am more tired than I realized. Why don't you talk to me. I will be certain to stay awake then."

"I guess I could do that." Fiona worried her lower lip with her teeth. In truth, she had hoped for just such an opportunity. She had been wrestling with a daring idea ever since the day of the gathering. This morning, when she had watched Adam show the Larkspur ponies with such amazing results, she had come to the conclusion she simply must get up the courage to mention it to him. What better time than now, when he was so pleasantly relaxed?

She took a deep breath. "It occurs to me we make a good team."

Adam opened one eye. "A good team? Balderdash! We make a *great* team."

"It is true. We are very different, but in many ways that is advantageous."

Adam's eyes remained closed, but his mouth curved in a mischievous smile. "I agree wholeheartedly."

"You have talents I lack. You are very adept at physical things—like chopping wood, for instance—and I have never known anyone who could communicate with animals like you do. It is a rare gift."

"Thank you."

"But I am strong in the very areas where you are weakest."

"You think me weak?" Adam sounded more amused than insulted.

"Well not weak exactly. But you have admitted to a penchant for gambling, which I most certainly do not have—and you are very careless where money is concerned, while I am extremely practical. So, we actually compliment each other."

"Ummmm."

So far so good. Fiona took another deep breath and forced herself to continue. "I enjoy talking to you; you are without a doubt the most mentally challenging person I have ever met. Furthermore, I am . . . that is I . . . oh dear, this is most embarrassing."

She stared straight ahead, afraid that if she glanced at Adam, she might find he had his eyes open and was looking at her in that knowing way of his. "Well, I can think of no other way to say it than to be utterly truthful. I am beset with the most amazing feelings when you kiss me—and I think you find kissing me rather pleasant too. Else why would you keep on doing so?"

She paused to gather her wits. "And if kissing each other is so pleasurable, it would seem logical that . . . that a certain enjoyment might be derived from the other more intimate things men and women do together. Do you agree?"

"Ummmm."

"I am so happy to hear you say so because that gives me the impetus to continue this rather frank discussion." She considered mentioning the "sign" the gods had sent and all it implied, but quickly discarded the idea. Adam obviously had an aversion to anything of a mystical nature.

Instead, she gritted her teeth and forged ahead. "What I am about to say will undoubtedly shock you even more than my confession about enjoying your kisses." She paused, but he made no comment, so she continued. "This is not the sort of speech a woman would normally make. But I have no choice since in a way our roles are reversed. While you are without funds or property, I own a farm that is the envy of every man in Exmoor. Ergo, being a proud man—which I can readily see you are—you would not feel free to propose any relationship between us of a permanent nature."

"Ummmm."

"Just as I thought! But can you not see it would be the perfect solution to both our problems. You cannot return to London because of your unfortunate addiction." She glanced at the watch which was a tangible reminder of the sordid life he had once led, and found the inspiration to carry on. "But you are much too intelligent a man to wander aimlessly about the country working as a farmhand—and since I cannot possibly manage Larkspur Farm by myself . . ."

With her last ounce of courage she blurted out, "I think we should consider marrying after I have observed a decent period of mourning. What do you say to that?"

Fiona waited, heart pounding, for Adam's answer. But all she heard was the sound of slow, steady breathing and an occasional "phfffft" redolent of wind whistling through a fireplace chimney.

She turned her head to stare down at the man to whom she had just bared her most intimate feelings—indeed her very soul—in the most embarrassing few minutes she had ever endured.

The insensitive clod was sound asleep.

Adam turned over the last of Oliver Pinchert's ponies to the buyer's stockmen after a successful bidding session, suffered the farmer's public display of gratitude, and did his best to ignore the angry mutterings of the other farmers who had not been so successful at selling their ponies.

He could see Fiona sitting on the end of the Larkspur sledge cart, clutching her reticule, exactly as he had left her more than an hour earlier. Even from a distance, he recognized the same belligerent look on her face that she had worn when she'd berated him for falling asleep in the midst of their conversation.

Devil take it, he was aware he had been unforgivably rude. But it was scarcely a hanging offense. What had they been talking about anyway? He had a vague memory of Fiona's saying something about their being a good team. Everything after that was a blur until she had awakened him, dangled his watch in his face and reminded him, in a most unpleasant tone of voice, that he was due in the arena. What could have happened in the few minutes he had dozed off to raise her hackles?

A sudden thought occurred to him. He must have talked in his sleep again. Damn and blast! That had to be it. He had obviously said something that sorely offended her. Probably some stupid reference to the lust he harbored for her. Well, whatever it was, he couldn't take it back. He would simply have to show her such a good time at the fair, she would forgive him his somnolent ravings.

With an outward air of confidence he was far from feeling, he pasted a smile on his face and strode the last few feet to where she sat. "Oliver Pinchert's ponies all sold at a price nearly as high as those with the Larkspur brand," he announced cheerfully.

"I was sure they would with you to show them."

"Yes, well whatever the reason, I am free for the rest of the day. What would you like to do first?"

"Do?"

Adam jingled the coins in his pocket suggestively. "We have money to spend, love. Since this is my first time at Plimpton Fair, I will let you decide where we should spend it."

She looked genuinely confused. "I have not the slightest idea."

"What amusement concession did you enjoy most at last year's fair? We could begin there."

"I didn't really see much of it. Someone had to guard the money we collected for the sheep and ponies."

Adam gritted his teeth. "So you stood guard while Ben and your husband celebrated at Hiram Blodgett's stall. Am I right?"

"You need not make it sound so awful. I was not the only farm wife who watched over her husband's profits—and I really did not mind in the least. I have never been one to care for idle amusement."

"How would you know?"

"I beg your pardon?"

"How would you know if you enjoy having fun, Fiona? From what I have learned of your past history, I strongly suspect you have never had any. However, I plan to change all that this evening."

Without waiting for her to comment on his declaration, Adam spanned her narrow waist with his two hands, lifted her from the cart, and set her on her feet. "But first, do you trust me?"

"What a silly question. Of course I trust you."

"Then give me that money you are clutching to your breast. I will put it in a pocket that is sewn into the inner lining of my jacket where no cutpurse can reach it. Then you will be free to enjoy yourself without worrying about it."

Fiona clutched her reticule even tighter and stared at him with wide, startled eyes. But just when he became convinced she was about to refuse his request, she handed it over to him.

He removed the sheaf of pound notes and put them in the pocket he had indicated. Then scooping up a few loose fragments of wool remaining from the bale that had earlier reposed in the cart, he stuffed them into the reticule and handed it back to her. "Any miscreant who was watching you earlier in the day with an eye to relieving you of your blunt will expect to see you carrying this," he said with a grin. "We would not want to disappoint him." With that settled, he offered her his arm and set off at a brisk pace toward the village square, where the amusement concessions had been set up.

Adam was a connoisseur when it came to fairs. As a boy, he had taken in every one that was held in London, from the spectacular holiday fair at Springfield to the oldest and grandest of them all, St. Bartholomew's. He had also spent a good deal of time at the country fairs in Kent, where his father's favorite estate was located. But Plimpton was the first farmers' fair he'd attended and he could see at a glance it was nothing like any of those. Here there were no human freaks or dancing pigs, no acrobats or tight-rope walkers, and certainly no colorful theatrical productions such as those put on each year at St. Bartholomew's.

But the rich aromas filling his nostrils told him Plimpton Fair did have the usual gingerbread and fruit tarts, and the traditional pig roasting on a spit. Furthermore, he could see two booths selling trinkets, a down-at-the-heels Punch-and-Judy Show, two foreign-looking chaps tumbling on a makeshift stage, and a portable peep show—as well as a gaudy red-and-yellow caravan he felt certain must hold a Gypsy fortune-teller.

On the opposite side of the square Hiram Blodgett dispensed his popular ale from a stand which stood next to a large tent, the purpose of which Adam couldn't imagine.

Not the most auspicious collection of amusements with which to show Fiona an evening of fun, he had to admit, but at least the people milling about the square appeared to be in a cheerful holiday mood.

He glanced down to find Fiona staring at the tiny Punch and Judy stage, as wide-eyed as the smallest child in the audience. "Shall we stop here first?" he asked. "It looks like the show has just begun." She nodded, too engrossed in the poorly staged performance to tear her gaze away.

Adam paid two pennies for the privilege of sitting on one of the four wooden benches set up before the little theatre. The only space left was scarcely wide enough for two people, which meant his hip and thigh were pressed tightly against Fiona's—a position he found both pleasurable and frustrating. He fully expected Fiona to object to the enforced intimacy, but she was so intent on watching the puppet show, she seemed oblivious to everything around her.

Adam stretched out his right leg to brace himself, fixed his attention on the stage, and immediately became engrossed in the argument between the two puppets.

This Exmoor Punch might lack the elegant appearance of his London counterparts, but he was obviously up to the same kind of mischief. First he accused a somewhat dilapidated-looking Judy of infidelity. Then after a brief tussle, dealt her a lethal blow to the head and tossed her through the window, to a chorus of boos and hisses from the audience.

Adam booed and hissed with the best of them, but Fiona remained strangely quiet—her gaze riveted on the stage, her face a mask of disapproval. Adam frowned. It was obvious she was not enjoying the age-old melodrama as much as he had hoped she would.

As always, the hangman arrived shortly after Punch had disposed of Judy. This one was a particularly fierce-looking puppet with bushy eyebrows and a full black beard. With a great deal of posing and arm waving, he informed Punch he must pay for his dastardly crime with his life. He even produced the rope, complete with a hangman's noose, to carry out the sentence.

The audience greeted this bit of theatrics with the usual cheering and stamping of feet. Fiona, however, did not cheer. To Adam's surprise, she leapt to her feet, pushed past him, and fled into the crowd of people watching the show from outside the theatre area.

"What the devil?" Adam sprinted after her. Pushing his way through the crowd, he caught up with her outside the Gypsy fortune-teller's caravan. "What is wrong?" he demanded. "Why did you leave so suddenly? Are you ill?"

"No, I am not ill. I simply have no desire to witness a hanging—even one that is merely part of a puppet show. The very thought turns my stomach. Though I must say, a miserable fellow like Punch seems destined to dance on a gibbet sooner or later."

Adam studied her troubled face with disbelieving eyes. "Good Lord, can it be you have never seen a Punch-and-Judy show?"

The sudden flush that suffused her cheeks answered his question. "Of course you haven't," he said softly. "I forgot you were always left to guard the profits."

Never had the differences in their backgrounds seemed so striking as at that moment. He had seen so much, done so much, lived with such reckless abandon—while Fiona was like a beautifully bound volume filled with empty pages on which the first words were yet to be written.

"We need to talk," Adam said, looking about him for some place where he could clear up Fiona's misunderstanding about the puppet show without publicly embarrassing her. The only spot not overrun with people was a narrow space between the Gypsy's caravan and the adjoining gingerbread stall. Taking her hand in his, he led her to it.

The space was smaller than he had estimated and unfortunately afforded no shade from the late-afternoon sun. But at least they had a relative amount of privacy.

Fiona stood with her back to the caravan, her ill-fitting widow's weeds looking darker and uglier than ever against the vivid backdrop. Beads of perspiration dotted her forehead and a lock of damp, flame-colored hair curled against her cheek. Gently, Adam tucked it behind her ear, then stepped back until he felt his shoulders press against the sun-warmed wall of the gingerbread stand.

"Punch-and-Judy shows may vary slightly according to the whim of the puppeteer," he explained. "But of one thing you can be absolutely certain: Punch will never hang. The fun of the show for the audience is watching the slippery fellow confuse the hangman with his nonsensical ravings while he plots to escape the punishment he deserves."

Fiona looked a bit skeptical. "How does he manage his escape?"

"He doesn't actually, for Punch is not the brightest of fellows. But all ends well when Judy returns, battered but very much alive, to bash the hangman over the head with the same club Punch used on her."

Fiona's eyes widened in obvious disbelief. "You cannot be serious. Why would she rescue the miserable bully? I would not lift a finger to save a man who had beaten me unconscious."

Adam chuckled. "No intelligent woman would, but it is the sheer nonsense of the story that has appealed to audiences in every city and hamlet of England since the time of Queen Anne. You really must learn to appreciate nonsense, Fiona. It is often all that saves one's sanity when reality becomes too overwhelming."

"You have seen Punch and Judy shows in London, I take it."

"Many times. In point of fact, I saw a particularly elaborate one as recently as this past February at the Frost Fair, when the Thames froze over. But my all-time favorite was the one I saw at Greenwich the year I became fifteen. What a wicked scoundrel that Punch was!"

He smiled reminiscently. "My brother, Ethan, and I were forbidden to attend the fair, so we ran away from home and spent three gloriously sinful days doing all the things our father had warned us we must never do."

"But why would your father object to a fair?"

"Greenwich is not just any fair. It is held in London's notorious East End and is patronized by every kind of lowlife from

Cockney bully boys and pimps to sailors and their gin house doxies. But we had the time of our lives. It was worth every stripe the du . . . my father put on our backsides when we returned home."

Adam reached into his pocket for a handkerchief to wipe away the sweat dripping into his eyes and remembered he had tossed the gravy-stained linen to the back of the sledge cart just before he had fallen asleep.

He ran the palm of his hand across his forehead instead before continuing. "I heard the famous Bow Bells for the first time when I was at that fair. To this day, whenever I hear a church bell ring, I remember Greenwich." *And the buxom, brown-eyed Cockney whore who, for half a crown, initiated both Ethan and me into the here-to-fore unexplored mysteries of sexual pleasure.*

Behind him the crowd at the puppet theatre gave a loud cheer, then began clapping their hands and stamping their feet in unison. Adam grinned. "From the sound of things, I would say Punch and his Judy are finally reunited and exchanging a passionate kiss right about now."

Fiona hung her head. "You must think me the most ignorant of women to have so little knowledge of what is apparently a very common thing."

"Never, love. I might judge you inexperienced in the ways of the world, but never ignorant. In truth, you are the most intelligent woman I have ever met—and the most unique. Knowing you has spoiled me for all others."

"I thank you for the compliment," Fiona said, "but unique is the last thing I wish to be. The women of my family have always been cursed with that unhappy quality. I want only to be ordinary."

Adam sensed the terrible loneliness behind Fiona's telling statement. He ached to take her in his arms and kiss her until the look of sadness disappeared from her lovely eyes. He could scarcely do so in the midst of a country fair.

He decided to tease her instead, hoping to coax her from her dark mood. "I know little of Exmoor so I can offer no advice as to how you might go about being ordinary here. In London, it would be an easy matter. You would simply have to buy yourself a frivolous new bonnet and take up reading Ann Radcliffe's novels. In no time at all you would acquire the vacant look and the meaningless prattle that are the trademarks of every ordinary London lady."

Fiona rewarded him with a smile for his efforts. "Life as a London lady sounds most tempting." Her expression sobered. "But who is this Ann Radcliffe you recommend so highly. Is she some sort of modern-day philosopher?"

Adam chuckled. "I have never heard her called that. But now that you mention it, her writings have influenced the thinking of a great many of England's females."

"Then I should like very much to read what this influential woman has written."

"And so you shall, love. Hatchard's Bookstore will be the first place I shall take you when we get to London," Adam said without thinking.

Fiona frowned. "You foresee our visiting London together?"

Adam swallowed hard. He was already in for a penny; he might as well try for a pound. "I do," he said, meeting her gaze squarely, "and in the not-too-distant future."

He expected her to give him one of her jaw-me-dead lectures for suggesting such a scandalous idea. To his surprise, she merely asked, "But what of your unfortunate addiction? I thought you dared not return to the scene of temptation."

He let out the breath he hadn't realized he had been holding and surreptitiously crossed his fingers behind his back. "With you to keep me on the straight and narrow, love, I feel certain I can withstand any enticement the London gambling hells may offer."

"Then we are not too far apart in our thinking after all," Fiona declared, her golden eyes sparkling with something that looked suspiciously like triumph.

"We are not?"

"As well you would know if you had listened to all I had to say this afternoon." She frowned. "By the way, just how much *did* you hear before you fell asleep?"

"Not nearly enough apparently," Adam said, thoroughly confused by the strange turn their conversation had taken. Could it be that convincing Fiona to put her future in his hands would not be as difficult as he had imagined? He sensed a subtle change in her attitude toward him—a change she inferred he would understand if he had stayed awake long enough to hear her out.

He hated mysteries, especially when they pertained to him, and Fiona was being infuriatingly mysterious. Well enough was enough. He had apologized for his rude behavior. What more did she want of him? Groveling was out of the question. He had his pride. He was, after all, the son of the Duke of Bellmont.

He was also very hot and very tired, and the aroma of fresh gingerbread wafting through the cracks of the hastily constructed stand at his back made him long for a taste of the sticky stuff.

"Devil take it, Fiona," he growled, "how long are you planning to punish me for dozing off at an inopportune moment? If the truth be known, I was exhausted from lack of sleep. I lay awake most of the night under that blasted sledge cart in which you slept—and my insomnia was not because I found the ground too hard. Now would you please repeat whatever it was you said to me this afternoon when I was . . . indisposed. Then maybe we can put this sorry matter to rest once and for all and get back to enjoying the fair."

For a long, silent moment, he waited for her to speak, his impatience growing by the second. Why were women—even the best of them—such difficult creatures?

"Are you or are you not going to tell me what I want to know," he demanded finally.

Fiona shook her head slowly from side to side. "I really cannot do that, Adam."

"Whyever not?"

An enigmatic, almost feline, smile flitted across her expressive face. "Because it took every ounce of courage I had to say something so . . . so shockingly intimate once. It will be a long time before I can bring myself to do anything that daring again."

Chapter Twelve

Shockingly Intimate! This infuriating woman, whom he desired with every fiber of his being, had finally said something "shockingly intimate" to him and he had slept through it!

Adam suspected he might find a certain humor in the situation if any other man he knew had made such a ridiculous blunder. But frustration and humor seldom walked hand in hand, and at the moment he was bedeviled by a monstrous frustration. For he was learning firsthand the truth of Creenagh's claim that Fiona was a "mule-stubborn" female. Nothing he had said in the last ten minutes had moved her to change her mind about repeating her revealing soliloquy—and he had said a great many things, some of which bordered on that groveling he had sworn he would never do.

But he would say no more. Even Wellington had had to pull back his forces when the enemy was too strongly entrenched—and when it came to digging in and refusing to budge, no brigade in Bonaparte's army could match the Widow Haines. There was nothing for it but to soldier on from one to another of the dubious amusements this back-country fair offered and hope she would mellow as the evening progressed.

But first, he was in dire need of sustenance. With Fiona in tow, he made his way to the pit where the pig turned slowly on a spit above a bed of hot coals, and paid two pennies for a plateful of the succulent meat.

From there the two of them made their way back to the gingerbread stand for wedges of the sweet, warm cake and waxed-paper cones of lemonade. Fiona ate and drank with the same gusto she had exhibited earlier toward the beef pastie—a good sign, Adam decided optimistically, as he licked the last of the gingerbread crumbs from his fingers.

"I think our next stop should be at the Gypsy's caravan to have your fortune told," he said, tossing the empty cones into the open wooden barrel beside the stand. He had dealt with Romany soothsayers before, and he planned to cross the Gypsy woman's palm with a shilling—a generous sum by any standards—to ensure Fiona a happy-ever-after fortune—preferably with a tall, dark man in it.

"I am not sure I want to do that," Fiona said, eyeing the gaudy red-and-yellow wagon somewhat dubiously. "It is not that I am superstitious about such things . . ."

Adam chuckled. "The thought never entered my mind. It is, after all, such an ordinary thing to do. Since every woman I have ever known has loved having her fortune told, I naturally assumed you would feel the same."

"Oh, well in that case . . ."

With Adam beside her, Fiona walked the few steps to the caravan to find Oliver Pinchert's two plump, plain-faced daughters leaving just as they arrived. Both girls ducked their heads and giggled when they saw Adam.

"Ye'll not be sorry ye come, Mistress Haines," the older girl whispered in Fiona's ear as she passed. "This Gypsy do tell the loveliest fortunes just by looking at the lines in the flat of a body's hand. Mine be ever so much nicer than last year."

Whatever qualms Fiona had harbored about availing herself of the Gypsy's talent instantly disappeared. Once again Adam was proved right. Having one's fortune told must indeed be the sort of thing ordinary women did. For Fiona had never met two females who better fit her concept of that blessed state than Oliver Pinchert's daughters. With a grateful smile, she accepted the coin Adam pressed into her hand and made her way alone up the three steps leading to the Gypsy's open door.

"Come in, come in young miss. Learn what your future holds." The Gypsy's voice had a low, almost masculine timbre and her strange, guttural accent gave even the simplest words an aura of mystery.

Ignoring the nervous flutterings in her stomach, Fiona stepped into the shadowy interior of the caravan. The air was close, despite the open door, and heavy with the smell of garlic. Once her eyes adjusted to the dim light, she made out a small table and behind it a heavyset, gray-haired woman seated in a high-backed chair.

At first glance, the chair appeared to be upholstered in some kind of fur, but she took another look and blinked in astonishment. In actuality, it was draped with the pelt of a black bear, the head of which loomed above the woman's swarthy face like a huge, grotesque hat.

"So, we have a pretty one this time. All the better." The Gypsy's full lips parted in a sly smile and it occurred to Fiona she must have been quite beautiful in a dark, foreign way before her features coarsened and her body ran to fat.

"Give me your penny, miss," she purred, "then let me look at your pretty little hand and I will tell you all you want to know."

Fiona placed Adam's coin on the table and too late realized he had given her one of his hard-earned shillings. She ground her teeth in frustration. The man really did need a keeper; he had no concept whatsoever of the value of money.

The Gypsy woman's dark eyes glowed at the sight of the coin. Quick as a hawk seizing its prey, her long, talonlike fingers snatched it up and deposited it in the pocket of her scarlet skirt. "Now your hand, miss, if you please."

Fiona placed her hand on the table, palm up, hoping the woman could read her fortune without touching her. She cringed at the thought of those grimy fingers grasping hers as they had the coin.

Her hope was in vain. But worse yet, the minute the woman's hand touched hers, bright, fiery sparks flew from their point of contact and a fierce tingling started in Fiona's fingertips, then spread up her arm. Startled, she raised her head to find the Gypsy's sloe eyes wide with shock. "Who are you?" the woman whispered. "Why have you come to me? There is nothing a poor Gypsy can tell one with the kind of witching powers you possess."

Fiona's first inclination was to yank her hand from the fortune-teller's grasp and run as fast as her legs would carry her. Curiosity kept her anchored to the chair. "You mistake me for another," she said. "Her blood flows in my veins and it is undoubtedly that which you sense. But I have no such powers; nor do I want any."

"So you say, but you are witch-spawned and there is no denying it." The old woman searched Fiona's face with narrowed eyes. "What is it you want of me?"

"I just want my fortune told, like any other ordinary woman. Tell me, please, what do you see in the lines of my hand?"

With obvious reluctance, the Gypsy lowered her gaze to Fiona's hand. "I see you are not a maiden," she said, tracing a blackened fingernail along one of the lines that marked the palm, "but the man whose name you bear was but a single drop of water in the sea of your life. For he possessed only your body, never your heart."

Fiona blinked, amazed that this stranger could so accurately describe her marriage to Buckley. Nervously, she watched the same fingernail trace another line. "But there is another man— one whom the gods have already made known to you. Against this man, your heart will have no defense."

She had heard enough. She didn't need a Gypsy to tell her that her feelings for Adam were getting dangerously out of control. She tried to free her hand from the Gypsy's hold, but to no avail. The dirt-encrusted fingers only tightened their grip.

The old woman's eyes were closed now and she swayed back and forth as if listening to some music only she could hear. "Because of this man," she intoned in a sing-song voice, "you will feel the passion you never thought to feel and see wondrous things you never thought to see."

Fiona's pulse quickened when she remembered Adam's prophesy that they would see London together.

"He will break your heart," the Gypsy continued. "But when all is said and done, you must accept what he offers, for unless you do, love will be lost to you forever."

She opened her eyes and dropped Fiona's hand as if the very touch of it scorched her flesh. "Now go and leave me in peace, for there is no more I can tell you."

"Thank you," Fiona said in a small voice and rose from the chair.

"Wait!" The Gypsy stopped her before she could step through the doorway. "My luck would turn evil as an adder's tongue if I took money from one such as you." She reached into her pocket and drew forth the shilling.

Fiona raised a hand in protest. "Keep the money; you have earned it—and never fear the source. It was given me by the man of whom you spoke, and his blood carries no taint of witchcraft."

The Gypsy received this bit of information with obvious skepticism, but in the end greed won out over caution and she pocketed the coin.

Adam was leaning against the counter of the gingerbread stand, finishing off yet another slice of the warm cake, when Fiona made her way down the rickety steps of the caravan. She found herself wondering if his appetite for the spicy stuff was really as inexhaustible as it seemed or if he just liked chatting up the pretty girls who sold it.

She took a closer look. The silly creature currently batting her eyelashes at him in such a revolting manner was Kate Blodgett, the youngest of Hiram Blodgett's four daughters. Fiona hoped Adam wasn't such a fool as to think she had singled him out. For, in truth, the little trollop was the most outrageous flirt in all of Exmoor.

The vicious thought shocked her. She despised people who judged others and she had always felt a healthy disgust for jealous shrews. When had she begun thinking like one?

Gathering her wits, she marched down the three steps of the caravan. "I have had my fortune told and I am ready to do something else," she announced as she swept past her handsome farmhand.

Adam brushed the crumbs from his lips and bestowed a final smile on the flirtatious gingerbread seller before turning his attention to Fiona. He could see she was upset about something. What, he couldn't imagine. No Gypsy would be so foolish as to tell a pretty young woman a fortune she didn't like—especially a Gypsy who had been grossly overpaid.

He caught up with her when she stopped at the edge of the crowd watching the tumblers. "So, love, what did you learn from the fortune-teller?"

"Very little that was not already known to me." She avoided looking at him, staring instead at the two dark-skinned men performing their tricks on the makeshift stage. "I fear you wasted your shilling, which by the way was a ridiculous sum to pay for such a service."

"Not if you enjoyed yourself."

"That is very generous of you and it was most . . . most edifying," she said in a tight little voice that told him she had not enjoyed it one whit.

So much for that. His earlier optimism about showing Fiona a good time was fading fast. Nothing had gone as he had planned so far.

"Shall we try the peep show next?" he asked hopefully. "The crowd around it seems to have thinned out."

Fiona nodded. "That would be very nice," she agreed, but she looked a bit vague, and it occurred to him she had not the slightest idea what a peep show was. He felt a sudden overwhelming tenderness for this lovely woman who had known so little of the simple pleasures of life. He found himself hoping against hope this little country peep show would hold the same magic for Fiona that he had found in the first one he had viewed as a young boy.

With his hand beneath Fiona's elbow, Adam cleared a path for them through the throng of people milling up and down the street. They were making good progress toward their destination when two rough-looking fellows heading in the opposite direction bumped into Fiona, then quickly disappeared into the crowd.

"I am sorry," she said when she stumbled against Adam. "Those two were not looking where they were going."

"On the contrary, I think they knew exactly where they were going and why. Look at your reticule."

She glanced down at the two straps she still clutched in her hand and gave a small, strangled gasp. They had been neatly severed just above where they had formerly attached to the reticule. "How did they do that? I never felt a thing."

Adam chuckled. "One never does when the cutpurse is good at his trade. Oh well, there is nothing lost. As I recall, the reticule was a bit ragged around the edges. My only regret is that I cannot see their faces when they open up their ill-gotten prize."

Fiona's face was pale with shock. "I am deeply grateful the money is safe. Larkspur Farm could not have survived long without it. But ragged or not, I shall miss my reticule. It was the only one I had."

"Then we shall have to find you another," Adam declared. "We can take a quick look at the trinket booths. Those I have seen at other fairs always carried that sort of thing."

"Now you are being silly. Such a thing would be much too expensive. I am certain I can find a scrap of fabric with which to make one."

Adam ignored her protest. Taking a firmer grip on her elbow, he led her to the first trinket booth and asked the proprietor what he had in the way of lady's reticules.

As it turned out, he had three on hand—two constructed of plain linen with cord drawstrings and one a brocade in an ugly shade of green, with braided velvet handles. "We will take the green one," Adam said when he saw how Fiona's eyes lighted up at the sight of it. Though if the truth be known, he doubted that any other lady of his acquaintance would consider carrying the tawdry thing.

"You have excellent taste, sir. The item is a trifle expensive, but worth every penny." The trinket salesman cleared his throat. "But seeing as how this is Exmoor, where money is particularly scarce right now, I can bring myself to part with it for . . . twelve shillings."

Fiona gave a small shriek of protest, but Adam ignored her and paid the fellow his asking price without demur. Then, draping the handles of the reticule over one of her arms and taking a firm grasp on the other, he set off once again for the peep show.

No sooner were they out of earshot of the trinket booth than Fiona lit into him, exactly as he had known she would, for spending a "fortune" on the blasted thing. "Easy come, easy go," he declared with a grin, because he knew it was the comment most likely to shock the little pinchpenny into a pursed-lip silence.

The peep show they approached a few minutes later consisted of a huge wooden box six feet long and four feet wide set atop a wheeled cart. The box was constructed of beautifully finished oak and the numerous eyeholes all around the perimeter were each encircled with a narrow polished brass plate. It was, in fact, so nicely put together Adam felt his hopes rise for the quality of the show inside.

As they drew closer, he spied a neatly lettered sign at the top of the box proclaiming, "See the Wondrous Sights of London. One penny admission."

The proprietor was a jolly-looking fellow with a rim of gray hair surrounding his shiny bald pate and a pair of twinkling blue eyes. His substantial girth was splendidly decked out in a burgundy velvet frock coat, gray watered-silk waistcoat, and a snowy cravat tied in the intricate mathematical.

"Good afternoon to you, young couple," he said, rising from his chair beside the peep show box. "You have picked a good time to view the show. We were busier than the Billingsgate Market on a Friday afternoon until half an hour ago. But 'tis suppertime for most folks now and you will have it all to yourselves."

Adam sorted through the coins in his pocket, found two pennies, and paid the requisite admission. "We are looking forward to it. If the show inside is as splendid as the box itself, it will be a rare treat indeed for a country fair."

" 'Tis that and more." A plump little gray-haired lady with the same twinkling eyes as the proprietor stepped from behind the box. "I am Mary Carmichael," she said, "and this is my brother, William." She smiled up at Adam. "I can tell from your manner of speech you are London born and bred, and from the West End of the great city as well, I would say."

"You have a good ear, ma'am. Adam Cresswell at your service, and may I present Mistress Fiona Haines."

"Pleased to meet you, ma'am." The little lady made a neat curtsy. "As Londoners, you are bound to enjoy what you are about to see. My dear brother has devoted a lifetime to carving his miniatures of the buildings of the great city and they are really quite remarkable."

"An unusual hobby, sir," Adam said, addressing the beaming proprietor. "How came you to take it up?"

"My sister and I were in the employ of the Earl of Barton for close to thirty years—I as his valet and she as his housekeeper. Perhaps you have heard of his lordship."

"Who in London has not. He is famous for his many philanthropies."

"True. A superior gentleman and the kindest of masters. But being somewhat of a recluse, he had little need of my services. Since I had so much time on my hands, I took up carving—"

"And I undertook the painting of brother's buildings," Mary Carmichael interjected. "It was a most delightful way to pass a cold winter's eve."

Her expression sobered. "We lost his lordship to the lung fever last winter. But he had provided for us most generously in his will, and my brother suggested we turn the carvings into a peep show and with it, tour all the parts of England we had always longed to see."

"Now that is enough of your blather, Mary. The young people have come to see the carvings, not hear the history of their construction." William Carmichael beamed at Adam and Fiona. "I will light new candles in the lamps so you'll not miss a thing."

This he did, and Adam directed Fiona to put her eye to one of the peepholes, while he put his to another. The sight that greeted him literally took his breath away. A miniature City of London lay spread out before him—every major building carved and painted in exquisite detail.

He looked up from his peephole and met Carmichael's eye. "This is absolutely magnificent. A true work of art and every bit as authentic as your sister claimed."

The two Carmichaels beamed from ear to ear at this praise of their work.

"I had heard London was a grand city, but I had no idea how grand," Fiona said, her eyes glued to her chosen peephole. "Tell me about the buildings, if you please, sir, for I have never been to London and I have no way of knowing one from another."

"I should like to be the one to tell her," Adam said. "There is so much to see, we would claim these peepholes for hours if it were all to be explained. But I think I know what would mean the most to her."

"A fine idea, young sir," Carmichael agreed. "And since you and your lady have so graciously complimented our work, I will make it easier for you to do so. If you will give me a hand, we can lift the top off the box so you can look at it as I do when I wish to enjoy my handiwork. Then we will leave you two to enjoy yourselves while sister and I partake of our evening meal at the table we have set up nearby."

A few moments later Adam, with Fiona at his side, stood atop the viewing ledge erected at the back of the box and surveyed the miniature city from a bird's-eye view. He could scarcely contain his elation. Fate had finally smiled on him. Fiona was already quivering with excitement; by the time he had finished pointing out the wonders of London, she would be eager to accept his offer of a charming residence in the city and the life of ease and luxury he could provide her.

With the pointer provided him by Miss Carmichael, he quickly indicated the Houses of Parliament, the Bank of England, Whitehall, and Carlton House. Fiona's eyes lighted up. "They are often mentioned in the London newspapers that are delivered every week to the Black Boar Inn, but I had no idea what they looked like."

"And this magnificent edifice over here is Westminster Abby, where every king and queen of England has been crowned since the time of William the Conqueror."

"It is incredibly beautiful." Fiona leaned over the edge of the box to better examine the most splendid structure in the remarkable collection. "Just imagine how huge it must be in reality."

"Now this street is one you must visit," Adam said, pointing to Bond Street. "Firstly because this building right here is Hookum's Lending Library and secondly because these stores lining both sides of Bond Street are where the ladies of London's West End do their shopping."

Fiona clapped her hands. "And where I can buy the frivolous new bonnet you said I must have."

"Exactly, and dozens of beautiful gowns and satin slippers to match each one."

Fiona laughed gaily. "Oh, Adam, you do say the most ridiculous things. Why would any woman need dozens of gowns? And satin slippers would be utterly impractical."

"Nevertheless, you must have a carriage dress if we are to drive through Hyde Park at the fashionable hour in my shiny new black curricle." He pointed to the park and the elegantly garbed figures in a tiny carriage pulled by two tiny matched bays. Beside them, two equally elegant gentlemen rode astride sleek thoroughbreds.

"I must indeed," Fiona said solemnly, but the mischief in her eyes told Adam she thought this all a great joke.

"And, of course, we shall want to attend the theatre," he continued. "See that building with the columns in front. That is the Royal Theatre at Covent Garden—one of the first places I shall take you after we arrive in London. Between it and Drury Lane, the most splendid entertainment you can imagine is available almost every night of the week during the Season."

"Will you really? I should like that very much. I have seen some of their playbills printed in Hiram's newspapers and longed to see a play or opera." She frowned. "It is a good thing we are only daydreaming, because I suspect such things must be frightfully expensive."

"Frightfully. But think how that clever mind of yours will be challenged. Why just before I left London, I attended the play *Hamlet, Prince of Denmark* by your hero, William Shakespeare."

"Hamlet? You cannot be serious. I know that play by heart."

Adam systematically worked his way across London, properly identifying each building as he went, with two exceptions: Newgate Prison and the Tower of London. The first was an abomination and the latter little better. In his opinion, the poor beasts presently on display at the tower were not much better off than the historical figures who had awaited their executions there in past centuries.

"I have saved the best for last," he said finally. "Can you guess what building I am pointing to now?"

Fiona's smile was wistful. "It has to be Hatchard's Bookstore." Once again she leaned over the edge of the box, this time to touch a finger to the miniature of the famous establishment. "That is where I shall go as soon as I arrive in London—and the first book I seek out will be a novel by Ann Radcliffe."

"Then once you have made your purchase, we shall drive over to Berkeley Square, park beneath the trees, and eat strawberry ices from Gunther's Pastry Shop like all the other ordinary London ladies and gentlemen."

"What a lovely daydream. I wish we could stay here for hours looking at this wondrous display. There are still so many buildings you have not identified." She made a sweeping gesture which included most of Mayfair. "What are all those structures built around open squares, for instance?"

"The town houses of the nobility, and I can name you the owner of each and every one." William Carmichael had stepped onto the ledge so quietly neither Fiona nor Adam had heard him.

"How fascinating. Would you name me a few?"

The old man rested his forearms on the edge of the box. "That rather odd-looking one with the stone gargoyles out front belongs to Frederick Wyman, the Marquis of Stamford."

Adam's heart thudded in his chest. The marquis was his father's next-door neighbor.

"The tall town house on one side of it belongs to Edward Fitzsimmons, the Earl of Camden."

A cold sweat broke out on Adam's brow.

"And the elegant building on the other side is the Duke of Bellmont's town house. I cannot recall his given name right off, but the family name is Cres . . ." William Carmichael's gaze locked with Adam's and his eyes looked about to pop from his head. Adam's scowl effectively silenced him before he could say the last syllable of the name.

Behind Fiona's back, Adam slipped the flabbergasted old man a stack of shillings he didn't bother to count. Carmichael's lips instantly clamped shut.

"Creston is the name you are searching for, unless I am mistaken," Adam said as calmly as his thundering heart would let him. He managed a weak smile for Fiona. "It is common knowledge in London. The duke is a well-known public figure, since he is one of the most vocal members of the House of Lords."

The next few minutes passed in a flurry of activity. In silent agreement, Adam and Carmichael replaced the top of the box—and just in time. With the supper hour over and evening coming on, a new crowd of customers had arrived to take a last-minute look at the peep show that was the talk of the fairgrounds.

With a heartfelt "thank you" to the ex-valet and his sister, Adam took Fiona's hand and led her away before the befuddled proprietor let something slip that would give the game

away. But he had come too close; his luck couldn't last forever. Two people at this fair already knew his identity and he
couldn't count on their silence. He had to settle things with
Fiona before she learned the truth from someone else.

There was no doubt about it. Tonight was the night he must
speak his piece.

A crowd of people was gathering outside the large tent next
to Hiram Blodgett's stand, and without thinking he gravitated
toward them. A greasy-looking barker in a yellow double-
breasted tailcoat that had seen better days stood outside the
tent, drumming up customers with his spiel, "Come meet two
survivors of General Wellington's war with the Corsican Mon-
ster. A penny is all you need to hear the hair-raising tales these
two brave lads who gave their all for good old England have to
tell of the fighting in Spain. Tales you will never forget as long
as you live."

Adam felt his blood run cold. "What the devil," he muttered
under his breath, and felt Fiona grip his arm.

"Come away, Adam," she begged. "You do not need to hear
this."

He shook her hand off and searched his pocket for coins. "I
want to see what is going on in that tent. Are you coming with
me, or would you rather wait out here?"

"I am coming with you."

Adam stalked to the entrance, paid the small boy collecting
the admission fees, and found a seat on one of the benches for
Fiona and him. He looked about for the "brave lads" but they
were nowhere in sight. What was in sight was a small, elevated stage with a backdrop approximately eight feet long and
six feet high depicting a bloody battle scene. The drawing was
poorly executed and could have been any of the battles the
English troops fought on the Peninsula. But crude as it was,
the artist had captured the carnage and the horror and the terrible finality of death that was war as Adam remembered it.

The pain he had managed to subdue the past few weeks rose
up to slash him with razor-sharp knives. His stomach felt
queasy and a strange array of small, black clouds floated past
his eyes. Whatever was going to happen here had better hap-

pen fast or he was going to humiliate himself mightily in front of God and Fiona and anyone else who happened to be nearby.

Once the benches were full, the barker returned, gave a short speech describing the battles of Ciuidad Rodrigo and Badajoz, straight from the newspaper accounts, Adam suspected. Then, with a flourish, he called forth the two ex-soldiers.

They were both in the uniform of the Light Infantry. One limped in on crutches, minus a leg; the other had an empty left sleeve pinned to the shoulder of his ragged, bloodstained uniform.

"Go on, lads, tell the folks all about the war and the brave English boys who fought it," the barker demanded, and for the next ten minutes the armless man did just that. Staring with dead eyes over the heads of the audience, he described the bloody battle of Badajoz in a toneless voice utterly devoid of expression.

The legless man's description of Ciudad Rodrigo was shorter, but equally as spine-chilling and to the best of Adam's recollection, grimly accurate. Except for a few whispered comments here and there, the audience greeted the two gruesome dissertations with shocked silence, then rose and filed out of the tent.

Adam watched the two men disappear behind the backdrop with a mixture of anger and sorrow. He sensed their humiliation at being put on display like freaks in a raree-show, and the desperation that had driven them to agree to participate in such a demeaning thing. England was overrun with ex-servicemen with all their limbs who could find no work to keep body and soul together. What chance would these poor mutilated devils have?

He turned to Fiona and saw the color had blanched from her face and her eyes glistened with unshed tears. "I want you to do me a favor," he said softly. "Keep the barker busy long enough for me to speak to the two soldiers."

"Of course." She instantly rose and walked toward the foot of the stage where the repulsive fellow was talking to two Exmoor farmers and their wives.

Adam reached inside his jacket and from another pocket similar to the one holding Fiona's money, withdrew four ten-

pound notes. Quickly, before the barker should see him, he
slipped around the end of the stage and pressed the notes into
the hands of the astonished soldiers. "Put this by for a rainy
day," he said, echoing Fiona's advice to him.

The one-legged fellow just stared at him with grateful eyes,
but the one-armed soldier found his voice. "Lord luv you, guvnor, it ain't stopped raining since the day I took the ball what
cost me my arm." He stuffed his half of the money into the
pocket of his uniform. "But this'll buy a few pints to push
back the clouds, and that's a fact."

Fiona breathed a sigh of relief when she saw Adam emerge
from behind the stage. The barker had taken her effort to engage him in a conversation as an invitation and he was getting
much too friendly for her peace of mind. He was, in fact, beginning to paw her in a way that made her stomach roil with
nausea.

Snatching her arm from beneath his white sausage fingers,
she mumbled a quick farewell and hurried over to where
Adam waited for her by the entrance to the tent. He had never
looked as good as he did this moment, when she compared
him to the dreadful barker. In truth, she was beginning to think
the gods were right; there was no other man on earth who
could hold a candle to Adam Cresswell—and no other man so
in need of a practical woman to keep him from spending every
cent he got his hands on.

Money meant nothing to him. First he had spent far more
than he should at the fair, particularly on her beautiful new
reticule. Now she felt certain the kindhearted fellow had
sought out the two unfortunate soldiers to give them the last of
his hard-earned shillings. He was, without a doubt, the most
generous of men, as well as the most careless of his own wel-
fare. The plain truth was, in his own way Adam needed her
even more than Buckley had.

The Gypsy fortune-teller's words rang in her ears. "You
must go to him, or love will be lost to you forever." What was
she waiting for? She had found the courage once to tell him
how she felt; she could find it again.

There was no doubt bout it. Tonight was the night she must
speak her piece.

Chapter Thirteen

Adam waited impatiently while Fiona collected the herb money due Creenagh from Hiram Blodgett. Now that he had definitely made up his mind to reveal his true identity and offer her the opportunity to live in London under his protection, he wanted to get on with it while the memory of all the city had to offer was fresh in her mind.

He could hardly wait to see the little country widow evolve into the charming woman she was meant to be. With her quick wit, she would soon gain enough town bronze to be at ease wherever he might take her—be it the theatre, the Bond Street shops, or on the strut in Hyde Park in his fine new curricle.

But Fiona's metamorphosis was not the only reason he was anxious to return to London as soon as possible. The sorry plight of the two infantrymen had started him thinking about the thousands of other ex-servicemen throughout England who were penniless and desperate. Someone had to speak for these men who had fought so bravely for their country, only to have those in power turn their backs on them once the war ended. The second son of a duke might not wield much influence by himself, but with his connections to his father and to Lord Castlereagh, he would at least be heard in the right places.

This was the challenge he needed to justify surviving the carnage in Spain when so many good men had lost their lives, and the sooner he met it, the better. Now all he had to do was bring Fiona around to his way of thinking and he could get on with his plans for the next few years of his life.

She was all smiles when she returned from her chat with the innkeeper and his customers, including Ben, who were finishing off the last keg of the ale Blodgett had brought from the Black Boar Inn.

"The herbs sold very well." She dropped a small cloth bag fat with coins into her new reticule. "People may not want anything to do with the Witch of Exmoor, but they are not above using her herbal remedies for what ails them."

Adam took her arm and steered her toward the Larkspur Farm sledge cart before she could be diverted again. "I am happy for Creenagh. Now she will have that spending money you spoke of."

Unconsciously he tightened his grip. "I need to say something to you, Fiona. Something important. I hope we can manage a few minutes alone while Ben is still occupied with Blodgett and his ale."

"I need to say something to you too. I have thought it over and I have decided I should repeat what I said earlier."

"The 'shockingly intimate' bit I missed when I fell asleep, I trust," he teased.

"As a matter of fact . . ."

Even in the waning light, he could see the blush that colored her cheeks. His pulse quickened. Unless he missed his guess, she was about to tell him she had tender feelings for him. Granted, the average woman would expect the man she was interested in to confess his feelings first—but the average woman had neither Fiona's courage nor her ignorance of social custom.

The more he thought about it, the more certain he became that was what the little minx had in mind. Why else would she be loath to look him in the face? He smiled, vastly pleased that things were going his way.

In his anxiety to hear what she had to say he hastened his steps until the two of them were practically running by the time they reached the sledge cart. Without further ado, he grasped her about the waist, lifted her onto the end of the cart, and hopped up to sit beside her. "You go first. I will say my piece later."

He waited while Fiona toyed with the braided velvet handles of her new reticule—waited while she methodically twisted and untwisted them with absentminded precision until he could stand it no longer. Prying the blasted thing out of her hand, he tossed it into the back of the wagon. "Now tell me what is on your mind, love."

Still she avoided his eyes. "I want to. I have thought about it all day, but now I find I am too embarrassed to do so."

Exasperated, Adam took her hand in his. It was ice cold, despite the warmth of the summer evening. "Would it help if I told you I hold you in great regard?"

Finally she met his gaze. "I hold you in great regard too, Adam," she said with a shy smile.

"And that I desire you more than any other woman I have ever known."

"You do? How amazing!" Her smile faded and she studied him with solemn eyes. "I am not very knowledgeable about such things, but certain feelings you arouse in me make me think that I . . ." Her blush deepened until her cheeks were as crimson as the strawberries in the Plimpton Fair tarts. "No," she amended, "I do not think it; I know it. I desire you too."

Adam wanted to shout his triumph to the heavens. In truth, it was all he could do to keep from taking her in his arms and kissing her in front of all of Plimpton Fair. He'd had little doubt about Fiona's attraction to him since she had responded so passionately to his kiss, but her shy confession conferred the final benediction on his plans for their future together.

He groaned. Little good that did him at the moment. Just thinking about the way her soft lips had opened to him with such uninhibited invitation made him ache with needs he couldn't begin to satisfy in an open cart in the middle of a fairground. "I think we may safely assume we are physically compatible and proceed from there," he said in a voice that even to his own ears sounded a bit strained.

"I find that very comforting. But there is more than that to a successful relationship between a man and woman. Do I offer you sufficient mental challenge to keep you from being bored with my company? You are, after all, much more worldly-wise than I."

Adam raised his right hand. "I swear on all that I hold sacred I have never met any woman who offered me the mental challenge you do, Fiona Haines. I cannot imagine ever being bored by you. And as for your lack of worldly wisdom, think of the fun I shall have teaching you all you need to know."

Fiona studied him thoughtfully. "How is it you always know to say the very thing that puts me at ease? But what of our ma-

terial differences? It does not bother you that I own Larkspur
Farm while you apparently have no worldly possessions except an expensive gold watch which I strongly suspect you
won in a high-stakes card game?"

"Not in the least."

"Then it does not bother me either." She favored him with a
smile so radiant, it eclipsed the rising moon he glimpsed over
her shoulder.

With a sigh of contentment, she leaned her head on his
shoulder and linked her fingers more tightly into his. "You
agree then, there is no reason why we should not become . . .
that is to say why we should not—"

"No reason at all." Adam slipped an arm around her and
drew her closer. By George, this was turning out to be far easier than he had expected. The little darling was offering to take
him as her lover when she thought him a penniless farmhand.
Imagine how thrilled she would be when he told her who he
really was and all he had to offer her. He found himself a little
dazed by his phenomenal good luck.

"But it is a big step, Adam, especially for you," she murmured. "I want you to consider it carefully before you commit
yourself."

Adam brushed the top of her head with a feather-light kiss.
"I have considered it all I need to, love. It is what I want. I
cannot wait to make you mine, and I promise you I shall do
everything in my power to make certain you never regret
putting your life in my hands."

"What a lovely thing to say. And I promise I shall do everything in my power to make certain you are never sorry you
have put your life in *my* hands."

Adam frowned. The wording of her fervent pledge had an
odd ring to it; for some reason he couldn't quite put his finger
on he felt a twinge of uneasiness. "We are both talking about
the same thing here, are we not?" he asked warily.

"Of course we are." Fiona raised her head from his shoulder
and regarded him with shining eyes. "Now that we have that
settled, I have one request to make of you." She glanced toward the village square. "Oh dear, I think I see Ben coming. I
shall have to speak rapidly; I do not want to share our plans
with anyone else right now."

"Good God no—especially not Ben."

"Right. It should be our secret for the time being. Ben is very fond of you. Once he knows what we intend, he will brag about it to everyone in Exmoor."

Adam sincerely doubted that Ben would brag about his beloved mistress taking a lover. He would be more likely to hunt up that ancient pistol he used to kill barn rats and put a bullet through the heart of the glib-tongued Londoner who had reneged on his promise.

Ben drew near enough so Adam could recognize the bawdy tavern ballad he was whistling. "Say what you have to say, love, but make it fast," he whispered in Fiona's ear. "The town crier is almost upon us."

"Aye." She slipped her fingers from his, scooted a few inches away from him, and folded her hands primly in her lap—the perfect picture of a properly virtuous widow.

"To put it as briefly as possible," she whispered, "Buckley was very good to me. I would never do anything to dishonor him."

Adam's uneasiness increased tenfold. He had come to realize that Fiona had a moral code all her own, which often disagreed with that of society. Still, all things considered, her statement did seem a trifle odd coming from a woman about to take a lover only two months after she had buried her husband.

She leaned forward and raised her voice just enough to be heard over the sound of Ben's boots shuffling through the gravel surrounding the sledge cart. "Believe me, Adam, I am every bit as anxious as you are to settle upon the future course of our lives. But I hope you will understand why I feel I must observe a decent period of mourning for my first husband before I marry you."

Marry!

Hell and damnation! The very word sent chills down Adam's spine. What had he said or done that made Fiona believe he intended to marry her?

He searched his memory but could find no answer to that puzzling question. In truth, shock numbed his mind and rendered him incapable of thinking coherently about anything.

Somehow he managed to spread Ben's quilt on the ground and help the jug-bitten old man lie down before he fell flat on his face. Somehow he managed to mouth the appropriate words in response to Fiona's shy, "Good night Adam," and stretched out on his own quilt before his legs gave out beneath him.

Then with Ben snoring beside him and Fiona sleeping in the cart above him, he finally acknowledged that he was in trouble. Serious trouble. And he had no one but himself to blame.

With blind, stupid arrogance he had formulated his plans for Fiona's future without heeding Creenagh's warning that she was obsessed with the idea of respectability. He was prepared to give her everything any woman could desire . . . except respectability.

Nor had he given much credence to Liam Campbell's claim that a sense of guilt had made her a little irrational where her late husband was concerned. He could see now that Campbell was right. Fiona would probably consider any offer he might make her short of marriage an insult to Buckley Haines's memory.

But much as he might desire her—even respect her for her courage and intelligence—he could never marry her. In his world, a nobleman who took a beautiful commoner with a questionable past as his mistress was considered a clever fellow; a nobleman who married such a woman was branded a fool.

He could well imagine the Duke of Bellmont's rage and horror if his second son married the illegitimate granddaughter of a moorland witch. Nor would the duke be alone in his condemnation. Adam knew how cruelly she would be treated by the vicious cats of the *ton*.

Furthermore, such a misalliance would close every door in fashionable London to him as well, including the doors he must open to find help for the thousands of desperate men he had vowed to represent.

Around him the boisterous holiday sounds of the fairground slowly decreased to a drowsy silence and the clouds of dust raised by beasts and humans settled back onto the village streets. One by one the candles illuminating the booths were extinguished until the only light still shed on Plimpton Fair came from the bright summer moon and the countless stars piercing the black dome of the sky above him.

With each passing minute the ache in his heart grew more intense until he felt as if some monstrous invisible hand had driven a jagged splinter of ice into its pulsing depths. But even more painful was the knowledge that he could not hope to extricate himself from this bumblebroth he had stumbled into without hurting Fiona—and that was the one thing, above all others, he had hoped never to do. He suspected he was in for another sleepless night and this time something far more disturbing than mere lust would keep his eyes open and his brain whirling.

For at long last he had been forced to face the truth he had steadfastly ignored since the idea of taking the lovely Widow Haines under his protection first occurred to him. She had managed by sheer grit and determination to escape the base mold into which generations of Derry women had been cast, and it mattered little what the gods had ordained, or even that she desired him as passionately as he desired her. Without her precious respectability, Fiona's proud spirit would wither and die.

Honor demanded that he release her from the commitment she had made to him and return to London alone. So he would do, because he was an honorable man. But with a wisdom borne of his belated soul-searching, he sadly acknowledged that his heart would forever remain in Exmoor.

Fiona was confused. She had thought their secret pact would bring Adam and her closer together. Instead, it appeared to have driven an invisible wedge between them that made her feel lonely and isolated and a little worried that once he had given serious thought to her proposal, he had changed his mind.

He had seemed so eager at first. But toward the end of their hurried conversation, he had grown strangely silent and the expression in his silver eyes had looked almost like shock.

He had not spoken a word the next morning either; just quietly hitched the ponies to the sledge cart while Ben nursed his aching head.

When he had kept his distance during the long ride from Plimpton Fair to the farm, she had reasoned he could do little else with Ben and the four Pincherts accompanying them. But now they had been home for two whole days and he had still said nothing more to her than "Good morning" and "Good night" and "Please pass the mutton." Not once had he shown the slightest inclination to kiss her, though she had done her level best to show him she was not averse to the idea.

True, the poor man had had little time for socializing in those two days. Nor had she for that matter; with the weather so miserable every chore took twice as long as usual. For the skies had opened up the morning after their return and they had been deluged with rain ever since. So much rain, most of her vegetable garden had washed away and the last time she had looked, the cow was standing in six inches of water inside the barn. The entire farm was a sea of sticky, oozing mud and she had spent most of the last forty-eight hours drying Ben's and Adam's clothes before the fireplace.

She looked up from her supper preparations to find the two of them on the front porch pulling off their boots and divesting themselves of their outer clothing—not an easy thing with Caesar wrapped around Adam's legs. The dog had not let his hero out of his sight since he had returned from the fair.

" 'Tis finally stopped raining, mistress, and thankful I be fer that," Ben declared. "Though 'tis a bit too late, to my way of thinking."

"Too late for what?"

"I'd a mind to sit in on the card game set fer Saturday night at the Black Boar, but 'twill take more than two days of sun to make the road 'tween here and there passable. I doubt even the surest-footed pony could muck his way through the mud this day."

"Well luckily no one here needs to risk life and limb traveling such roads now that Plimpton Fair is behind us." Fiona put two pans of twice-risen bread dough on the baking rack in the fireplace, gave the hot coals a stir with the poker, and straightened up just in time to glimpse an odd, almost haunted look on Adam's face.

There was definitely something wrong. She felt a cold frisson of fear travel her spine. Had she been mistaken in how he felt about her? Had he thought it over and decided marriage was too restrictive for a man used to the free wheeling ways of a gambler?

He had only to say so and she would instantly free him from

his commitment. She had already spent six years in a one-sided marriage; she had no desire to find herself in another—particularly when this time she would be the only one in love.

Adam saw the look on Fiona's face and knew she had sensed he was deeply troubled. These past two days had been the worst kind of hell and if Ben's assessment of the road was correct, there were at least three more such days to be endured before he could say the words that would turn the budding love she had confessed for him to hatred.

Three more days of reading the invitation in her eyes and fighting the urge to take her in his arms and carry her off to that lumpy little bed of his in the attic. Three more days of the agony of thinking this is the last time I shall ever see her pat Caesar on the head or laugh at some caustic remark of Creenagh's or do something as mundane as sew a patch on the knee of Ben's breeches. Then like the lying jackal he was, he could slink off to London and seek his own kind.

If he had ever doubted that Fiona held his heart in her capable little work-roughened hands, he doubted no more. He wondered if those gods of hers took malicious pleasure in giving him this glimpse of the heaven he could never attain.

Once supper was over, he excused himself and with Caesar at his heels, headed for his attic bedchamber as he had done the past two nights. Fiona stopped him halfway up the narrow staircase. "Wait, Adam. I know you must be tired from all the extra work the storm has caused, but I really need to speak with you . . . alone."

Reluctantly, he retraced his steps. "That might be hard to manage in a cottage this size." He glanced toward Ben and Creenagh sitting on opposite sides of the fireplace.

"It has stopped raining. We can talk on the porch." Without waiting for him to agree, she headed for the door.

Adam had no choice but to follow her. Pushing Caesar forward with his foot, he stepped outside and drew a deep breath of the clean night air. The moon was out for the first time in three nights. It cast an eerie, silver light on the water-soaked wood of the porch and the muddy farmyard beyond it.

Fiona wheeled around to face him once he had closed the door behind him. "What is wrong, Adam?" she demanded in her usual blunt way.

"Wrong?"

"Do not try to fob me off. You have not been yourself ever since . . . since our talk two nights ago. If what we discussed is repugnant to you, you have only to say so and we will forget the conversation ever occurred."

"Repugnant? Good Lord, Fiona, how could you even think such a thing? I admit I have a problem or two with the idea of our marrying, but never that. Whatever the future holds for us, I shall both desire and admire you until the moment I draw my last breath."

She took a step toward him. "Then the gods were right. For I feel the same about you."

He backed up a step. "The gods be damned for the cruel pranksters they have turned out to be."

Frantically, he cast about for the right words to say what must be said in the least hurtful way. He had hoped to put this confrontation off until just before he left; he could see now that was no longer possible.

"People are not always what they appear to be," he began, then stopped short as Caesar stiffened beside him and snarled deep in his throat.

"What is it, boy? What do you hear?" Adam reached down to rub Caesar behind his ears and found them flattened against his head.

Fiona stepped to the porch railing and peered into the dark farmyard. "I think I see something, or someone, just beyond the gate. We had best investigate."

"Let me get my pistol first, just in case. Whoever it is would have to be desperate to travel the road as it is tonight."

Moments later, pistol in hand, Adam sloshed down the muddy path to the gate. Fiona followed close behind him and a growling Caesar bounded ahead, his ruff raised ominously.

Adam sighted a moonlit figure outside the gate. "It is only a pony," he said with a sigh of relief.

"A moorland pony?" Fiona moved up to stand beside him. "How odd. I have never known them to wander this close to the cottage before."

Adam took a closer look. "This one is domesticated. It is saddled and from the steam rising from its flanks I would say it has been ridden recently and ridden hard." Adam opened the gate, stepped forward to catch hold of the dangling reins, and stumbled over what looked like a mound of clothing lying close to the pony's hooves. Caesar sniffed it, and the mound gave a soft, distinctly feminine moan.

"What the devil! It's a woman." Adam knelt down and gently turned her over. Ugly purple bruises marred one swollen cheek and surrounded both closed eyes. Her upper lip was split open and vivid fingermarks circled her throat.

Fiona knelt beside him. "Who can she be?"

"It is hard to tell with her face in the condition it is. But she looks vaguely familiar."

Fiona made a closer study of the woman's battered face. "Good heavens! This is Molly Blodgett, the innkeeper's oldest daughter."

"And your brother's sweetheart," Adam said grimly.

Fiona swallowed hard. "Yes. What in the world could have happened to her?"

"She has obviously been severely beaten by someone who is an expert at the sorry business." Adam slipped one arm beneath the girl's shoulders, the other beneath her knees. "Run ahead and open the door so I can carry her inside."

Fiona followed his order without question, grateful Adam had once again taken charge of a difficult situation.

"Take her down the hall to my bedchamber," she directed a moment later when he stepped through the doorway with Molly in his arms. Quickly gathering the stack of clean cloths she used to dry the dishes and the bucket of water she had carried in from the well before supper, she hurried after him. Creenagh had reached the bedchamber before her and was already bending over Molly's unconscious form.

Together they stripped off the young woman's heavy woolen cape and found huge bloodstains on both her blue skirt and white apron.

"I will go stable the pony," Adam said and promptly left the room.

Fiona pulled a clean sheet from her bureau drawer, and Creenagh and she slipped it beneath Molly before they removed any more of her clothing. "Just as I feared," Creenagh said when it turned out her petticoat and bloomers were soaked in blood.

"So much blood," Fiona murmured, leaning against the bed-post while she struggled to control her nausea.

" 'Tis always the way of it when a woman loses a babe."

"A babe?" Fiona gasped, wondering if Liam was aware he had planted his seed in the girl. Like all of Hiram Blodgett's daughters, Molly had a reputation for being no better than she should be. But as far as Fiona knew, she had been true to Liam since they had begun walking out together some six months earlier.

But who could have beaten her so unmercifully? Liam was careless and irresponsible, but he had never shown any evidence of having a cruel streak.

"Stay with the lass whilst I mix the juice of sea grass and endive with a bit of hysop," Creenagh said, heading for the chamber door. " 'Twill stop the flow of blood if anything can."

"She will be all right then once she drinks your brew?"

Creenagh shrugged. " 'Tis too soon to tell. She'll live or die depending on how much of her lifeblood be already lost."

Fiona sat on the edge of the bed and took Molly's cold hand in hers. She had always liked the pretty, sunny-natured girl, despite her reputation as a flirt. If the truth be known, she thought Molly much too good for a care-for-nothing fellow like Liam.

Molly stirred and opened her eyes. "My babe?"

Fiona gave her fingers a gentle squeeze. "I am so sorry."

Tears welled in Molly's eyes. "I guess I knowed it. What chance did it have, poor wee thing?"

Fiona brushed the girl's unruly black curls off her pale brow. "Who did this terrible thing to you and what possessed you to travel the road to Larkspur Farm when it was in such terrible condition?"

"Liam," Molly whispered.

"Liam beat you?" Fiona's voice shook. "I find that hard to believe. He has never been a violent man."

"No! No! Liam would never beat me. 'Twas them excise officers trying to make me tell them where he be. But never a word did they get from me for all their punching and kicking."

She made an effort to sit up, but she was too weak from loss of blood. "Please, Mistress Haines, help me," she begged, sinking back onto the pillow. "I must find Liam."

"I am sorry. He is not here."

"I know that. He be visiting the man as is his pap, for all he never give Liam his name. But I couldn't make it that far so I come to you."

"Are you saying Liam is at Lynmouth Bay with the Earl of Stratham?" Fiona winced as the words passed her lips. She had never thought to speak aloud the name of the heartless wretch who had sired her and her half brother.

"Aye. This be his second visit to the earl on account of he be ailing." Molly's fingers grasped Fiona's with surprising strength. "Find him, Mistress. Warn him the excise officers will hang him if they catches him."

Fiona had always known that Liam was involved in smuggling. But then so was half the population of Exmoor and Cornwall, and the rest of the citizens looked the other way when the "gentlemen" plied their trade. Gently she withdrew her aching fingers from Molly's paralyzing grip. "Not to worry. No one is ever hanged in Exmoor for smuggling."

" 'Tis not smuggling he be accused of, but landing a French spy on our coast when England were at war, and that be a hanging crime."

"But that is ridiculous. Liam may not be the most praiseworthy of men, but he is certainly no traitor. Who would start such a vicious rumor?"

Molly's eyes drifted shut. "I cannot say for sure, but I suspect 'twere that spawn o' the devil, Dooley Twig." Her voice faded to a whisper. "I were walking out with him afore I took up with Liam, and he swore he would get even with Liam for stealing me from him."

Fiona heard a sound behind her and turned to find Adam standing in the doorway. The angry scowl on his face told her he had heard Molly's story and found Twig's method of revenging himself on a rival as disgusting as she did.

"Keep her talking if you can," he warned. "If she loses consciousness, Creenagh may not be able to bring her back."

Fear spiraled through Fiona. Grasping the girl's plump shoulders, she gave them a gentle shake. "Please try to stay awake, Molly, at least until my grandmother returns." She shook her again but to no avail; Molly had lost consciousness.

Moments later Creenagh returned with Ben close behind her. She took one look at her patient and shook her head. "I am not sure I can save the poor lass. Whoever 'twas beat her did a fine piece of work."

"Try, Creenagh. She is much too young to die." Fiona's voice broke in a sob. "I will hold her head up so you can spoon some of your brew into her. Then maybe some rich mutton broth to give her strength."

Adam laid a hand on Fiona's shoulder. "I will help Creenagh. You go make that broth."

"And I will fetch Hiram at first light. 'Tis only right he be here," Ben declared. "I knows the road to the Black Boar as well as I knows me own name. A bit of mud will never stop me."

Once Ben and Fiona had departed from the room, Adam lifted Molly's head and shoulders off the pillow and slid in behind her on the bed so her upper body rested against him. With half his mind, he monitored Creenagh's efforts to spoon-feed her herbal concoction to her patient; with the other half he contemplated this latest bizarre development in what he had begun to think of as the Exmoor saga.

Once again fate had intervened before he could make his much-needed confession to Fiona. He was beginning to wonder if he would ever find the opportunity to say his piece and return to his own way of life.

One thing was certain; he would not be leaving for London as soon as he had planned—not if his softhearted little love was about to go haring off to some place called Lynmouth to save her brother from the hangman's noose. But once he saw her safely through this latest trouble, he would end his masquerade once and for all. Surely not even Creenagh's capricious Celtic gods could be so callous as to expect a London-born nobleman to dwell much longer in this hellish provincial limbo they had created.

Chapter Fourteen

Miraculously, Molly Blodgett survived the night. Fiona thought they had lost her shortly before midnight and again in the wee hours of the morning. But Molly was a healthy young woman and a scrapper to boot. Somehow she held on to a thin thread of life until Creenagh's healing herbs began to take effect.

Now an hour before dawn, as Fiona changed into her heavy riding skirt and warm jacket, she sensed the girl's anxious gaze was fixed on her. "Not to worry, Molly," she said, moving to stand beside the bed. "I will find Liam and warn him of the danger he is in. In the meantime, my grandmother will take good care of you. If you need anything, you have only to ask."

"Aye, Mistress Haines. I'll not be afeared of the witch ever again—not after what she done for me this night." Tears welled in Molly's eyes and she turned her head toward the room's one window. "Will Liam be leaving England, do ye think?"

"He will probably have to until this ridiculous business about the French spy is cleared up. But you need never fret about Liam; he always lands on his feet wherever he goes."

"Aye, that he does. But likely I'll not see him again and I'll miss him sorely. For all his rapscallion ways, he could make a body feel so . . ." She sighed. "There was never another man made me feel the way Liam did when he touched me."

"Such a man is both a blessing and a curse," Fiona agreed, and realized it was not only Liam Campbell she had in mind. A few months ago she might have judged Molly harshly for giving herself so cheaply to a known scoundrel, even as she had judged all the Derry women before her for succumbing to masculine wiles.

But a few months ago she had not shivered with delight at Adam Cresswell's kiss nor listened enthralled when he spun his tales of the wondrous things to be found in Londontown. Was what Molly had done any more shameful than practically begging a man to marry her—a man who admittedly "had a problem or two" with the idea?

The handsome black-haired devil who had driven her to such a disgraceful pass was seated at the table with Creenagh when she entered the kitchen. He looked up from the bowl of porridge he was eating long enough to ask, "How is the patient?"

"Weak but awake. Unless something untoward happens in the next few hours, she should soon be on the mend."

"Glad to hear it." He finished off his porridge and set the bowl aside. "Then I hope we can leave for Lynmouth as soon as you have your breakfast. The sooner the better, as far as I am concerned."

"We? I do not recall asking you to go with me."

He raised an eyebrow in that insufferably arrogant way of his. "Did you think I would let you make such a journey alone?"

"Since when has a mere employee been privileged to let me do anything?" It was a petty remark. She cared not. His admitted reservations about marrying her had been both hurtful and humiliating.

"The lad be right, Fiona," Creenagh declared. " 'Tis not safe for a woman to be riding the moors alone."

Fiona cast her grandmother a withering look. "This from a woman who spent the last six years living in a cave in the most godforsaken part of said moors."

Creenagh exchanged a knowing look with Adam. "Ye'll recall, Londoner, I told ye the chit be pigheaded as they come."

"She is angry with me and rightfully so." The note of sadness in Adam's voice shocked Fiona and silenced any cutting remark she might have made.

He rose from the table and faced her squarely. "You are correct, of course. As your employee I have no right to tell you what to do. Therefore, I terminate my employment as of this minute and tell you as a friend, I plan to accompany you to Lynmouth."

Fiona's heart thudded painfully in her breast, but she made no further objection. She might be a fool where Adam was concerned, but not so much a fool that she would waste any more time on an argument she could never hope to win.

Dawn would be breaking any moment now and it was imperative she be on her way. If Dooley Twig was behind this scurrilous attack, as Molly suspected, he would be certain to direct the excisemen to Liam's sister now that they had failed to get the information they wanted from his sweetheart. Twig had even more reason to hate her than her brother. Not only had she refused his suit, but thanks to Adam she had bested him at Plimpton Fair as well.

Without another word she stuffed a loaf of bread and a wedge of cheese into a small cloth sack and marched out the door.

Ben was already saddling his pony when Adam and she arrived at the stable. He bid them farewell just as the topmost rim of the sun blazed into view, and rode off down the muddy trail to the Black Boar Inn.

A few moments later, Adam and Fiona locked a protesting Caesar in the barn and headed in the opposite direction. "So you are playing the lady today, Fiona." Adam eyed her riding skirt and bonnet and the sidesaddle she only rode when she absolutely had to. "I had expected to see you in your breeches." His voice held an odd note, almost as if he were disappointed.

She found herself remembering the first time they had set out together across the moors to fetch Creenagh to Larkspur Farm. Then she had been wearing her comfortable breeches and ridden astride. Today, because of her destination, she felt it necessary to wear a proper skirt, which necessitated using the sidesaddle she despised. Had it really been only a few weeks? It seemed as if her life had revolved around Adam forever—a condition that would undoubtedly change the minute they returned from their trip to Lynmouth. For not only had he managed to wriggle out of his commitment to marry her; he had turned a simple disagreement into an opportunity to quit his job as her farmhand as well.

It was all too obvious Adam was leaving Larkspur Farm, as Ben had predicted he would, and she felt numb with pain at the thought of spending the rest of her life without him.

He pulled up alongside her when they had ridden due north a little over an hour. "Where is this place we are headed for and how long will it take to get there?"

"Lynmouth Bay borders the Bristol Channel, which lies just beyond those hills on the far horizon. With steady riding at a fair pace we should reach the Aerie in another four hours."

"The Aerie, I take it, is the home of the Earl of Stratham."

"It is."

"And the earl is Liam Campbell's natural father."

"He is," Fiona said in a chilling tone of voice that challenged her inquisitor to add the earl was her natural father as well.

Adam promptly lapsed into silence. He had enough trouble ahead of him; he saw no reason to needlessly invite Fiona's wrath.

For the next three hours they rode across the open moor, drawing ever closer to the purple hills that ringed the Exmoor coastline. Twice when they stopped to rest the ponies, Adam tried to strike up a conversation with Fiona, but each time she answered him in terse monosyllables or not at all.

He could have borne her anger; in truth he deserved it for the less than subtle way in which he had let her know he was not interested in marrying her. But she had a wounded look about her that increased his feeling of guilt tenfold—more so because she was putting on such a brave show of indifference.

What a love she was. He wished he could take back the careless words that had hurt her so deeply. More than that, he wished . . . but he had convinced himself weeks ago that no good would come of thinking about what could never be.

Still, for the first time in his life, he found himself daring to wonder what would be so earthshaking about the second son of the Duke of Bellmont's marrying beneath him—very far beneath him, considering the woman he had in mind was the illegitimate granddaughter of an Exmoor witch and a by-blow of the notorious Earl of Stratham. Of course, both his father and Ethan would declare the idea unthinkable, and those stiff-necked arbiters of polite society, the patronesses of Almack's, would probably never recover from the shock.

But why should he be obligated to honor such hidebound restrictions? He was not the heir to the title. He could never even inherit one of the many properties belonging to the dukedom, since they were all entailed. Nor, despite what his father might contend, was it his responsibility to provide the duke with a suitably blue-blooded grandson to carry on the title in the distant future. That was Ethan's province.

Then by all that was holy, he should be free to marry the one woman with whom he could imagine spending the rest of his life.

And so he would!

His father would undoubtedly rant and rave when he was presented with Fiona as a daughter-in-law . . . much as he had ranted and raved over the many other ways in which Adam had defied him over the years. But he would eventually adjust to the idea when he had no other choice.

As for the efforts on behalf of the nation's ex-servicemen, Adam had to admit he might have to talk a little longer and be a little more convincing if his standing in London society was diminished by an unsuitable wife. But the cause was too just to be ignored. Sooner or later those in power would have to listen to him.

Now that he had made the daring decision, he felt as if an anvil had been lifted off his shoulders. Thank God he had accompanied Fiona on this mission of hers. It had given him the opportunity he needed to reassess his priorities—an unexpected benefit, since his initial reason for insisting he journey to Lynmouth with her had had nothing to do with their future together. Though he would never say as much to Fiona, he had cause to believe she would need all the support she could get if saving her brother necessitated her coming face-to-face with her natural father.

Adam had been a green lad on his first holiday from Eton the year Dierk Wolverson, the Earl of Stratham, had come to London seeking a bride. A giant of a man with flaming red hair and a mouth as foul as that of any dockside sailor, Stratham had disrupted one entire Season with his shocking presence.

For though he was rich as an India trade nabob, not even the most ambitious of the *ton*'s matrons had been willing to submit their daughters to the tender mercies of the "Barbarian," as he was dubbed by London society. There was a rumor he had fallen madly in love with one of the *ton*'s incomparables, but she had rejected him out of hand, and her father threatened to shoot him if he ever approached her again. Adam could scarcely believe such an unmitigated boor could have sired a daughter as lovely and refined as Fiona.

So engrossed was he in his ruminations, it took him a moment to realize they had finally arrived at the base of the coastal hills. The sun directly above him proclaimed the hour of noon, and his rumbling stomach verified it as surely as if he had checked his watch.

Here the moorland road entered a deep combe that was bordered on both sides with walls of stone rising from the valley floor like the bulwarks of a medieval castle. The road narrowed slightly, but though it was wide enough to accommodate two ponies, Adam held back, letting Fiona take the lead.

For the next few minutes they followed a swiftly flowing stream, the banks of which were covered by masses of brilliantly colored primroses and wild hyacinths. An excellent spot for a picnic, in his opinion, but to his dismay, Fiona pushed on relentlessly.

"What is that roaring I hear?" he asked, when a little farther on a sound like distant thunder filled his ears.

"A waterfall. This part of Exmoor is famous for thcm," Fiona said over her shoulder. "I have been here only once before with Liam when I was twelve, but I remember the one up ahead as being quite spectacular. We can stop there for our noonday meal if you wish."

Adam readily agreed. At least she was finally talking to him. Maybe she would mellow even more once they had rested and eaten the inevitable bread and cheese. He hoped so. Considering his unfortunate remark, he had his work cut out for him if he hoped to convince her he'd had a change of mind. A good-natured Fiona would be much easier to deal with than his taciturn traveling companion of the last three hours.

A great jut of iron gray rock rose up from the valley floor a half mile or so ahead and once they wound their way around it, he caught his first sight of the waterfall. A majestic torrent of white water, it plunged hundreds of feet into a deep, rocky pool.

Dismounting, he gazed around him at the incredible beauty of his surroundings and finally at the lovely woman standing beside him. He breathed deeply of the cool, spray-filled air and felt a profound contentment that had been missing in his life for far too long. He smiled to himself, wondering if this was what his aunt had had in mind when she had advised him to go to Exmoor to find his peace of mind.

He touched Fiona's arm to gain her attention. "Magnificent," he shouted over the deafening roar. "I had no idea I would find anything like this in Exmoor."

Fiona could see Adam's lips move, but his words were drowned in the thundering water. It mattered not; she sensed his awe, read the same exhilaration on his face that the wondrous spectacle inspired in her, and knew he was the one person in all the world she would have chosen to share this moment with her.

As she watched, a sunbeam painted a vivid rainbow in the cloud of spray circling the plummeting water. "Magic," she said to herself, half expecting to see the white pony appear on the tree-lined cliff above her. Out of the corner of her eye, she saw Adam searching the same cliff, as if he too felt the magic of this incredible place.

She studied his raven black hair, his strong profile, the thin white scar that spoke of other, deeper scars he carried in his heart and mind—and some age-old womanly instinct told her this was the only man she would ever love. Her heart twisted with pain at the realization that like all the Derry women before her she was destined to love a man who would never marry her.

He turned his head to stare down at her, and the desire that flared in his silver eyes matched her own aching need. Never in all her life had she longed for anything as much as she longed to feel his warm, sensuous mouth pressed to hers just one more time.

"Kiss me, Adam," she whispered, but though she sensed he read her lips, he made no move to take her in his arms. She wondered if he was so worried she might somehow trap him into the marriage he opposed, he was afraid to touch her.

For one insane moment she wished she really was the witch the Gypsy fortune-teller had accused her of being. Maybe then she could cast a spell over him that would compel him to do as she desired.

As if the wish were its own fulfillment, she suddenly felt the same odd tingling in her fingers that the Gypsy's touch had created. Her breath caught in her throat. Could it be she had mystic powers she had never realized?

Did she dare use them on Adam?

Was it fair to bewitch a man to make him kiss her?

Even as she asked herself those questions, she knew she could not resist the temptation to just once try her hand at casting a spell. What did she have to lose? For all practical purposes, she had already lost her one true love.

She closed her eyes and with every fiber of her being willed Adam to kiss her. Before she could draw a deep breath, she was in his arms, with his lips claiming hers in a kiss more wildly passionate than any they had previously shared.

Without another thought, she gave herself up to the waves of pleasure washing through her. Of their own volition, hands that had been pressed to Adam's chest slid up the strong column of his throat and into his spray-damp hair. Instantly he deepened the kiss to explore her mouth with an intimate expertise that made every nerve in her body hum like a tautly stretched wire.

One strong arm tightened around her waist, molding her feminine softness to his strong male body in a way that left no doubt in her mind he was fully aroused. The other cupped her breast possessively.

With Adam's lips on hers and his long, elegant fingers kneading her breast to a throbbing peak, she suddenly felt gloriously, triumphantly female. Then he lifted his head and bereft of his lips, Fiona opened her eyes. One look at the dazed expression on his face and her magic bubble burst. With a chilling intensity, sanity returned to taunt her with what she had done. She wanted this man with all her heart and soul— but not if she had to cast a spell to get him.

With a sob, she broke from his embrace and fled to her waiting pony. Quickly mounting, she turned the animal back onto the trail that led to Lynmouth and left the man on whom she had practiced her neophyte witchcraft standing, mouth agape, behind her.

Adam couldn't imagine what had gotten into him. One minute he had been firm in his determination to keep his hands off Fiona until he could make her a respectable offer of marriage; the next he had grabbed her, hauled her up against him, and kissed her with fierce, unbridled passion. Worse yet, he had fondled her as if she were some cheap little dolly-mop he had picked off the London streets. Had she not escaped him when she did, he would probably have thrown her to the ground and taken her then and there.

She must despise him. He felt certain she had been crying when she mounted her pony and fled from him in terror. Sadly, he acknowledged he had never before driven any woman to tears. Even his ex-mistresses looked on him as a trusted friend. Then why in the name of God had he chosen to treat the only woman he had ever wanted to marry so shabbily?

He clenched his fists in frustration. Devil take it, how could a man who had always prided himself on his ironclad control make such a cawker of himself?

Well, there was nothing for it but to find her and apologize. She had enough problems right now without his adding to them.

He caught up with her nearly a mile down the road. She had tied her pony to a convenient bush and disappeared beneath the trailing branches of a huge willow tree that grew on the bank of the same stream they had followed since they'd left the moors.

Quickly he dismounted and pushed his way into her shady hideaway, stopping far enough away from her so she would have no reason to think he was about to attack her again. "Hell and damnation, Fiona, I have no idea what got into me. Can you ever forgive me?"

"Th . . . there is nothing to forgive."

"Of course there is. I acted like the worst kind of bounder."

"You did not know what you were doing."

"Let me assure you, I always know what I am doing." Though come to think of it, he had surprised himself as much as he had undoubtedly surprised her.

"It was not your fault, Adam. Believe me."

She really was a love. No other woman he knew would be so forgiving. "You are making things worse by being so sweet about it," he said contritely. "I would feel much better if you would tear a few strips off my hide, as I deserve." To his surprise his feeble attempt at levity brought on a new spate of tears.

He couldn't bear to see her like this. At the risk of frightening her further, he drew her into his arms until her head rested on his shoulder. Awkwardly, he patted her heaving back. "I hope you know I would never hurt you, Fiona," he whispered in her ear.

She burrowed her face into the hollow between his chest and his shoulder. "I hope you know I would never purposely hurt you either, Adam." She raised her head. "Or embarrass you. Or force you to do something you did not want to do."

Adam studied her earnest face somewhat warily. He was beginning to get that uneasy feeling again—the same one that had preceded her unexpected proposal of marriage. What was she leading up to this time?

He put her from him, but kept his hands on her upper arms. "Are you by any chance trying to tell me something, love?"

She nodded. "It all started because I wanted you to kiss me. Very much."

He smiled. "And I wanted to kiss you. But all things considered, I decided it best I wait until after—"

"I could tell you were not going to do it. Which is why I was driven to do what I did."

"What exactly did you do?" he asked absentmindedly, still wrestling with the puzzle of why he couldn't remember what had happened to make him act so contrary to his nature.

Fiona gulped. "I cast a spell over you."

"You did what?" Adam felt certain he could not have heard what he thought he had.

"Maybe we should wait until after we eat to discuss this. I have noticed you are always in a better mood when your stomach is full."

"We will discuss it now." Adam scowled. "Tell me again, slowly and distinctly, exactly what it was you did."

"I cast a spell over you," Fiona repeated in a voice that quivered ever so slightly. "Just a little one to make you kiss me," she amended, as if qualifying her amazing statement would make it more palatable.

"Are you claiming that you are a witch like your grandmother, and that you practiced your black art on me?"

Fiona's nod was barely perceptible.

"That, madam, is the most preposterous thing I have ever heard," Adam declared, until he recalled the inexplicable compulsion that had come over him.

He clenched his fists in frustration. "Hell and damnation, you are serious about this, aren't you?" How much of this blasted hocus-pocus did Fiona expect him to tolerate? Disappearing ponies, quirky Celtic gods, and an eighty-year-old woman who could pass for a young girl were more than enough for any ordinary, God-fearing man to have on his plate. Now this!

"Did it never occur to you to mention your little . . . eccentricity when you proposed marriage to me?"

Fiona avoided his eyes. "I was not really aware of it then. I just decided to give it a try when I recalled the Gypsy fortune-teller had accused me of having mystical powers."

"What prompted her to do that?"

"I think it had something to do with the fact that sparks flew when she touched my fingers."

"Good God!"

Fiona looked so miserable, Adam was tempted to take her in his arms and assure her everything would be all right. Unfortunately he doubted his words would ring true. "I have always had a horror of anything bordering on the occult," he said stiffly.

She winced. "I can understand that."

"Then perhaps you can understand what a shock it is to realize I have been considering marrying a woman who might very well be a witch."

"Have you really—been considering marrying me, that is. I thought you had 'problems' with the idea."

"I did. God knows I certainly do now." Adam knew his mounting exasperation was due as much to his own equivocating as to anything Fiona had done. "So help me, if it were not that I think I have fallen in love with you—"

"Oh, Adam!" Fiona's eyes looked like candles had just been lighted behind them. It was all Adam could do to keep from blinking. Devil take it, he was dressing the woman down and she looked like he had just presented her with the royal jewels.

He shifted his weight from one foot to the other, then planted both firmly on the mossy ground and faced her squarely. In truth, he couldn't help but be flattered that she had wanted to kiss him so badly, she had resorted to witchcraft to bring it about. But he could see he must begin as he meant to go on with Fiona or she would soon get entirely out of hand.

"I have to tell you, this latest development gives me pause for thought," he said in the no-nonsense tone of voice he had used when he'd found it necessary to reprimand one of the men in his command. "Even the most congenial of married couples has an occasional quarrel. How could I be certain you would not, in a fit of pique, turn me into a toad or some such thing."

Fiona looked highly insulted. "I would never do anything like that—even if I could. As a matter of fact, I have decided to give up practicing witchcraft. I shall never need it now that I know you love me."

Adam groaned. This entire scenario was growing more bizarre by the minute. "I commend your decision," he said gravely, "and should we marry, I would feel obliged to insist you live by it." He frowned. "But I would hope you based it on a more logical reason than that. You have always struck me as a very practical woman. Never say you are going to start dealing in such fairy tales as *Love Conquers All.*"

"Oh, but it is not a fairy tale, as I am living proof." Fiona's smile was dazzling. "Since the moment Molly told me where I must find Liam, I have been dreading a possible encounter with the Earl of Stratham. But no more.

"I shall march up to the ogre's door and deliver my message without the slightest qualm. There is nothing the earl, or anyone else, can do that will hurt or humiliate me ever again—because the only person in all the world whose opinion I truly value has just confessed he loves me."

Chapter Fifteen

With her newfound self-confidence buoying up her spirits, Fiona was ready and eager to push on to Lynmouth Bay once Adam and she had eaten their simple noon meal.

He had seemed uncommonly touched by her declaration that his love had set her free from her anxiety about facing the man who was her natural father. At least he'd taken the time to give her a tender kiss before he'd begun eating his bread and cheese. Considering his voracious appetite, that seemed a most propitious sign.

They had ridden no more than an hour through a leafy forest of oaks and hawthorns, when a softness in the air and a tang of salt warned they were nearing the coast. "It looks as if we may be in for some rain," Adam said, pointing to the bank of ominous gray clouds hovering on the horizon. "I hope we can find an inn where we can stay the night. We could never make it back to Larkspur Farm before dark, and I doubt you will want to accept the Earl of Stratham's hospitality."

"I doubt he will offer it," Fiona said dryly. "But you are right. I would sooner sleep on the open moors than be beholden to *him* for a night's lodging."

"Let us hope it doesn't come to that. Is there no town between here and the Aerie?"

"We should come to Lynton very soon now, but I was here so long ago I cannot remember if I saw an inn." No sooner had the words left her mouth than the road on which they were traveling emerged from the forest, and the sleepy little town lay spread out before them.

It had changed little since last she'd seen it. Perched somewhat precariously above the wooded cliffs where the Lyn gorge cut back into the hills, the entire town commanded a sweeping view of the Bristol Channel.

"Unless my eyes deceive me that rather picturesque wattle and daub structure up ahead is what we're seeking," Adam said as they rode down the town's only street. As they drew near, Fiona spied a neatly lettered sign above the door proclaiming it to be The Lamb and Lion Inn and Alehouse. Though not a single carriage could be seen in the immaculate innyard, a plump, gray-haired woman in a starched apron and snowy mobcap was busy sweeping the steps as if she expected travelers to arrive at any minute.

Adam brought his pony to a halt. "Now that looks promising. Should we bespeak rooms and an evening meal before we go on to the Aerie?"

Fiona had never stopped overnight at an inn. Mentally she counted the few coins in her jacket pocket and wondered how dear such an unexpected extravagance might be.

"I have sufficient funds with me for a meal and a night's lodging if that is what's worrying you," Adam declared when she failed to answer his question. Without further ado, he dismounted, looped his pony's reins around the nearest bush and approached the woman wielding the broom.

Fiona gritted her teeth. Once again he had taken charge without so much as a by-your-leave.

"It is all arranged," he said a few moments later when he rejoined Fiona. "And a lucky thing too. The coach to Ilfracombe, which stops the night here, is due within the hour."

Fiona swallowed the angry protest she had been about to make over his high-handed behavior. It was hard to argue with a man who was right. "I should have paid for our lodging," she grumbled. "You are only here out of concern for me."

Adam's only response was one of his arrogant looks that plainly said what he thought of that idea. She found herself wondering how a common gambler had managed to perfect a look one would normally attribute to a highborn aristocrat. Once they were safely married, she planned to discuss that annoying habit with him, as well as his tendency to automatically take control of every situation in which they found themselves.

At the moment, however, she intended to devote all her energy to getting this sorry business with Liam over and done with as soon as possible. Only then could she move forward with hers—and, of course, Adam's—plans for the future.

With that in mind, she urged her pony forward past a dozen or more shops ranging from a saddle and tackle shop to a purveyor of ladies' undergarments, past a pretty stone church and vicarage and a bevy of neat little thatched roof cottages.

The last building they came to as they were about to leave the town was a blacksmith's open forge, with a smithy hard at work. "I just realized this is the first blacksmith I've seen since I arrived in Exmoor," Adam said, when they stopped to let the ponies drink at the watering trough just beyond the forge.

"That is because they are few and far between on the moors. Unlike the pampered horses you Londoners spend good money to maintain, Exmoor ponies need never be shod. Their hooves are naturally iron-hard and perfectly adapted to the terrain they travel."

Adam heard the boastful note in her voice and smiled to himself. Fiona was the most independent woman he had ever met and she obviously considered her beloved ponies' lack of dependence on man a decided attribute. He suspected she viewed her own independence with equal pride.

He shook his head. A man would have to be mad or, at the very least, madly in love to consider taking on a wife who presented him with so many problems. Even the most strong-minded woman should realize she was meant to be her husband's helpmeet, not his competitor. He would have to have a serious discussion with her on this subject once they were safely married. But right now he must concentrate on getting this sorry business with Liam Campbell behind them so he could get on with his—and, of course, Fiona's—plans for the future.

A mile or so beyond the outskirts of the town the road split into two branches. One wound downward toward Lynmouth Bay; the other continued along the edge of the cliff. Fiona took the high road.

"This leads to the Foreland Point lighthouse," she called over her shoulder. "The Aerie lies halfway between the bay and the point."

"The sooner we reach it, the better. From the look of that sky, I'd say a storm is definitely brewing," he called back. The clouds directly above them had turned a threatening slate gray in the short time since they'd left Lynton and a rising wind whistled through the few scraggly trees bordering the cliff.

From far below came the sullen roar of surf breaking on shingle and a lone gull circled above the shore and headed out to sea. Then without warning, a brilliant flash of lightning split the sky, spooking both ponies. Even as Adam struggled to bring his animal under control and make certain Fiona was safely managing hers, he heard a clap of thunder so near, it seemed to rattle the very ground on which they rode. A moment later he felt the first splatter of rain against his cheek.

The cliff was barren of trees here and the road curved sharply upward across the screes. With a firm hand on his pony's reins, Adam topped the crest of the small hill behind Fiona, and found himself looking at what had to be the Aerie.

Like the eagle's nest for which it was named, it clung to a rocky promontory some two hundred feet above the crashing waves. With its vast moss-shrouded walls and octagonal angle turrets, its narrow slot windows, and battlemented chimneys, it looked more like a medieval stronghold than a nobleman's manor house.

As they rode closer, Adam realized there was no door on the exterior wall. The only entrance to, or exit from, the fortress-like structure appeared to be a tall, arched tunnel which led to an inner courtyard. The domicile of the Earl of Stratham was without a doubt the coldest, most unwelcoming place he had ever seen.

A gust of wind whipped a tendril of hair loose from Fiona's already untidy braid and the rain plastered it against her cheek. She stared at the massive stone structure before her and despite the brave words she'd uttered earlier, felt a shiver of apprehension. When Liam and she had come here years ago, they had hidden in the woods along the cliff and stared at it from a distance.

Now, viewing it up close, she had to wonder what kind of man would live in such a cheerless place—and why, if Molly was to believed, Liam had visited it twice in recent weeks.

She brought her pony to a halt just outside the entrance to the arched tunnel and Adam promptly pulled up beside her. "I need to stop a moment and gather my wits before I pound on the earl's door," she said. "I assume it's somewhere through that tunnel."

Adam nodded his agreement. The thoughtful frown on his handsome face told her he found the Aerie every bit as grim as she did.

She had seen the nobleman who owned the ominous-looking structure only once, the year she was ten. He had ridden through the village on his great black stallion—a huge man with a shock of flaming red hair encircling his head like a wreath of fire and massive shoulders that strained the seams of a fine linen shirt not unlike the ones Adam always wore.

To this day, she remembered how his loud, mocking laughter had boomed down the village street when all the mothers rushed their daughters inside their cottages and bolted the doors.

For weeks afterward, the village children had taunted Liam and her unmercifully because it was no secret they were by-blows of the evil, red-haired earl. Liam had blacked the eyes of half a dozen boys who made the loudest catcalls, then promptly dismissed the incident as unimportant.

Not so Fiona. It was then she'd made a vow that when she grew up she would be so proper and respectable no one would ever dare ridicule her again.

She glanced at the rain-drenched man patiently sitting his pony beside her, and smiled. Respectability with Buckley had required that she ignore all the womanly instincts deep inside her. But with Adam she would have it all—a proper marriage and the wild and wonderful passion Creenagh praised so highly as well.

He returned her smile with one of his endearing lopsided grins and she felt her heart do its usual flip-flop. "Well, love," he asked, eyeing her tenderly, "are you ready to face the dragon?"

Fiona leaned forward in the saddle and planted a quick kiss on the scar slicing his cheek. "With you by my side, sir knight, I say fie on all dragons!"

The surly-looking servant who answered their knock at the door, once they finally located it inside the bleak inner courtyard, added his own unique touch to the rather macabre ambi-

ence of his place of employment. His sparse gray hair was collected at his nape with a greasy-looking leather thong and his
face had so many wrinkles it resembled one of the famous
Dodslet Brothers' hand-drawn maps of London. The faded
blue livery draping his scrawny body lacked two buttons and
bore stains reminiscent of numerous past meals.

Still, despite his disreputable appearance, he had that unmistakable air about him that Adam had always thought of as
upper servant snobbery. He perused the two wet, bedraggled
people on his doorstep as if taking their measure, and the sneer
on his face plainly said he judged them beneath contempt.

"The Earl of Stratham ain't receiving," he snarled and shut
the door in their faces before they could state their business.
Luckily Adam's foot was firmly lodged against the doorjamb.

"Mistress Fiona Haines has an urgent message for Mr. Liam
Campbell," Adam announced calmly. "We were given to understand he is visiting the earl."

The old fellow turned purple with rage. "Maybe he is and
maybe he ain't. Wait where you are and I'll ask 'im."

"We will wait inside." With a firm grip on Fiona's arm,
Adam pushed the door open and strode past the fuming servant into the great hall of the Aerie.

In the arrogant manner he'd inherited from generations of
Cresswells, he demanded, "Inform Mr. Campbell we wish to
see him immediately."

Something about Adam must have alerted the surly fellow
to the fact that he was not dealing with a simple farmer, as
he had first thought, because the fellow shuffled toward an
open doorway on the left side of the hall as fast as his carpet-
slippered feet would carry him.

Fiona's eyes were as round as the proverbial saucers. "Just
look at this place," she whispered, slipping her hand into
Adam's once the servant was out of sight. "It could easily be
the castle belonging to Mr. Shakespeare's *Macbeth* or that
dreary one in Denmark where the young prince went mad."

Adam had been too angry to notice much before now. He
was not accustomed to being subjected to insolence on the part
of a servant—particularly one who looked like a minor character in a Drury Lane comedy. He glanced about him and experienced the odd sensation that he had somehow stepped into

another, much earlier century when he passed through the door of the Aerie.

Walls of solid stone stretched toward a shadowy ceiling some thirty feet above him. These same walls were hung with ancient, faded tapestries depicting long-ago battle scenes, and shields emblazoned with a snarling lion crouched to spring, as well as every kind of medieval weapon known to man.

A fireplace large enough to accommodate a horse and carriage took up the better part of the far wall; three suits of rusted armor stood beside a broad oak staircase, and a dozen or more moth-eaten bear skin rugs decorated the vast stone floor.

"Cozy little place, isn't it," he remarked.

Fiona felt the urge to giggle. Leave it to Adam to put things into perspective. A moment before she had been awed by the grand scale of the earl's ancient manor house. Now she saw it for what it was—a drafty old monstrosity that had outlived its time.

She looked up to find the servant had reappeared and was indicating they should follow him. Silently, he led them to the doorway through which he had disappeared moments before. "Mistress Fiona Haines and . . . companion to see Mr. Campbell," he announced in his reedy voice and with a last malevolent glance at Adam, shuffled off.

The small wood-paneled room they entered was stifling, chiefly because, despite the mild June weather, a roaring fire blazed in the huge stone fireplace. Fiona's gaze instantly flew to Liam, who stood next to the room's one tall, narrow window, a glass of brandy in his hand.

His ginger brows drew together in a frown. "Welcome, sister. I had never expected to see you here."

"I can say the same of you . . . brother," she said, keenly aware that the hooded eyes of the man slumped in a chair before the fire were riveted on her. She assumed he must be the Earl of Stratham, but this cadaverous creature with rusty gray hair and sunken cheeks bore little resemblance to the virile man she remembered.

"Who is this woman who addresses you with such familiarity?" The earl spoke to Liam, but his gaze lingered on Fiona.

"Mistress Fiona Haines—my half sister and your daughter, my lord."

"This saucy-tongued creature is one of my by-blows?" The earl straightened in his chair and immediately his emaciated frame was racked by a fit of coughing. "Who was your mother, girl?" he asked when it finally subsided.

Fiona felt Adam's fingers tighten on her arm as if offering his support. "My mother's name was Eithne Derry," she said in a firm, clear voice. "She died giving me birth."

"Derry? The name strikes no chord. But I was a rutting bull in my salad days, and one country lass was much like another."

Fiona was torn between laughing and crying. So much for her mother's grand passion. Her lover didn't even remember her. She wondered if any of the noblemen who had seduced her predecessors had better memories than this boor.

The earl raked her with a gaze that turned her blood cold. He had the look of death about him and it was all she could do to keep from turning about-face and fleeing from his presence.

"You're comely enough, but if you've come here hoping to be mentioned in my will, you've wasted your time. Not even I am rich enough to provide for every bastard I sired in my youth."

Fiona glared at this shell of a man whose every word was laden with venom. "You flatter yourself, my lord. You own nothing I covet. If the truth be known, you are rich in the things I do not need and poor in the things I count important." Fiona raised her chin to a haughty level. "Will your tawdry possessions to someone who wants them."

"You've a tongue on you sharp as a Scotsman's dirk; I'll say that for you, girl. 'Tis the Wolverson blood in your veins." For one brief moment the earl's gaunt face came to life. Then exhaustion claimed him and he sank back into his chair.

Adam squeezed Fiona's arm and she raised her head to find him grinning at her as if he found this bizarre conversation with her natural father a huge joke—one they would laugh about together later over their supper at the inn. Gazing into his wicked silver eyes, she found it a joke as well. Thanks to this wise and gentle man who loved her, she felt as if the weight of shame and bitterness she had carried all her life was suddenly lifted off her shoulders.

"So, Fiona, what is this urgent message Dobson tells me you have for me?" Liam's face was flushed, his voice a little too hearty. He was obviously embarrassed by the old man's surly behavior.

Fiona glanced at the earl, whose eyes had closed. "It is of a private nature."

"You may speak freely. I assume your 'companion' is already privy to the information." Liam cleared his throat self-consciously. "And I have no secrets from my father."

Fiona shot Liam a quick, searching glance. Since when had he and the Earl of Stratham been on such close terms?

"I am here at the request of your friend, Molly Blodgett," she said in a tight voice. "She begged me to warn you that two excise officers are looking for you with a view to hanging you. It appears someone, probably Dooley Twig, has accused you of landing a French spy on the Exmoor coast during the war."

"Nonsense. How did Molly come up with such a taradiddle?"

"I suspect it occurred to her while the officers were beating her to within an inch of her life to make her tell where you were. Which, by the way, she did not."

Liam slammed his glass of brandy down on a nearby table. "The devil you say. Is she all right?"

"She will live, thanks to my grandmother and her healing herbs, but she lost her babe."

Liam paled noticeably. "Moll was with child?" He struck the table with his fist. "By God, I'll make those lily-livered bullies pay for what they did to her—and that lying bastard, Dooley Twig, as well."

Cursing under his breath, he strode toward the door, but Adam stepped forward and barred his way. "Cool down, Campbell. You will accomplish nothing but your own hanging if you go storming back to the village before this business is straightened out. Were I you I should not want to give Twig that satisfaction."

The exertion of the past few minutes had robbed the earl's sunken cheeks of their last bit of color, but he roused himself sufficiently to say, "This stranger, whoever he may be, speaks the truth, Liam. Best you leave England for the time being. My yacht, the *Seagull*, lies at anchor in the bay with her crew aboard. Sail it to Ireland and stay at my estate outside Dublin until my solicitor can contact the proper people to clear your name."

Liam's gray eyes sparked with rage. "If you think I will let this attack against me go unanswered, you know me not, my lord."

"You will have plenty of opportunity to get even with your enemies once you have inherited my title, you young fool, and a great deal more power with which to do so." Stratham scowled. "Need I remind you that day is not far off."

Liam shook his head. "No, my lord, I know it all too well. For that reason, if no other, I could not bring myself to go haring off to Ireland right now."

Stratham closed his eyes and rested his shaggy head against the tall chair back. "Do not delude yourself that because I have named you my heir, I feel any sentimental attachment for you, Liam Campbell. For I do not. Nor do I need you to help me die. I have lived alone all my life; I am quite capable of dying alone as well."

He gestured weakly. "Now begone all of you and let me do so in peace."

The rain had slowed to a dreary drizzle by the time Adam and Fiona left the Aerie. Liam rode with them as far as the fork in the road. Just before he started down toward the bay and the ship that would take him to Ireland, he reined in his pony. Adam watched Fiona bring her pony to a halt beside her brother and promptly pulled up next to her.

"I owe you both a debt of thanks for coming all the way to Lynmouth to warn me of Dooley Twig's treachery and the danger I am in because of it," Campbell said, breaking the moody silence he had maintained since the earl's terse dismissal.

Fiona smiled. "Despite our differences, you are my brother. I may not always like you, but I cannot help but love you."

"Well said, Fiona. I feel the same about you." Campbell shifted in the saddle as if he were uncomfortable. "I suppose you are wondering how it came about that the Earl of Stratham declared me his legal heir."

"It was a surprise to say the least," Fiona admitted.

"To make a long story short, his solicitor contacted me and said the old man was dying and since he had no legitimate issue, he was interviewing all his known male bastards to determine which one he should name his heir." He shrugged. "With the war over and the Corsican on Elba, the smuggling business was a bit slow, so I decided I might as well try my luck at the Aerie.

"I was just one of a dozen or more red-haired bastards to darken the earl's doorstep to hear old Dobson, the butler, tell it. But I could see right away Stratham liked it that I was educated and could speak proper English, which apparently was more than most of his by-blows could do."

Campbell stared at the gray, churning water of the Channel far below them, a pensive look on his handsome face. "I think he liked me too, despite what he said this afternoon. For we'd talked no more than an hour when he declared he'd order his solicitor to draw up the papers that would make me his legal heir. You may find this passing strange, Fiona, but in an odd sort of way, I liked him too. Or maybe it was just that we understood each other. With all his wealth and properties, he is as much an outcast of society as I am."

"The Earl of Stratham is that saddest of all human beings," Adam agreed, "a man born out of his time. He would have made a great Saxon warrior or an eighth-century Viking, when such huge, brutish men were in vogue. In our more civilized time, he is judged a barbarian by polite society."

Adam fixed Liam Campbell with a meaningful gaze. "Imagine, if you will, the humiliation such a proud barbarian would have suffered at the hands of his noble peers if he dared shop for a bride at the London Season like other men of title."

Campbell's eyes widened as if he had just been struck by an illuminating thought. "I suspect such an experience would have made him bitter—so bitter he would find a way to take his revenge on those who maligned him, even if it took him a lifetime to do so."

Fiona glanced from Adam to her brother and back again. "I cannot fathom how either of you could have gained so much understanding of the earl on such short acquaintance."

She sighed. "Still, I will admit that for the first time in my life, I feel more pity for him that hatred. For there is something terribly sad about a man who cares so little for any other human being he prefers to live and die alone." She paused. "While I found little to like in him, I felt guilty leaving him to the mercy of that dreadful servant."

"It was what he wanted," Campbell said, but his voice shook slightly.

A sudden gust of wind whipped Fiona's bonnet off her head; only the ribbons tied beneath her chin kept it from flying over the cliff. A moment later, Adam felt a spit of rain. "You'd best be on your way before a storm comes up that keeps you in the harbor," he advised Liam Campbell. "Every minute you delay you put your life at risk."

"Aye, I know that. But it galls me to run away like a whipped dog."

Adam smiled, remembering a time before the campaign in Spain when he too was a hothead. "As Fiona's favorite bard would say, 'The better part of valor is discretion.' I recommend you take your father's advice and exact your revenge on your enemies when the odds are in your favor."

"And so I will." Campbell leaned across his pony's head and kissed Fiona on the cheek. "Good-bye little sister. Tell Moll to wait for me; I will get back to her as soon as I can."

"Are you certain that is what you want me to tell her?" Fiona asked. "When next you see Molly you'll likely be the Earl of Stratham. Earls and tavern wenches have little in common."

"If you're saying I cannot marry her as we once discussed, that is true. For as part of our agreement, the earl made me promise to take a noble-born woman as my wife. One particular woman, as a matter of fact. A small price to pay for all he offered in return." Behind Fiona's back, Campbell's gaze locked with Adam's, and Adam sensed that somehow this arranged marriage was tied in with the old earl's revenge on those in the *ton* who had humiliated him so many years ago.

"If you can never marry Molly, then have the decency to stay away from her," Fiona scolded. "You will only break her heart if you do not."

"On the contrary, little Prim and Priss, while I may not be able to put a wedding ring on her finger, I can make her my mistress and give her all the pretty things she could never have otherwise."

"But another less affluent man could give her his name and the home and children every woman longs for." Fiona's brow knit in a troubled frown. "The girl loves you, Liam. She nearly lost her life trying to save you. Making her your whore seems a shabby way to repay her for her loyalty."

Liam's expression hardened. "Damn you and your everlasting sermonizing. That is one thing I'll not miss when I take up my new life." With a defiant toss of his head, he galloped off down the road toward the bay, but Adam knew, from the look on his face, that Fiona's barb had struck home.

He breathed a silent prayer of thanks that circumstances had prevented him from offering Fiona what she saw as a life of shame and degradation. He knew now he would have destroyed any chance he might have for a future with her.

"Have patience," he told himself, as he urged his pony forward toward Lynton and the inn where they were to stay the night—and prayed that saying the words aloud would somehow make the doing of it easier. For his passionate little witch was as straitlaced as any psalm-singing Methodist lady—and just thinking about the intriguing combination made him ache with desire.

Chapter Sixteen

The inn was crowded with guests when Adam and Fiona arrived there a short time later. Adam had hoped to arrange for a private parlor, but there was no such thing to be had at the Lamb and Lion that day. In the end, they dined at a long table in the taproom with eight travelers off the coach. This was a far cry from what Adam was accustomed to when stopping at a roadside inn, but Fiona declared herself enchanted with the novelty of eating a meal with a group of strangers.

From the haunted look he spied in her eyes now and again, he suspected a good deal of the enchantment stemmed from her need to keep busy at the business of living so she wouldn't have to think about the man who lay dying alone in his gloomy ancestral home.

The supper the inn provided was a simple but well-prepared meal of roast beef, potatoes, and garden vegetables, with an excellent syllabub for dessert. Adam, as usual, ate heartily. But he couldn't help but notice that Fiona spent more time pushing the food around her plate than eating it. Furthermore, for someone who found dining with strangers so intriguing, she was strangely silent.

He suggested they take a walk after their meal and enjoy the sunset. It was either that or spend the evening listening to two sheep farmers bewail the falling demand for West Country mutton and wool.

Retiring early was not an option. For, as it turned out, their sleeping accommodations were no better than the dining arrangement to Adam's way of thinking. He had requested two bedchambers, explaining his snoring kept his wife awake, so he wouldn't have to admit Fiona was traveling alone with a man not her husband. But with the inn full to overflowing, the landlord explained apologetically he could spare them no more than one bedchamber with a truckle bed set up behind a dressing screen.

Adam had visions of another sleepless night fraught with frustration. But with determined cheerfulness, Fiona pointed out that the room's one window offered a magnificent view of Bristol Bay. "And," she added, "it would be lovely to fall asleep to the sound of the surf."

The storm had blown over by the time they set out on their walk, leaving the sky a brilliant azure and every tree, flower, and blade of grass looking as if it had just been freshly washed. They strolled arm in arm past the row of shops, stopping to gaze into each window. They visited the pretty little church and listened to a brief discourse on its history by the vicar. They stopped to admire the blossoms in one of the cottage gardens and finally passed by the smithy's cold forge to stand on the edge of the cliff and watch the last rays of the sun bathe the waves of the Channel in a deep crimson glow.

Were it not for the fact that with each passing minute Fiona grew more silent and more withdrawn, it might have been a very pleasant interlude at the end of a hectic day. "A beautiful view," Adam ventured in an attempt to draw her out of her shell.

"The most beautiful I have ever seen," she agreed. "I wish I could stay here forever. Like this. With you." She turned her head and searched Adam's face with troubled eyes. "But I cannot. I have to go back."

"Of course you do, and the moors have a unique beauty all their own."

Fiona shook her head. "No, you don't understand. I have to return to the Aerie. I cannot leave the earl to die alone."

By the time they reached the ancient monument to the past, it was immersed in the shadows of evening and Fiona found it even more gloomy than when she'd viewed it earlier in the day. The windows seemed smaller and darker than she remembered, the moss on the walls more encroaching, the waves crashing on the rocky shore far below louder and angrier.

She shivered, deeply grateful for the caring man who had accompanied her on her mission. Adam had made no protest when she'd declared her intention to stay with the earl until his spirit departed this earth. It was almost as if he had already sensed her need to see this chapter of her life to its close.

Together they rode through the tunnel into the courtyard, dismounted, and tied their ponies to the rusty remains of a landau carriage. As one, they turned toward the entrance door— determined, if necessary, to force their way past the truculent servant—only to find the door standing wide open.

"Something is wrong," Adam said, drawing his pistol. "Wait here while I investigate."

Fiona's heart lurched in her breast at the very thought of being left alone in the shadow-darkened courtyard. "I will not," she protested. "I am going with you."

An ominous silence greeted them when they entered the great hall. Fiona looked about her, but there was no sign of the surly servant they had seen earlier.

She felt Adam's hand on her shoulder. "The earl may already be dead," he said quietly. "Freebooters have been here." He pointed to a sword hanging on the wall to their right. "I remember admiring the gem stones in the hilt this afternoon. As you can see, they are missing now."

"Good heavens! I wonder where his lordship is. We must find him." Fiona started toward the staircase.

"Wait." Adam caught her by the arm. "I suspect he is somewhere on this level. From what I saw of him this afternoon, I doubt he could climb the stairs, and that fellow, Dobson, didn't look strong enough to carry him."

They found him lying on the floor of the same small chamber in which he had sat when they'd come looking for Liam. He had evidently collapsed while trying to crawl to a massive leather couch at the opposite end of the room. Adam knelt and pressed his fingers to the earl's throat to find a pulse.

Fiona watched, her heart thudding against her rib cage. "Is he—"

"He's alive, but just barely. Can you give me a hand if I lift him onto the couch? Even skin and bones as he is, he's a handful." With Fiona lifting the earl's slippered feet and Adam his shoulders, they hoisted him onto the couch and slipped a pillow beneath his head.

Fiona could see a fine film of perspiration on the unconscious man's chalky features. "Watch over him while I find some cool water and a cloth," she directed Adam.

"I'll find them. Best you stay with him in case he regains consciousness." Adam dragged a chair next to the couch for her to sit on and promptly disappeared.

After what seemed an interminable time, he returned with a wooden bowl full of water and an apologetic look on his face. "It took me a while to find the kitchen and even longer to find the pump. This mausoleum is twice the size of Carlton House." He set the bowl on the floor beside her and extracted his handkerchief from his pocket. "This will have to do as a cloth; the only ones I could find were far from clean."

Fiona dipped the handkerchief in the water, wrung it out, and was in the process of bathing the earl's face when he opened his eyes. "Who . . . what . . ." He blinked. "You! I told you I didn't want you," he said in a voice no more than a hoarse whisper.

Fiona dipped the handkerchief in the water again, this time placing it on his forehead. "That was scarcely a revelation, my lord. You have never wanted me."

He stared at her, obviously taken aback. "You're too late," he spat out venomously. "My servant has already stolen any valuables small enough to carry."

"A bitter disappointment, my lord, but one I shall endeavor to live with." Once again she moistened the cloth, but this time she pressed it to his parched lips.

She looked up to find Adam standing beside her, a glass of brandy in his hand. "Campbell left this on the table. Perchance the earl could use it."

Fiona cast him a grateful glance. Then slipping her arm beneath the old man's head, she held the glass to his mouth. "No more laudanum," he murmured. "I'll sleep soon enough."

" 'Tis brandy my lord, not laudanum."

He took a sip, then another, and Fiona watched a faint trace of color tint his gaunt cheeks.

"Enough of your fussing," he grumbled a moment later. "Now leave me in peace."

"I think not, my lord. The last time I did that you ended up facedown on a stone floor."

"You're a fool," the earl muttered, his eyes drifting shut. "Just like your mother before you. The foolish woman actually believed she loved me."

Fiona swallowed the lump in her throat. "So you do remember her after all, my lord," she said softly, but she doubted the earl heard her.

With maddening slowness, the long hours of the night crept by. Adam fell asleep in a nearby chair sometime after midnight, but by sheer determination, Fiona managed to stay awake.

The earl dozed and woke time and again. But each time the waking period was shorter than the last and though the deep-set eyes that searched Fiona's face held a look of recognition, he seemed unable to speak.

Then just before dawn, he woke again and miraculously, appeared to have rallied. His eyes were bright and his lips worked as if he were trying to say something. Instinctively, Fiona covered his hand with hers and leaned closer. "What is it, my lord? What are you trying to say?"

His lips moved, but no sound came out. He rested a moment, then tried again. This time, slowly and distinctly, he said, "Daughter."

But even as the word registered in Fiona's mind, the light in his eyes faded and flickered out, leaving them eerily glazed and lifeless. Gently, she brushed her fingertips over the hooded lids and closed them for all eternity.

Then rising from the chair in which she'd sat her nightlong vigil, she crossed to where Adam slept and spoke his name.

He woke instantly, stretched, and stood up. "The earl?" he asked quietly.

"My father is dead," Fiona said and flung herself into his outstretched arms to sob her heart out.

Adam left Fiona asleep in the chamber they had bespoken at the inn while he searched out the local magistrate to report the earl's death and arrange for his burial. Luckily the magistrate was a competent official and one of the few men whom Stratham had called his friend. He agreed to notify the earl's solicitor in Ilfracombe of his client's death and to inform him of the heir's whereabouts in Ireland.

He also hired a trustworthy fellow to act as caretaker of the

Aerie until such time as the new earl could take over, since the light-fingered Dobson had been seen departing on the same early-morning coach as the overnight guests at The Lamb and Lion.

That left only the actual burial to put behind them before Fiona and he could leave Lynton. The brief service was conducted by the local vicar and except for the magistrate, Fiona and he were the only people who witnessed the Earl of Stratham's interment in the Wolverson family crypt. By eleven o'clock that morning they were back on the road that led to Larkspur Farm.

They spoke little the first hour, but it was a companionable silence. Only once did Fiona refer to the death of the earl. "No words I learned from Vicar Edelson are adequate to express my gratitude to you for standing by me during these difficult hours just past," she said simply and with that brought the traumatic episode to closure.

Adam sensed that she and the earl had arrived at some kind of understanding before the old man died. How or what it was, he had no way of knowing, but there was some indefinable air about her now that spoke of a woman at peace with herself.

In truth, this journey that had been thrust upon them had turned out to be good for both of them. For in different ways, they had each found the serenity that had been missing in their lives.

"I paid the innkeeper's wife two shillings to pack us a picnic lunch," Fiona said as they emerged from the forest to ride beside the stream Adam remembered from their previous day's journey. "An exorbitant sum, but the price included a small basket. It is in my saddlebag."

Adam raised an incredulous eyebrow. "How extravagant of you, Mistress Haines."

"Not at all," she said indignantly. "I am never extravagant. The basket I use to gather eggs is falling apart; I could see right away this one would be a perfect replacement."

"Ah, I might have known."

"Well we cannot travel all the way to Larkspur Farm without food in our stomachs, can we? And I thought we could take our noonday meal beneath our lovely willow tree." She blushed. "The one where you confessed you loved me."

"A romantic interlude? But, Mistress Haines, I distinctly remember your telling me you were not the least bit romantic."

Her blush deepened. "Do give off teasing me, Adam. You know very well that you arouse feelings in me unlike any I have ever before experienced."

"Ah, but it is so nice to hear you confess it." He stared thoughtfully at the trees lining the bank of the stream. "But can we find that exact same tree again? There are any number of willows in this area."

"I will know it." She averted her gaze, as if loath to look him in the eye. "I will feel the magic we created when last we were beneath it."

"Come now, Fiona," he scoffed. But for once he found the mysticism in which his little witch dealt more pleasurable than annoying. There was something very satisfying about being the only man in whose touch she found magic.

"This is it," she said a few moments later, and without the slightest hesitation stopped beside a willow that looked no different from any other as far as he could tell. He took her at her word, dismounted, and tied his pony to the same bush as she had tied hers.

"Do you feel the magic?" she asked as they brushed aside the trailing branches to stand within the shady canopy of the ancient tree. "I feel it here." She pressed her hand to the gentle swell of her bosom and turned to him with glowing eyes and softly parted lips that told him she desired him as much as he desired her—indeed that she was his for the taking.

He wanted her. God, how he wanted her. Not just her lithe young body, but her heart and mind and soul as well. She completed him in a way no other woman ever had. She filled the terrible emptiness in his heart with her compassion—lighted the darkest corners of his mind with her laughter.

He could scarcely remember the jaded libertine who had ridden up to her gate a few short weeks ago. That care-for-nothing fellow would have taken what she offered with no thought of how vulnerable she was after her emotional vigil at the earl's deathbed, or how much she might regret tomorrow what she did today. But luckily that fellow no longer existed.

"What I feel," he said softly in answer to her question, "is an overwhelming desire to take you in my arms and kiss you as you've never been kissed before. But if I do, we both know it will not end with just a kiss—and I could not, in good conscience, make love to you, when I have not been entirely honest with you."

Her look of rapture quickly changed to one of puzzlement. "You make it sound so serious. Maybe we should have our picnic first. Things always seen less dismal when one has a full stomach."

"No." Adam seated himself at the base of the tree trunk and drew her down beside him. "I have tried to tell you this so many times and always something has happened to interrupt me. This time I intend to finish what I have to say."

He would not tell her everything at once, of course; that would only confuse her. Better a little now, a little later, so she could gradually learn all that marrying him would entail.

Trustingly, she nestled in the circle of his arms, her head on his shoulder. "Very well, tell away, but I shall never forgive you if you destroy the magic."

He swallowed hard. "To begin with, my father is a nobleman."

Fiona stiffened. "A nobleman? You mean like an earl?"

"A duke, actually. I am the son of the Duke of Bellmont."

She raised her head and stared at him, her eyes wide with shock. "The Duke of Bellmont whose town house was in the Carmichaels' peep show?"

He nodded. "The same."

Fiona felt the happiness that had been steadily growing within her for the past hour shrivel and die. As if blinders had been ripped from her eyes, so many things about Adam that had puzzled her suddenly made sense. His natural arrogance, his tendency to take control—even his elegant gold watch and fine linen shirts and handkerchiefs. He was so obviously an aristocrat. What a blind, stupid fool she had been.

A double fool, she reminded herself, when she realized she had done exactly what every Derry woman before her had done: she had lost her heart to a nobleman she had no hope of marrying. What had made her think she could escape the curse that had plagued the women of her family since the beginning of time?

"If what you say is true, why have you pretended you wanted to marry me?" she asked, making no effort to hide her bitterness.

"I have pretended nothing, Fiona. I am very serious about wanting to marry you."

"Do not compound your lies. Even I know the son of a duke cannot marry the illegitimate daughter of another nobleman, much less the granddaughter of an Exmoor witch."

"That would be all too true if I were the duke's heir and responsible for providing him with a blue-blooded grandson to carry on the title. But that is my older brother, Ethan's, responsibility. I am only the duke's second son."

"Second son or no, I cannot believe your noble father will approve your taking a woman with my background to wife."

Adam had the grace to look a little sheepish. "Knowing the duke, I expect he will rant and rave and carry on like a madman."

Fiona sighed. "So I thought."

"But he will come around eventually. What else can he do? He cannot have my marriage annulled once it is consummated." Adam's sensuous lips curved in a wolfish grin. "Which I plan to do the minute I have my ring on your finger."

Fiona's cheeks flamed as visions of Adam's powerful body united with hers in the most intimate of ways flashed through her mind.

"Nor can my father threaten to disinherit me. I was born disinherited. My brother Ethan is heir to the title and all the properties connected to it. Were it not for an inheritance I received from my maternal grandmother, I would be penniless."

"But how unfair! Your father must be the cruelest of men. I cannot imagine Oliver Pinchert giving everything he owned to one son and leaving the others with no way to make a living."

"It has been my observation that the aristocracy is rarely as logical as the common man. But to give the devil his due, it was not my father's choice to make. The wealth and properties of the dukedom have been entailed to the firstborn male of each generation since the first duke was granted his title by the King some two hundred years ago."

"No wonder you took to gambling."

"As to that . . ." Adam cleared his throat. "I was actually

more serious about my career in the army than as a professional gambler. But that is another story."

Fiona rose to her feet and pushing aside the willow branches, moved to stand on the bank of the stream. She sensed Adam following her. "I suspect there are a great many other stories you are not telling me," she said dryly. "Such as how and why the second son of the Duke of Bellmont found his way to a remote place like Exmoor."

A sudden thought struck her, and she whipped around to face him. "You were the lord with whom Buckley played cards the night he was killed!"

Adam's agonized expression told her she was right in her assumption. "I learned of the accident a few days later and I knew I had to find his widow and give her the money he had lost to me," he explained. "When you mistook me for an ex-soldier looking for work, I couldn't resist the challenge of proving to myself I could do an honest day's labor like any common man. Little did I know that in the process I would lose my heart to a lovely Exmoor witch . . . and a herd of wild moorland ponies."

"Surely you are not claiming you will be content to chop wood and herd ponies for the rest of your life."

"No, Fiona, I am not. I could not do so even if I wished it. There is work I must accomplish in London. The Tories in power must be made to realize they cannot turn their backs on the thousands of brave men who fought to save England from the clutches of the Corsican madman. I mean to see that they are. If you agree to become my wife, you will have to accustom yourself to spending most of the year in London, with only a month or two at Larkspur Farm each summer."

Fiona stared at him in shocked disbelief. "You must be as mad as Bonaparte. I know nothing about how to go on in London society. I would disgrace you at every turn."

"If I can learn to survive in Exmoor, you can learn to survive in London," Adam said matter-of-factly. "It should be child's play compared to what you have already managed to accomplish under your Vicar Edelson's tutelage."

Fiona felt her heart leap with sudden hope. Still she had to ask, "But why would you want to marry a woman who presents you with so many problems?"

"A good question." He cocked his head as if giving the subject serious thought. "Could it be I am bewitched?"

"How dare you suggest such a thing." Fiona's bosom heaved in anger. "I have not . . . I would not—"

"Then there can only be one answer," Adam interjected, hauling her into his arms and claiming her mouth in a deeply passionate kiss.

"Yes, it is just as I feared," he moaned as he raised his head a moment later. "I am in love with you."

He watched her eyes darken with emotion; her lush lips soften invitingly. She leaned into him and instantly his body throbbed with desire for his intriguing little witch. "Be careful, love," he whispered. "Do not tempt me too much or I shall forget my vow to wait until we share our respectable marriage bed to make you mine."

Her bemused gaze traced his features one by one until, with unconscious sensuality, it settled on his mouth. "I love you too," she whispered, "and I will learn to walk through fire if that is what it takes to be the proper wife you deserve."

"Then, love, there is nothing anyone on God's green earth can do to stand in the way of our glorious future together," he whispered back, and once again molded his burning lips to hers.

The miles seemed to fly by as they rode across the moors to Larkspur Farm once they finished their picnic lunch. Adam could never remember when the sky had been so blue or the grass so green—or when he had felt so much like laughing aloud from the sheer joy of living.

All his fears about telling Fiona the truth of who he was and what he was doing in Exmoor had come to nothing. She loved him and nothing else mattered.

Each time they stopped to rest their ponies he kissed her and with each kiss she grew more daring in her response until the tentative brush of her tongue against his threatened to send him up in flames. There was no doubt about it, his shy little widow was rapidly turning into the consummate seductress.

Four ponies were tied to the fence when they rode into the Larkspur farmyard and another stood in the traces of a sledge cart. "I recognize the cart as Hiram Blodgett's," Fiona said. "But I've no idea who could have arrived on the ponies."

They stabled and fed their own ponies, then hurried toward the open door of the cottage in time to hear the irate innkeeper shout, "Cowardly muckworms, that's what ye be, and I'll have ye up afore the magistrate fer what ye done to me girl. If he don't hang ye, I'll do the deed meself."

Fiona exchanged a look with Adam. "The excise officers," she whispered and stepped through the doorway in time to witness a scene of utter bedlam. Hiram Blodgett was waving his fist in the face of a stumpy little man with stringy brown hair and beady eyes, while Ben Watson, with pistol drawn, held the other excise officer at bay. Oliver Pinchert and his eldest son, Simon, also with pistols at the ready, appeared to be guarding the entrance to the hall leading to her bedchamber.

"There she be," the taller of the two excise officers shouted when he spotted Fiona. Pushing past Ben, he pointed a finger at her and declared, "In the name of His Majesty's government, Mistress Fiona Haines, I demand ye tell us the whereabouts of yer brother, the traitor Liam Campbell."

Fiona swept the pawky fellow with a look of pure disgust. "In the first place, my brother is no traitor and you, sir, are an idiot if you have let pond scum like Dooley Twig convince you he is."

"So I told 'em, not five minutes ago," Oliver Pinchert declared.

"In the second place," Fiona continued, "with our father recently dead, Liam is the new Earl of Stratham. Were I you, I would mount my pony and keep riding until I was long gone from Exmoor. Liam has sworn to take his revenge on you and your craven partner—and that lying scoundrel Twig as well—and he has the wealth and power to do so."

Adam managed to keep a straight face as the two excise officers gathered up their official papers and scurried out the door like frightened rabbits. Whatever qualms he'd had about Fiona's holding her own against the spiteful cats of the *ton* promptly disappeared. She could obviously take care of herself.

"Now what be this tall tale ye told about Liam Campbell?" Hiram asked as soon as the door closed behind the excisemen.

"Unbelievable as it seems, it is the truth," Fiona said, "as Adam will attest."

"Then 'tis a story me girl will want to hear, so the telling of it should be in yer bedchamber where she lies." Without further ado, Hiram disappeared down the hall, with Ben, Creenagh, and the two Pincherts close behind him.

Adam sensed Fiona's reluctance to join them. "Molly has to be told sometime," he said, drawing her into his arms.

"You are right, of course. But I'll not tell her Liam plans to see her again. Bitter medicine is best swallowed all at once." She slid her arms around his waist and for a brief instant laid her head on his chest. "It seems especially cruel to smash another woman's hopes when I am so happy myself."

Adam gave her a quick hug. "The sooner you get it over with, the better for all concerned," he said, and taking her hand, led her down the hall to her bedchamber.

"Well don't that beat all," Blodgett exclaimed when, without going into any detail, Fiona explained that the earl had had papers drawn up declaring Liam his legal heir shortly before he died. "The next·time ye walks out with the lad, ye'll be on the arm of a bloody earl, Molly me girl."

Molly's face was as white as the pillow cover beneath her head, ·her eyes dark with despair. "Now ye're talking foolishness, Pap. Earls don't walk out with tavern maids."

Her gaze swept the collection of people crowding the small room and landed on Oliver Pinchert's son. "And now, Simon Pinchert," she said in a voice that trembled only slightly, "if ye'll stop yer gawking long enough to carry me to me pap's sledge cart, I'd like to go home where I belong."

Adam smiled to himself as he watched the tall, red-faced young farmer sweep her up from the bed, quilt and all, and stride down the narrow hallway. It appeared Liam Campbell was not the only one who knew how to land on his feet.

A short while later, Fiona and he stood outside the gate and watched the Blodgett cart, with the two Pincherts riding behind it, disappear down the road toward the Black Boar Inn.

"Well that is that," Fiona said. "Let us hope we may have a little peace and quiet for a change."

"Peace, yes but quiet, no," Adam said, slipping an arm around her slender shoulders. "I know it is sooner than you'd wished, but I hope you will agree to having our marriage banns posted for the first time Sunday next, so we can marry and leave for London by the middle of August."

"So soon?" Shock sharpened Fiona's voice. "But I cannot just walk away from the farm. Ben isn't capable of handling it, even if I can find him a capable helper."

Adam had known he would face opposition. He was prepared to use any weapon he needed to win this particular conflict. He drew her into his arms and kissed her tenderly. "Then we should hire a capable manager," he murmured, dropping another feather-light kiss on the tip of her pretty little nose. "I must start campaigning on behalf of the men I served with in Spain as soon as possible. Some, like those two we saw at Plimpton Fair, won't last the winter without help."

One hand slid to her waist, the other cupped her chin while his lips once again explored hers with sensual expertise. "And don't even consider suggesting I go on to London alone and wait for you to join me, because I will not consider it," he said when he finally raised his head.

"Oh dear, I was afraid you would say that." Fiona tried to slip from his arms, but he only tightened his hold on her. Once again, Adam was taking charge and this time she wasn't sure she was ready to do what he wanted her to. She felt him nip her ear lobe with his strong, white teeth, and suddenly found it necessary to take a number of deep, sustaining breaths.

She heard herself say, "Maybe I could talk to Simon Pinchert about managing Larkspur Farm for me."

"There! I knew you would think of something." Adam's triumphant grin spread from ear to ear. "Simon would be ideal. He strikes me as a very capable young man. We will ride to the Pinchert farm tomorrow morning to make him an offer right after we visit the vicar to arrange to have our banns read. That way you will have close to a month to show Simon all he needs to know."

Fiona took a firm grip on the top rail of the fence to keep her trembling legs from collapsing beneath her. Adam reminded her of one of the "brooms of the gods," the name the old ones had given the fierce winds that blew across the moors in the winter, sweeping up everything in their wake. She felt both exhilarated and terrified by the idea of being married to such a man.

She watched him gaze across the moors toward the vivid sunset painting the western horizon, a satisfied look on his face. "By tomorrow at this time we will have everything pertaining to our future together settled," he said smugly, just as a horse and rider crested the rise over which Hiram Blodgett and his retinue had disappeared but minutes before.

"Now who can that be arriving here at this late hour of the day?" Fiona asked. "One thing is certain; he's a stranger, from the look of the elegant thoroughbred he's riding."

Adam shaded his eyes against the sun. "What the devil! It's John Bittner."

"He is a friend of yours?" Fiona asked, watching the slender, gray-haired fellow draw near.

"A friend and much more. A former tutor who was my batman all four years I spent on the Peninsula. Best batman any officer ever had. Saved my life twice—once at Ciudad Rodrigo and again at Salamanca." Adam chuckled. "Now he's the sorriest excuse for a valet you would ever care to see."

"You're a hard man to find, Major," Bittner said as he rode up. He dismounted stiffly. "I have seen enough of the West Country moors to last me the rest of my life."

"And you're a welcome sight, John." Adam pumped the older man's hand enthusiastically. "But why did my father send you after me. He should have sent one of the young grooms."

"It was not your father who sent me, but your aunt, the Lady Tansy. She thought the news would come easier from me, what with our history together in Spain and all."

"News?" Adam stared at his old friend through narrowed eyes. For some inexplicable reason, an odd chill crawled up his spine. It was a feeling he had experienced but once before at Salamanca—the day he'd been ordered to lead his company into the battle that had lost him so many of his comrades.

"Well spit it out, man, whatever it is," he said more sharply than he intended.

John Bittner glanced at Fiona. "It might be best if we were alone when I told it, Major."

Adam caught Fiona by the hand and drew her to his side.

"Mistress Haines is my betrothed. You can speak freely in front of her."

"Yes, sir." Bittner saluted smartly, as if Adam had just given him an order. "There is no way to tell it but straight out. There has been a terrible thing happen, sir. The Duke of Bellmont's carriage was waylaid by highwaymen on the way to his estate in Kent."

"Good Lord! Was he hurt?"

Adam saw the bleak look on his former batman's face, and felt the chilling tentacles deep inside him spread into his chest and turn the breath in his lungs into sharp, painful splinters of ice.

"It grieves me sorely to have to tell you that your father, the duke, was shot and killed by the blackguards, sir, and your brother, the viscount with him."

"Killed? The both of them?" Adam echoed numbly. Vaguely, he heard Fiona's gasp, felt her fingers grip his. But not even she could pierce the black cloud of pain that had descended on him with his friend's unbelievable words.

He realized John was speaking again and forced himself to listen as best he could, though his head seemed filled with a sound like rushing water.

"Lady Tansy asked me to beg you to return home as soon as possible, sir," John said in the careful voice Adam had heard him use when talking to a gravely wounded comrade. "As you can imagine, things are all at sixes and sevens with Lady Eudora and your five nieces—and the duke's man-of-affairs and solicitors are awaiting your instructions, as are the stewards of the various estates."

"My instructions?"

"Yes, Major." Bittner frowned. "I can see it has not yet registered with you, sir, but the fact is you are now the eighth Duke of Bellmont."

Chapter Seventeen

"You are now the eighth Duke of Bellmont."

Fiona closed her eyes and repeated the fateful sentence Adam's former batman had spoken some twelve hours earlier. Silently, she counted the words. Eight in all. For some reason she could not begin to explain, it seemed vitally important that she know the exact number of words it had taken to sound the death knell on her hopes for the future. Hopes that she now realized had been doomed from the moment she'd first conceived of them.

How the old gods must be laughing at the foolish mortal who had dared to believe she could circumvent the ancient curse they had imposed on all women in whose veins Derry blood flowed.

It had been but a few minutes since Adam had disappeared over the rise in the road and already she missed him desperately. As if rooted to the spot where they had spent their last few moments together, she stood beside the gate of her farm—seeing nothing, hearing nothing but the echo of his final farewell.

"I will write as soon as I have my affairs in order," he had promised and taking her in his arms, had kissed her with a desperate passion that tore yet another gaping hole in her wounded heart. But he had made no promise to send for her. For, of course, they both knew the Duke of Bellmont could not offer marriage to a common farm woman from Exmoor, much less one with a background as tainted as hers—and the man who now held that title was too honorable to offer anything less.

She remembered how glibly she had decreed that Molly Blodgett should cut Liam from her life rather than stoop to becoming his mistress, and wondered if she would have had the strength to refuse Adam if he had offered her a slip on the shoulder.

She felt strangely detached from reality and from Ben and Creenagh, who had said their own sad farewells to Adam. Though she'd shed no tears nor made no protests, she felt a kinship with Caesar, locked in the barn and howling his lungs out for his beloved hero. For while her mind had accepted that she would never see Adam again, her foolish heart refused to believe that bitter truth.

"Best ye come tend to Caesar, Mistress. The poor beastie will be doing himself harm, throwing his weight against the barn door like he be doing."

Fiona turned to find Ben standing behind her, his weathered face etched with a deep sadness. "The Londoner will be sore missed by all at Larkspur Farm," he declared, "and I be thinking he'll miss us as well."

The old man shook his head slowly from side to side. "I knowed right off the lad were special. But a high-and-mighty duke! 'Tis past believing I taught such a one to chop firewood."

And past believing such a man could have loved the grand-daughter of the Witch of Exmoor. But he had loved her. Of that Fiona felt certain, and though that knowledge made her loss even more unbearable, it had left her with a sense of pride in herself that she would carry with her until the day she died.

With a weary sigh she took Ben's advice and made her way to the kitchen to find the meaty bone with which she had planned to make soup. With that and a few dozen scratches behind his ears, she would assuage Caesar's anguish. She just wished she could find as simple a panacea to ease her own.

Adam arrived in London to find, to his relief, that Lady Eudora and her five daughters had departed for her father's estate in Surrey, leaving only Lady Tansy and him to occupy the town house. A fortnight after his return, he paid Eudora a visit and assured her that she and the girls would always be provided for in the manner Ethan would have wanted. Other than that, he found little to say to his sister-in-law. What could one say to a woman who grieved for a husband who had never loved her?

He departed from his brother's tearful widow more determined than ever that he would never do to any woman what Ethan had done to Eudora. If he could not marry the woman he loved, he would remain single and let the title pass to his sister's oldest son.

Furthermore, though his aching body cried for release from his long abstinence, he could not bring himself to touch his mistress when he finally visited her. He longed to make love to Fiona; the thought of lying with another woman turned his blood to ice. He promptly severed the relationship with a suitably expensive bauble, a sheaf of bank notes, and an introduction to a titled friend of his who had always admired the beautiful courtesan.

Aside from those two obligatory visits, his first month in London was chiefly devoted to meetings with his father's solicitors regarding the transfer of the title and properties of the dukedom. When that was accomplished, he retired the old duke's man-of-affairs with a generous pension and appointed a distant cousin to the post. Then he visited each of the five estates he had inherited and determined they were in the hands of capable stewards.

In short, he did everything expected of him as the new Duke of Bellmont. Only then did he visit his father's and brother's graves and allow himself to grieve for the family he had never had.

After two interminable months in London, his affairs were in order but his life was in chaos. For the one thing he could not bring himself to do was write the promised letter to Fiona. A dozen times he started it; a dozen times he crumpled up the paper and tossed it into the fireplace.

There was something so final about words on paper, and while his mind had accepted that Fiona could never be his, his foolish heart refused to believe the bitter truth.

July dragged by, day after tedious day, and August crawled along after it with no word from Adam. The agony Fiona had suffered the first fortnight after he left slowly subsided into a constant gnawing ache in the spot where her heart had once been. Not that she had actually expected him to write; she had merely clung to a small, foolish hope he might do so.

She could not even fault him for breaking his promise. He was, after all, one of the richest and most powerful men in England now that he had become the Duke of Bellmont. He would have far more important things to do than correspond with a woman he had known but a few brief weeks—a woman he would likely never see again.

She suspected the romantic notions he had entertained as a hired farmhand must now seem like nothing more than a crazy dream to a man who sat in the House of Lords and dined with the Regent. In truth, with the passage of time, those magical weeks they had shared were beginning to assume a dreamlike quality in her mind as well.

She woke one morning determined to once and for all put the past behind her. Only then would she stop grieving for a future that could never be. Ironically, that same day Liam arrived at Larkspur Farm and promptly scattered all her good intentions to the winds.

Astride a sleek chestnut thoroughbred and dressed as befit his new station in life, he was an elegant sight to see. With a purple tailcoat, a purple-and-silver striped waistcoat, and a pair of yellow breeches that hugged his long legs like an extra layer of skin, he was the most colorful creature Fiona had ever seen, and in her eyes, every inch the fine London gentleman. She found herself imagining how Adam would look in such splendid attire, and the pain in her heart immediately increased tenfold.

"Good morning to you, little sister," Liam said, doffing a high crown beaver similar to the ones the pony buyers from Plymouth had worn.

Fiona set the pot of snap beans she was preparing for supper down on the porch beside her and rose to greet him. "Good morning to you, Liam, or should I say 'my lord'?"

"Call me what you wish. Nothing has ever stopped you from doing so in the past." Liam waited until she had seated herself again on the porch bench, then spread his handkerchief on the top step and sat down. He had obviously been taking lessons in manners since last she'd seen him.

"I have just come from saying my good-byes to Molly," he said, a wry look on his handsome face. "It appears my concern for the faithless chit was ill-placed. She informed me the vicar will read first banns for Simon Pinchert and her Sunday next."

Fiona snapped a few more beans before looking up. "It is best," she said finally. "Simon will make her a good husband, and I suspect your ego is suffering more than your heart."

Liam shrugged. "True. But it leaves me at loose ends temporarily." He surveyed Fiona speculatively. "Which brings me to the point of this visit to you. I am in your debt in more ways than one, and I believe I have thought of a way to pay you back in some small measure for your warning about the excise officers, as well as for easing our father's last hours."

"It is not necessary."

"Nevertheless, Ben Watson told me how your 'farmhand' turned out to be a high-and-mighty duke, which leads me to believe you are rather at loose ends yourself right now, little sister. So, here is what I propose: I am going to London to buy myself a curricle and matched pair befitting my new station in life—and to judge the 'lay of the land,' so to speak, before I make my offer to the bride I am required to marry. I want you to come with me."

Fiona dropped her pot of beans, sending them scattering across the porch. "Have your wits gone begging? Of what earthly use would I be to you in London."

Liam grinned. "None whatsoever, but it is a grand place and one you should see. We'll stay at the Pulteney—I've been told it is one of the finest hotels in London—and we'll see all the sights the great city has to offer." Laughter danced in his golden eyes. "Just think of the fun we'll have."

"Now I know you have gone mad," Fiona said, diligently picking up each and every bean. "Have you any idea what all that would cost?"

"It matters not. I stopped at my solicitor's office in Ilfracombe Tuesday last and learned I am an exceedingly rich man. I daresay even richer than the new Duke of Bellmont."

"Well I am not rich and I have nothing I could wear in London, so I must decline your generous offer," Fiona said firmly. Though, in truth, the thought of seeing all the wondrous places Adam had pointed out in the peep show made her heart pound with excitement.

"I'll not take no for an answer, you silly baggage. Of course you'll need a new gown or two and I'll spring for the blunt. My good friend, Bridey McClanahan, can take you to the dressmaker who sews the gowns for the girls at Madam Blanche's place."

Fiona felt herself weakening. "Who is Madam Blanche?"

"The abbess of the finest bawdy house in London's East End."

"Thank you very much, but I believe I would rather look like the country bumpkin I am than a London whore," Fiona said indignantly.

"Never fear, Bridey will see you're turned out properly. Ladies and lightskirts dress exactly alike in London," Liam declared with such assurance, Fiona decided he must know what he was talking about.

The temptation was too great. When would another such opportunity come her way? "Well then," she declared, "if you are really serious about wanting me to go with you, I shall be happy to do so."

Thus it was that the following Friday morning Fiona found herself dressed in her one good Sunday gown and sitting opposite Liam in the coach to London while it jounced and jolted its way across the moors. Heart pounding and head awhirl, she clutched the only elegant thing she owned—her beautiful new green reticule—and contemplated all she would see and do once she reached London.

She would not, of course, try to contact Adam. He had made it all too clear he'd forgotten her as quickly as Molly had forgotten Liam. For all she knew, his banns were already being read linking him with some highborn London lady. She wished the poor woman luck. She would need it, casting her lot with a man whose feelings were as shallow as a moorland creek in August.

As for her, she would not waste one precious minute of the time she spent in London pining over Adam Cresswell. First she would buy a fashionable bonnet at a Bond Street shop, then walk in Hyde Park, maybe even attend the theatre. But best of all, she would spend one entire day browsing in Hookum's Lending Library and Hatchard's Bookstore. She might even buy a book or two by Ann Radcliffe with the small hoard of pound notes she had stashed in her reticule.

With her nose pressed to the window, she watched the miles slip by as the powerful horses raced toward the city she had dreamed of seeing all her life. Her eyes were dry, her lips firm, her hands steady. She felt certain that none of her fellow passengers, including Liam, had the slightest idea that deep inside her, her heart wept for her lost love.

Adam had been back in London a little over two months when he made the mistake of having dinner with a good friend at White's. Like wildfire, the word spread through the *ton* that the elusive new Duke of Bellmont was appearing in public and every day scores of invitations to quiet dinners and other social events befitting a man still in mourning were delivered to his town house. He tossed them all, unopened, into the nearest fireplace.

"I do not know what to make of you, Adam," Lady Tansy complained as the two of them sat in the sunny breakfast room one morning in early September. "You have become a virtual hermit since returning from Exmoor. You would show your father and brother no disrespect by accepting a dinner invitation or even attending the theatre now and again. I myself have put off my depressing blacks and taken up wearing grays and lavenders."

Adam looked up from the newspaper he was reading. "I prefer to stay at home."

"Oh dear, I had hoped the trip to Exmoor would help you find peace of mind. It appears to have had the opposite effect." Lady Tansy toyed with the shirred eggs on her plate. "I wonder, Your Grace, if I might be permitted to ask a favor of you."

Adam felt the hair rise up the back of his neck. Only twice before had Lady Tansy addressed him with such formality, and both times she had talked him into doing something he didn't want to do. What was the old dear up to now?

"What is your wish, Aunt? If it is within reason, I shall be happy to grant it," he said warily.

Lady Tansy clapped her hands. "What a dear you are, and it is a perfectly reasonable request." She surveyed Adam with her bright birdlike eyes. "Have you heard of Lord Elgin's marbles?"

"The Phidian sculptures he brought back from Greece? Of

course I've heard of them. Better yet, I viewed them when I first returned from Spain."

Lady Tansy hung her head. "I have never seen them, and I do so want to. Would you take me to view them this morning?"

Adam did his best to hide his irritation. "I will if you really wish me to, my lady. But if this is merely a ploy to force me out into society, I can think of any number of things you might enjoy more."

Spots of guilty color bloomed in Lady Tansy's cheeks, but she ignored his pointed remark. "If you are afraid I shall faint at the sight of a nude figure, I assure you I shall not."

Adam smiled. "The thought never entered my mind. As for the sculptures, individually they are exquisite works of art, despite the fact that many are broken or missing an arm or leg. But they are temporarily housed in a timbered outbuilding behind Burlington House and piled one upon another in the most haphazard fashion. I fear a fastidious woman such as yourself will be more offended than enthralled by the collection as it stands today."

Lady Tansy's delicate features assumed a stubborn mien. "I would still like to see them. But first, I have a few notes I must write."

He was beaten and he knew it. In more ways than one, his aunt reminded him of Fiona.

As he'd feared, the fine weather had brought a crowd of spectators to view the celebrated marbles, most of whom, oddly enough, were friends of Lady Tansy's. In the hour it took them to view the marbles, he was introduced to a half dozen of her bosom bows and each one had a daughter, who confessed she had been longing to meet His Grace, the Duke of Bellmont.

He bore it all with a weary patience, but he couldn't help but compare the colorless creatures to the fiercely independent woman he loved.

"I can see there is no point in staying here any longer," his aunt finally conceded. "You may escort me to the carriage."

Adam offered his arm, but just as they reached the door, he came face-to-face with a tall man with hawkish features and a head of faded brown hair, whom he recognized as one of the

Oxford dons under whom he had once studied. "You probably don't remember me, sir," he said, offering his hand. "I read Shakespeare with you one term a number of years ago."

The don studied him intently. "Cresswell? Of course I remember you. A fine student with an unusual affinity for the tragedy of King Richard III, unless my memory fails me."

"Remarkable, sir. I am amazed." Adam introduced his aunt and found himself wishing it could be Fiona meeting the noted scholar. How she would love to discuss her beloved bard with this undisputed expert.

"So, sir, you've come to view the wonders of ancient Greece," he remarked, loath to end the conversation.

"On the contrary, my interest lies in the museum's small, but excellent, collection of Celtic artifacts—in particular statues of the Celtic gods. Fascinating study. Are you familiar with such ancient deities, Cresswell?"

Adam felt the ache in his heart intensify. "I have what you might call a speaking acquaintance with them, sir."

"Then by all means join me. Unless changes have been made since I was here a year ago, the pieces are hidden away in that room to the left of us."

His curiosity piqued, Adam escorted his aunt to his waiting carriage, then joined the don in the small antechamber where he was examining a stone plaque on which were carved the heads and torsos of three women. "Eriu, Fodla, and Banbha, Ireland's triadic goddesses of the earth and fertility," he explained. "As you can see, the art of the Celts is much more primitive than that of the Greeks or Romans."

Indeed, Adam found the rather crudely chiseled stone statues a bit of a shock after the fluid beauty of the Grecian marbles. Still, there was something oddly appealing in the stark lines and bluntly executed features.

The don moved on to two statues approximately three feet high, both very obviously and very spectacularly male. "Nodens, the water god," he said, indicating the first. "And this fierce-looking fellow is Taranis, the god of war and thunder."

Beyond the two stood a statue of a woman riding sidesaddle, and Adam's eyes were instantly drawn to the familiar "toad eyes," and wide forehead of her mount. He turned to the don. "Who is the lady riding the Exmoor pony?"

"Epona, the goddess of all equines. But how did you recognize the animal she is riding?"

"I am well acquainted with the moorland ponies," Adam said without elaborating.

"Amazing creatures and the logical mount for a Celtic goddess since they are the only direct descendants of the original wild horse—as well as an integral part of British history. Did you know the war chariot of Boadicea, the queen of the Iceni, was pulled by an Exmoor pony when she fought the Romans for control of what is now Norfolk."

"No, sir, I did not," Adam said, smiling at the don's enthusiasm for Fiona's beloved ponies.

"Or that King Henry VIII decreed that all small horses in Britain should be destroyed," the don continued, warming to his subject. "The idiot's excuse was that they could not carry a man in armor, but I suspect it was more that he was too fat to ride anything but the largest of draft horses. The ponies survived in Exmoor because the stubborn residents defied him and hid them on the moors."

Adam chuckled. "Considering what I know of one of those stubborn residents, I can well believe it." His gaze shifted to the face of the goddess and he felt as if the breath had suddenly been sucked from his lungs. Crude as the carving was, he could see that her face, down to the last feature, closely resembled Fiona's. It was not inconceivable that some long, lost ancestress of hers had posed for this sculpture of the goddess.

He stared, transfixed by the sight of this replica of his beloved's face, until the terrible ache in his heart drove every thought from his head except his all-consuming need to see her, to touch her . . . to spend the rest of his life with her by his side.

Muttering a quick farewell to the don, he strode from the museum and joined his aunt, who sat beneath her lavender silk parasol in his curricle. Taking the reins from his tiger, he urged his pair of matched grays forward at a good clip.

With his usual skill, he maneuvered his way through the crowded streets of London, all the while wrestling with the idea that was taking shape in his troubled mind.

"If you are angry at me for contriving to introduce you to some eligible young ladies, please do get on with your scold,"

Lady Tansy said finally. "But I only did so because it grieves me to see you leading such a lonely existence."

Adam glanced at the attractive woman who sat beside him. "Not half as much as it grieves me, Aunt, which is why I have decided to do something about it—something I fear will shock you to the core."

"I imagine I shall recover in time." Lady Tansy laughed softly. "I have grown accustomed to being shocked by you, nephew. You have never been what one could call conventional."

"I have also never before been the Duke of Bellmont. It does make a difference." Adam loved his aunt. He hated to upset her, but he knew now that no matter what it cost him, he must have Fiona as his wife.

"I fell deeply in love in Exmoor," he said, neatly manipulating the turn onto Bond Street. "I thought I could give her up once I inherited the title; I know now I cannot live without her, and I will not insult her by offering her carte blanche. I am going to Doctor's Commons tomorrow to procure a special license, and I shall leave for Exmoor Friday next—the day after my speech in the House of Lords about the plight of England's ex-servicemen. I only hope she will still have me after the way I have neglected her these past two months."

"This woman you love is the farmer's widow, I presume."

"Yes." Adam geared himself to face his aunt's objections. As one of the pillars of London society, she was bound to have a great many.

To his surprise she merely said, "Dukes do not often marry commoners. Naturally, there will be a scandal, but it will quiet down eventually if the family stands behind you."

Adam frowned. "I doubt my noble relatives will feel moved to back me in this. Fiona is a woman of great intelligence, courage, and passion; she is, in fact, everything I have ever wanted in a wife. But she is also the bastard daughter of the Earl of Stratham—"

"Good heavens!" Lady Tansy pressed her gloved fingers to her lips. "I remember 'The Barbarian.'" She shuddered. "A dreadful man."

"Furthermore, she is also the granddaughter of the woman

known as the Witch of Exmoor," Adam continued, "and I suspect something of a witch herself."

"Oh my, let us hope that does not become common knowledge in the *ton*." Lady Tansy peered at Adam from beneath her parasol. "Are you absolutely certain you are in love with this woman?"

"I have never been more certain of anything in my life."

"Well then, you must marry her, of course, no matter what anyone says. Luckily, since you are the duke, it is your choice to make. I was forbidden to marry the young cit I loved and there was nothing I could do about it. Had I eloped with him, my father would have seen to it he lost the small shipping business he had worked so hard to build."

She sighed. "I saw him years later with his wife and children—children who should have been mine. I doubt I shall ever recover from the pain I suffered that day. Do not waste your life as mine has been wasted, nephew."

Adam felt as if a great stone had been lifted off his shoulders. Lady Tansy was the only one of his relatives whose good opinion he cherished. Now, if Fiona would just forgive his stupid waffling, he could escape this miserable limbo he had been imprisoned in this past two months and take up living again.

London was even more bewildering than Fiona had anticipated. The buildings were so huge, the noise so overpowering, the smells rising from the garbage-strewn streets so dreadful. With multitudes of horses and carriages constantly racing about, one put one's life at risk just crossing a street. But most bewildering of all were the people of London. There were so many of them and most of the them seemed to go out of their way to be unfriendly. The doorman of the Pulteney Hotel had actually barred them from entering until Liam crossed his palm with a five-pound note.

Liam's friend, Bridey McClanahan, was the exception; she was as friendly as a mongrel puppy. But Fiona couldn't help but notice she had a rather coarse way of speaking, and the dark little seamstress's establishment she recommended looked nothing like the Bond Street shops Adam had pointed out in the peep show. Still, the gowns she and the odd little

seamstress insisted were the height of fashion were so bright
and colorful they warmed Fiona's beauty-starved heart.

It scarcely mattered that the woman for whom they were
originally sewn had been a bit more generously proportioned.
Fiona paid the exorbitant price the seamstress asked with the
money Liam had given her and stepped from the shop feeling
every inch a queen in her green-and-yellow-striped walking
dress, despite its sagging neckline. For the green stripes were
the exact same shade as the lovely reticule Adam had bought
her.

Now all she needed was the frivolous bonnet he'd insisted was
the mark of a true London lady. She politely declined Bridey's
offer to take her to her milliner. Adam had specified Bond Street
as the place to buy bonnets and to Bond Street she was determined to go.

"Lord luv us, you'll not catch me rubbing shoulders with the
West End toffs," Bridey declared as she hailed a hackney
coach and told the driver Fiona's destination. "You'll have no
trouble finding your way back to the Pulteney," she said. "For
every jarvey in London knows it well."

Bond Street was an unbelievably long drive from where
Bridey and Fiona had parted company and the elegant shops
lining it a far cry from the dark cubbyhole where Fiona had
purchased her walking dress and what the seamstress had assured her was a proper gown for the theatre, which she carried
in an unwieldy parcel. But if the drab apparel the Bond Street
shoppers were wearing was an example of the wares to be
found in those shops, then Bridey had served her well. She
could tell, from the way people stared, that they were im-
pressed by her colorful gown.

When she finally found a bonnet shop, the bonnets on display were sadly disappointing. "Have you nothing more exciting than these plain straw things with just a flower or two on
the brim?" she asked the clerk who waited on her.

The woman sniffed as if she had just caught a whiff of something foul. "Our bonnets are both tasteful and *au courant*," she
declared haughtily. "But wait." She studied Fiona's gown with
narrowed eyes. "I believe I have just the thing that would suit
you in the back of the shop."

A moment later she returned with a lemon yellow bonnet

decorated with a splendid green feather that stood half an arm's length above the brim—and miracle of miracles it was very nearly the color of her reticule. Fiona's pulse quickened. If there was ever a frivolous bonnet, this was surely it. Without so much as a blink of her eye, she paid the incredible price of twenty shillings, donned her new bonnet, and took her leave of the sour-faced clerk.

It was time to return to the Pulteney. Liam would think she was lost if she tarried much longer. She glanced up and down the street, but the hackney she had previously hired was gone and she could see no others.

She started to cross the street, then quickly backed up as a shiny black open carriage bore down on her. The stylish driver was dressed in a frock coat the exact color of his pair of matched grays, and when Fiona took a closer look at the splendid fellow, she felt her mouth drop open in astonishment.

It was Adam and he was not alone. His passenger's face was hidden by her parasol, but Fiona caught a glimpse of a dainty gray-gloved hand and a gown of some iridescent lavender material so elegant it made her fine new walking dress seem tacky and overbright.

She ducked her head to keep him from recognizing her and raised it only when he had passed, to stare after him with eyes misted by tears. Imagining him with another woman had been hurtful enough; seeing her by his side in the beautiful new curricle he'd talked about in Exmoor was completely devastating.

Fiona's tears were flowing faster now and she searched in vain for some place where she could escape the curious scrutiny of passersby. Then she remembered Adam had mentioned that Hookum's Lending Library was on Bond Street, and set out in search of a building resembling the one he had pointed out in the peep show.

She spotted it a short distance from the bonnet shop, and with a cry of relief, dashed across the busy roadway toward it, heedless of the shouts of angry drivers and horsemen and the neighing of startled horses. For what better place could she find to bury her bitter despair than between the pages of a book.

Chapter Eighteen

Adam returned Lady Tansy to the town house and immediately sent word to the stable he wanted Starfire saddled. A few moments later, dressed in his buckskins and riding jacket, he set out for Hyde Park to work off some of his nervous energy with a brisk ride.

Luck was with him. It was well before the hour when those members of the *ton* wishing to see and be seen made their daily pilgrimage to the park. Furthermore, an unseasonal fog had descended without warning on London's fashionable West End. As a result, he had the bridle paths to himself.

Making the most of it, he urged Starfire into a brisk trot and followed the Serpentine deep into a part of the park he could never remember visiting before. Wisps of fog hung in the trees and hovered over the river like feathers scattered by a puff of wind, and an odd silence mantled the area, as if all life had been momentarily suspended. Indeed, even the birds had ceased their chirping.

He slowed Starfire to a walk, but the mare seemed unusually skittish—spooked by something or someone he could neither see nor hear. "What is it, girl?" he asked in the soothing voice that never failed to calm her.

Then even as he gently massaged the top of her neck from ear to withers, he saw it out of the corner of his eye—a mysterious flash of white moving through a grove of leafy birches off to his left. Curious, he brought the mare to a complete halt and watched as a shockingly familiar figure emerged from the trees.

"What the devil!" Adam stared with unbelieving eyes at the shimmering image of a white Exmoor pony standing in the middle of the Hyde Park bridle path some fifty feet ahead of him. As he watched, mesmerized, the animal raised its head, whinnied, and slowly faded into the swirling mist that surrounded it. A moment later the fog lifted, leaving the park bathed in the golden light of a warm September sun.

Stunned, he held his nervous mount in check and struggled to make sense of what had just occurred. The pony had been no illusion on his part; Starfire had obviously seen it as well. But he couldn't imagine why it had appeared to him alone when Fiona was hundreds of miles away? Always before they had observed it together.

A sudden thought started his pulse racing. If the pony was in London, it must follow that Fiona was also. But how did she get here? And why had she come? The thought of the naive country widow wandering the streets of London alone struck terror in his heart. With grim determination, he brought his emotions under control and calmly asked himself where in the vast city she might be found.

He ruled out Hyde Park, despite sighting the pony there. Likewise, he doubted his proud little love would call at his town house when he had neglected her so shamefully for more than two months. Indeed, once he located her, he would probably have to swallow a healthy portion of crow to get back in her good graces.

Then he remembered their discussions about Hatchard's Bookstore. Of all the diversions the city had to offer, that would surely be the most tempting to Fiona. Without further thought, he wheeled Starfire around, galloped back through the park, and headed for Picadilly.

Arriving at his destination, he tossed his reins to the ragged urchin who tended the horses belonging to Hatchard's patrons, whipped open the door, and strode into the busy store. The noisy chatter of clerks and customers instantly ceased as he stopped short and searched the startled faces around him.

"Stars and garters, 'tis his grace, the Duke of Bellmont!" a female voice squealed.

Instantly a clerk stepped from behind the counter and bowed obsequiously. "Good afternoon, Your Grace. May I help you locate a book, Your Grace?"

"Actually, I am looking for a person, not a book. A young countrywoman with flaming red hair," Adam said without thinking; then cursed himself for a fool. By nightfall everyone in the *ton* would have heard that the Duke of Bellmont was prowling London in search of a red-haired woman. "Never mind," he muttered to the goggle-eyed clerk. "I can see she's not here." So saying, he wheeled around and bolted out the door.

Retrieving Starfire's reins, he tossed the urchin a shilling and mounted the now docile mare. Sick with disappointment, he sat for a moment, contemplating where to search next. Fiona was in London. He could feel it in his bones—and he had been so certain he would find her at Hatchard's. Books were more important to her than anything else.

He felt a tug on his boot and looked down into the grimy face of the boy who had tended his horse. "Lookee 'ere, guvnor," the ragged lad said in the accent that pegged him a Cockney, "seein' as 'ow ye tipped me so fine, I'll twig ye to somethin' could save ye some blunt."

The boy winked broadly. "I've 'eard tell 'ookum's Liberry on Bond Street 'as ever so many books and they lets coves like ye borrow em for less'n 'alf the price these caper merchants at 'atchards asks."

Hookum's Lending Library. Of course. If his penny-pinching widow planned to spend any time in London, she would undoubtedly patronize the library and save her precious shillings for that rainy day she was so worried about.

"Good thinking, lad," he said and tossed the little Cockney what was probably the first half crown he had ever laid eyes on.

Adam made the trip from Picadilly to Bond Street in record time, found another lad to watch over Starfire, and rushed up the steps into the library. Unlike Hatchard's, it was eerily silent and virtually empty. The only patrons appeared to be three old men reading quietly at a sturdy oak table in front of the book stacks.

But Fiona was here. He sensed her presence with a surety that made his skin prickle.

"Good day, sir. How may I help you?" the white-haired librarian asked when he stepped up to the desk.

Adam knew better than to make the same mistake he'd made at Hatchard's. He favored the old man with a smile.

"Could you please tell me where I might find Ann Radcliffe's novels?"

Astonishment momentarily rearranged the wrinkles on the librarian's face, but he quickly recovered. "Mrs. Radcliffe's books are usually requested by young ladies," he said in a voice bordering on disapproval.

"As a matter of fact, I have a young lady in mind."

"Ah, then you may find what you seek in stack number five." The old man peered at Adam through his spectacles. "I see you are a gentleman of quality, sir. Therefore, I feel I should warn you a young woman of somewhat questionable appearance has been perusing our collection of Gothic novels for the past hour. We do not normally encourage such creatures to avail themselves of the library, but I could not bring myself to refuse her admittance. She was weeping, you see . . . rather copiously. I shall, however, show her the door if you feel she will distract you."

"She will not bother me in the least," Adam said, barely able to contain his glee. The young woman of "questionable appearance" had to be Fiona in her deplorable widow's weeds.

He hastened toward the designated stack; pleased it was far enough from the front desk to allow him and Fiona some privacy—only to stop short when he reached it. The woman he found there had her back to him, but it was all too apparent she was not Fiona. She was, in fact, the bold-as-brass lightskirt he'd earlier glimpsed plying her trade on Bond Street. There was no mistaking her gaudy striped dress and hideous plumed bonnet.

Bitterly disappointed, he was about to turn away when he noticed the familiar reticule on the bookshelf beside her—the ugly green reticule he had purchased at Plimpton Fair.

Good God! It was Fiona! But why was she decked out like a Haymarket harlot? He took a quick breath and a step forward. "Fiona?"

At the sound of her name, she whipped around, a copy of *The Mysteries of Udolpho* clutched to her bosom. "Adam!" she gasped. "What are you doing here?"

"I might ask the same of you, my love. You were planning to eventually let me know you were in London, I hope," he said, on the theory that the best defense was an offense.

Fiona lifted her chin defiantly. "I did not feel free to do so since you hadn't bothered to write," she said stiffly.

"I told you I would write when I had my affairs in order. It took longer than I had expected." It was only a small lie, and in a good cause. "But there is no harm done since I found you before I left for Exmoor."

Fiona stared at him in mute dismay. "You were going back to Exmoor? Whatever for?"

"To claim my bride, of course."

"Do not speak so foolishly, Adam," Fiona scolded in a voice that wobbled embarrassingly. "We both know that a woman with my background could never be a proper duchess."

"Then be my improper duchess. You told me once you would walk through fire if that was what it took to be my wife. Was that an idle promise? Or have you simply lost your courage?"

"No. I have not," Fiona declared indignantly. "But I fear you have lost your common sense. I might have managed to muck my way through as the wife of Lord Adam Cresswell, but as a gambler you must know the stakes were raised the minute you became the Duke of Bellmont."

She sighed. "I would cause you nothing but shame and scandal if I agreed to marry you now. Good heavens, look at me. My new walking dress seemed so pretty and bright at first, but I can see now it is all wrong—and my bonnet too, though I cannot blame Bridey for that since I picked it out myself."

"Bridey?" Adam raised an eyebrow in that infuriatingly autocratic way of his.

"Bridey McClanahan, a friend of Liam's. She took me to the seamstress who makes the gowns for all the girls who work for a lady named Madam Blanche."

"Ah, that explains it." Adam moved to within an arm's length of her and Fiona suddenly found it difficult to draw a deep breath. "Dresses and bonnets can be replaced, Fiona," he said in the same soothing tone of voice she'd heard him use on an excitable pony. "One only need find a proper modiste. As for anything else you need to learn, I am confident you can handle it. Look at what you have already accomplished."

Fiona sighed. "I cannot make my birth legitimate by reading a book, nor make my grandmother someone other than the Witch of Exmoor by memorizing passages from your Christian

Bible. You should marry an elegant lady like the one I saw riding in your carriage this morning."

"Lady Tansy?" Adam's eyes held a decidedly wicked glint. "Much as I adore her, I fear such an alliance would cause an even greater scandal than marrying the granddaughter of the Witch of Exmoor . . . since she is my father's sister."

"She's your aunt?" Fiona said weakly.

"Exactly and the only lady with whom I have associated since returning to London. The truth is I have not looked at another woman since the day I first laid eyes on you, Fiona Haines. The devil with society and its restrictions. I am the Duke of Bellmont and I will marry whomever I wish."

"But I will not marry you, Your Grace, and that is my final word."

"And I will not live without the woman I love, and that is my final word. So, since you refuse to marry me if I am the Duke of Bellmont, I have no choice but to renounce the title in favor of my eldest nephew."

Fiona glowered at him. "An idle threat, Your Grace. No man in his right mind would give up such a title and the wealth attached to it."

"It is a title I never expected or wanted. If I must choose between it and you, I will sign the papers to transfer it this very day." He shrugged. "A pity though, since the lad is something of a nodcock. His only talent appears to lie in tying an intricate cravat and gambling away his generous allowance."

Fiona frowned. "He doesn't sound like someone who would make a very good duke."

Obviously deep in thought, Adam ran his hand idly over the spine of one of Mrs. Radcliffe's books and Fiona shivered as if his long, elegant fingers were traveling her own spine.

"If the truth be known, the young idiot will make an atrocious duke," he said grimly. "He will take no responsibility for his tenant farmers and their families, and worse yet, he will never use the power of the title to better the lot of the thousands of ex-soldiers wandering our nation's highways hungry and homeless."

"But you will do those things and more," Fiona said, and knew she spoke the truth. "You will make the wisest, most compassionate duke in all of England, and thousands of people will be better off because of you."

Adam untied the ribbons of her bonnet, laid it aside and drew her into his arms. "I will do my best, love, as long as you are by my side."

Fiona smiled in spite of herself. "That, Your Grace, is out-and-out blackmail."

"I prefer to call it fate," he said, and lowered his mouth to hers in a deeply passionate kiss.

"We were meant to be together," he murmured moments later. "Believe it or not, I would not be here with you now had I not, this very morning, encountered a Celtic goddess and a mystic white pony."

Fiona raised her head from his shoulder. "What nonsense. I cannot credit a skeptic such as yourself suddenly embracing the ancient gods and the mysticism you have so firmly denounced in the past."

"As a matter of fact, I haven't," he admitted. "Nor will I ever believe that what you call the mystic pony is a sign from some long-forgotten Celtic god. But because of you, I have come to believe in something else I have scoffed at all my life."

She could see he was deadly serious. "Indeed, and what is that?"

"The power of love," Adam said, nuzzling his face in her hair. "It took me two long, miserable months without you to realize that for me the mystic pony is merely a manifestation of the love we share—and the miracle of that love is that we see with our hearts, not our eyes. For only with our hearts can we see beyond the puny limits of human reality."

Fiona's eyes misted with tears. But this time they were tears of joy. "Oh, Adam, what a wise and wonderful thing to say. I shall remember your lovely words all the rest of my life."

His mouth curved in the crooked grin that had been her undoing from the very beginning. "That should not be too difficult, my love, since I plan to repeat them to you every year on the anniversary of our wedding day."